The Grumpy Firefighter Next Door

A Best Friend's Brother Small Town Romance

A Seaholly Beach Novel

Avianne Ash

Copyright © 2025 by Avianne Ash

All rights reserved. No part of this publication may be reproduced, distributed, or transmitted in any form or by any means, including photocopying, recording, or other electronic or mechanical methods, without the prior written permission of the publisher, except in the case of brief quotations embodied in critical reviews and certain other noncommercial uses permitted by copyright law.

Published by Sapphire Bridge Press

ISBN: 9798273694606

The story, all names, characters, and incidents portrayed in this production are fictitious. No identification with actual persons (living or deceased), places, buildings, and products is intended or should be inferred.

Contents

1. Chapter 1: The Community Center . . . 1
2. Chapter 2: The Firehouse . . . 9
3. Chapter 3: Rachel's Cottage . . . 17
4. Chapter 4: The Grind . . . 25
5. Chapter 5: The Hardware Store . . . 31
6. Chapter 6: Ryan's Cottage . . . 39
7. Chapter 7: The Easel . . . 45
8. Chapter 8: The Firehouse . . . 53
9. Chapter 9: The Grind . . . 59
10. Chapter 10: Coral Pier . . . 67
11. Chapter 11: Rachel's Cottage . . . 73
12. Chapter 12: The Firehouse . . . 81
13. Chapter 13: Rachel's Cottage . . . 87
14. Chapter 14: Ryan's Cottage . . . 97

15.	Chapter 15: The Firehouse	105
16.	Chapter 16: Mrs. Henderson's House	113
17.	Chapter 17: Beverly's House	121
18.	Chapter 18: The Firehouse	127
19.	Chapter 19: Rachel's Cottage	135
20.	Chapter 20: The Boardwalk	145
21.	Chapter 21: The Grind	153
22.	Chapter 22: The Firehouse	161
23.	Chapter 23: The Easel	169
24.	Chapter 24: Ryan's Cottage	175
25.	Chapter 25: Seaholly Beach	183
26.	Chapter 26: Mrs. Henderson's House	193
27.	Chapter 27: The Community Center	201
28.	Chapter 28: The Firehouse	209
29.	Chapter 29: Rachel's Cottage	217
30.	Chapter 30: Coral Pier	225
31.	Chapter 31: Ryan's Cottage	233
32.	Chapter 32: The Firehouse	241
33.	Chapter 33: Beverly's House	249
34.	Chapter 34: Mrs. Henderson's House	257
35.	Chapter 35: The Community Center	263
36.	Chapter 36: Ryan's Cottage	273

37. Chapter 37: The Easel — 283
38. Chapter 38: The Firehouse — 291
39. Chapter 39: The Cottage — 299
40. Chapter 40: Coral Pier — 307
41. Epilogue: One Year Later — 315

Chapter One

The Community Center

Rachel

"Miss Rachel! The microwave is breathing FIRE!" Jayden hollered, his paintbrush frozen mid-air. "ARE WE GONNA DIE?"

"It's a DRAGON!" Emma shrieked, abandoning her self-portrait to point at the purple smoke billowing through the kitchenette door.

The microwave wailed like a banshee. Not the dignified beep it was supposed to make when your popcorn was ready, but a full-throated shriek.

I stood frozen in the community center's main hall, covered head-to-toe in grape acrylic. Sixteen seven-year-olds painting with all the restraint of Jackson Pollock on a sugar rush had splattered less paint on themselves than I had. Purple streaked my hair, smeared across my cheekbone, down my jeans and flannel sleeves.

"COOL!" "IT'S MAGIC SMOKE!" The chorus rose around me as the purple cloud thickened.

I grabbed a stack of construction paper and flapped it at the smoke detector like a deranged bird. The purple fog thickened. The alarm pulsed in triple-time. The kids fanned smoke back at me with their masterpieces, howling "Put it out!" even as they cheered the fire on.

"What do we do, Miss Rachel?" Mia asked, eyes wide.

"We stay calm." My voice cracked on the last word as another plume of purple smoke rolled out.

"You don't LOOK calm!" Jayden announced.

I lunged for the ancient window crank, elbowing purple smears onto the glass as I pried it open. A coastal gale blasted in, sending paint-splattered napkins flying. Some kids seized the moment to hurl their self-portraits like frisbees through the gap.

"BEST DAY EVER!" someone shrieked.

I half-tripped into the kitchenette, yanked open the microwave, and extracted a charred lump of popcorn. Dumped it in the sink. Turned on the tap. A geyser of grape-scented steam erupted.

The roar of "WHOAAAAA!" from the main hall drowned out every thought.

I rummaged under the sink for the fire extinguisher and blasted white foam at the smoking appliance. The internal sprinklers triggered. A feeble drizzle turned the spilled paint into purple sludge.

The kids went wild. Applause. Impromptu standing ovations atop art carts. One budding performance artist reenacted my every move like a BBC nature documentary.

Half mortification, half odd pride.

Sure, I'd nearly leveled the room, but I'd stopped the blaze and no one was dead.

The front doors banged open.

"RACHEL BROWN!" Brenda's voice cut through the chaos, high and frantic. "What on EARTH—oh my stars!"

The community center's receptionist stood in the doorway, one hand clutched to her cardigan, the other gripping her reading glasses. Her gray curls had gone a bit wild.

"Brenda, I can explain—"

"The alarm! The smoke! Are the children hurt?" She rushed forward, sensible flats squeaking on the wet floor, eyes scanning the room for injuries. "Oh honey, you're covered in paint. Are you burned?"

"No, no, everyone's fine. Just a small kitchen fire. Very small. Mostly under control."

"Mostly?" Her voice went up an octave.

"It was a DRAGON!" Emma announced.

"Miss Rachel saved us!" Tommy added, waving his purple-stained self-portrait.

Brenda pressed a hand to her heart, then seemed to register the full scope of the disaster. Paint everywhere. Foam. Purple sludge. The acrid smell of burnt popcorn mixed with synthetic cheese. "Oh dear. Oh my. The director is going to... and the parents... Rachel, sweet girl, what happened?"

"Popcorn. In the microwave. I forgot about it."

"You forgot..." She cut herself off, took a breath, and smoothed down her cardigan. "Okay. Okay. Let's just... we need to call the fire department."

"Already done!" Jayden announced, pointing out the window where flashing lights were pulling into the parking lot.

Brenda's eyes went wide. "They're already here?"

"The alarm auto-calls."

My stomach dropped to my paint-splattered sneakers.

Great. Now the whole town would know about this.

"Are you gonna get FIRED, Miss Rachel?" Mia asked, voice small and worried.

"What? No, sweetie, I'm not—"

"My mom got fired once," Jayden said. "She cried a lot."

"Nobody's getting fired," Brenda said quickly, but her eyes darted to the purple chaos. "Let's just... everyone stay calm."

The heavy doors clanged open again.

Ryan Rodriguez stepped through in full gear. Helmet, gloves, boots. He scanned the purple-hazed chaos like he was searching for survivors of a natural disaster.

His gaze landed on me.

Time hiccupped.

Not Maya's brother. Anyone but him. The guy I'd accidentally flirted with during the hurricane cleanup before Maya pulled me aside with that gentle warning about his fresh heartbreak.

The kid-chaos faded. Squeals and paintbrush clatters, going fuzzy at the edges.

His jaw loosened. The hard professional lines of his face softened, and for half a heartbeat, warmth flickered through. His eyes tracked over me. Paint-splattered, messy, surrounded by purple carnage. One corner of his mouth twitched.

Behind him, his crew exchanged looks. Nudged each other. Grinned.

Heat crawled up my neck.

"Oh!" Brenda pressed a hand to her heart again, but this time her cheeks went pink. "Oh my. Hello, officer. I mean, firefighter. Sir."

Ryan's attention snapped to Brenda, then back to the room. "Everyone okay here?"

"Yes, yes, we're fine. Just a small kitchen incident. Nothing serious. Rachel handled it beautifully."

I shot her a grateful look.

Then the pack of seven-year-olds launched themselves at the firefighters in an explosion of excitement.

"LOOK AT THE FIRE TRUCK!"

They swarmed Ryan, bouncing on their toes, voices layered in a cacophony of questions and observations.

"Do you slide down the pole?"

"Can I try on your helmet?"

"How much water fits in the truck?"

One small hand shot up in the front. "Are you Miss Rachel's boyfriend?"

The words hit like ice water.

Brenda made a small squeaking sound.

Ryan's eyes went wide for half a second before his professional mask slammed back into place. "I'm, uh—"

"He's Maya's brother!" I blurted out, then immediately wanted to sink through the floor.

"Who's Maya?" Emma asked.

"My friend."

"So he COULD be your boyfriend," Jayden decided with the iron logic of a seven-year-old.

Ryan's ears went pink.

His crew was losing it. Shoulders shaking, barely containing their laughter.

Ryan cleared his throat. "New year, new station. Didn't expect purple smoke on day one."

Tommy pushed through to the front, purple paint smeared across his cheeks, waving his self-portrait. "Look what I made!"

Ryan crouched down to Tommy's level. The corner of his mouth twitched again, fighting a smile. "That's really good, buddy. Is that you?"

"Yeah! Miss Rachel taught us about self-portraits. See? That's my nose."

"I see that." Ryan's voice went softer.

My throat squeezed.

"Alright, kiddos," one of the other firefighters said, "let's give the chief some room to work, yeah? Who wants to see the truck?"

The kids erupted in cheers and stampeded toward the door, leaving Ryan, his crew, Brenda, and me in the purple aftermath.

Brenda was practically vibrating. "Can I get anyone water? Coffee? We have coffee in the—oh. Well. We HAD coffee."

Ryan straightened. "We need to check the kitchen. Make sure there's no lingering fire hazard."

"Of course, of course." Brenda gestured toward the kitchenette. "Right this way."

Ryan headed for the kitchenette. His boots thudded on the floor. His jaw tightened as he took in the smoking microwave, the foam, the purple sludge.

He stopped. Looked at the microwave. Looked at me. "You know, Rachel, safety is important."

I waved a purple-stained hand. "I thought I was keeping things exciting."

Brenda gasped softly.

Ryan's mouth twitched. He was fighting it, trying to hold onto that grumpy professional mask, but I could see it cracking at the edges.

His crew appeared in the doorway, grinning. "Hey, isn't this your sister's friend? The artist?"

One of them nudged Ryan. "Pretty sure she remembers you from the hurricane cleanup."

"You two know each other?" Brenda's voice went up, delighted and curious.

"We've met," Ryan said, voice flat, but his fingers flexed at his sides.

He turned back to the microwave, shoulders rigid, but his hands gave him away. Tension thrumming through them, knuckles pale as he gripped the counter.

My heart kicked against my ribs.

Stop it. He's off-limits. Maya said so.

But my traitorous brain kept replaying the way his eyes had softened when they landed on me. The way his mouth fought that smile.

I dragged my gaze away and focused on the paint in my hair. The purple splatters across my flannel. The absolute disaster of my life.

Yeah. This was fine. Totally fine.

Brenda was chattering nervously at the crew, asking about fire safety and response times and whether they'd like some cookies from the break room, the one that wasn't currently a disaster zone.

Ryan did his inspection, poking at the microwave, checking the outlet, nodding to himself.

He straightened. "You'll need to replace this. Don't use it again."

"Noted."

Our eyes caught. Held.

The air between us thickened.

"Rodriguez!" one of his crew called from outside. "We're rolling out!"

The spell broke.

Ryan's shoulders dropped half an inch. He turned toward the door, boots scraping the floor, then paused and glanced back. "Next time, try not to burn down the town."

His voice came out gruff, but his eyes held that playful glint.

My heart did a stupid little flip.

"I'll do my best."

Brenda clasped her hands together, watching him go with stars in her eyes. "Such a nice young man. And a firefighter! Rachel, honey, you didn't mention you knew any firefighters."

"I don't. I mean, I barely—we just met during—it's not—" I gave up.

The fire trucks rumbled away, taking Ryan Rodriguez and his stupidly warm eyes with them.

I stood in the middle of the purple chaos, paint-streaked and mortified, my pulse still hammering.

Brenda patted my shoulder. "Don't you worry about the director, sweetie. I'll handle it. These things happen."

"Thanks, Brenda."

"But maybe next time, set a timer?" She smiled gently.

"Yeah. Timer. Good call."

Perfect timing. Set off a fire alarm, look like a disaster.

And the hot firefighter had to be Maya's brother.

She moved toward the kids, herding them back to their projects.

I grabbed a rag and started wiping down the counters. Through the windows, afternoon light was already fading. January days ended early. Trying to look productive. Trying not to replay every mortifying moment of the last thirty minutes.

I looked up. Brenda had returned, cleaning supplies in hand, but her expression had gone soft. Knowing.

"That young man couldn't take his eyes off you, dear. Maya's brother, right? Such a catch."

My stomach flipped and dropped.

Because I know exactly why that's complicated.

Chapter Two

The Firehouse

Ryan

"Whoa, down boy!"

Dirty paws hit my pristine uniform. The puppy launched himself at my legs again, tail whipping like a metronome on caffeine. Drool flew everywhere.

"Hey, watch the uniform!" I caught a whiff of wet dog mingling with lingering smoke from the firehouse. Not exactly how I planned to make my entrance.

Laughter erupted from the crew, voices bouncing off the walls.

"Looks like someone's making an impression!" Cooper called out, grinning.

I glanced down at my uniform. Mud and slobber. Perfect canvas. "First day and I'm covered in filth."

The little guy didn't seem to notice my irritation. He pranced around, energy contagious despite my frustration. I wiped my hands on my pants, trying to salvage a shred of dignity.

"You've got a new best friend, Ryan!" Cooper's laughter spilled out.

I shot him a glare, but my mouth twitched. The puppy darted away, a blur of fur disappearing around the corner of the firehouse. I sighed and wiped more slobber from my hands.

This chaotic, messy welcome was the exact opposite of the fresh start I'd envisioned. I had hoped for a smooth entry, free from complications. Just the job. So much for that plan.

The crew helped me clean up, their laughter filling the air.

"So, about your artist girlfriend." Martinez grinned from ear to ear.

Heat crept up my neck. "She's not—"

"Heard you like your women covered in purple paint." Cooper winked.

I shot him a glare. "Maya's friend. That's it."

"Does Maya know you're making moves on her friends?"

The whole crew erupted.

I tried to maintain my professional demeanor, but their relentless teasing chipped away at my defenses. Each jab felt like a playful poke, reminding me how unprepared I was for this kind of attention.

"So what about Rachel Brown?" Martinez leaned forward, eyes gleaming. "She seemed pretty into you at the community center."

The crew exchanged knowing glances, grins widening. My fingers curled into fists at my sides. Memories of her flooded back. The way she smiled. The spark in her eyes when she talked about her art. The paint in her hair. Hard to deny the attraction, even as I tried pushing it aside.

"Leave it alone." My voice came out flat.

"Oh, he's got it bad," Cooper announced.

"She set a microwave on fire. That's not exactly relationship material."

"She's an artist. That's just her chaotic, creative fuel." Martinez waggled his eyebrows.

"Chaos is the last thing I need."

"Maybe it's exactly what you need," Frank spoke from the corner.

I turned away and focused on the training exercises. Sunlight poured through the firehouse windows. I gripped the heavy hose, its weight tugging at my muscles as I maneuvered it into position.

"Let's see how you handle this, Rodriguez!" My trainer barked, voice sharp yet encouraging.

I nodded. Adrenaline coursed through me. Each pull of the hose was a reminder of my past, a burden I couldn't shake. Nights lost in messy relationships. The fallout from dating my lieutenant's ex-wife. That chaos had left me feeling betrayed, isolated.

"Keep your stance wide, and don't forget to breathe!"

I adjusted my feet, grounding myself. Took a deep breath. Forced down the tension twisting around my lungs. I could do this. Keep my head down. Focus on the job. Avoid complications.

I aimed the nozzle. Water surged forth, spraying a fine mist. The cool spray hit my face, stark contrast to the heat building inside me.

This time will be different. Professional. Clean. Uncomplicated.

Chief Patterson waved me over, expression serious. I stepped away from the crew, heart thudding.

"We need to talk about a big project." His voice was steady.

"What's going on?" I braced myself for news about training or equipment.

"There's a high-profile mural project coming up. Part of a community initiative. The town council is watching closely." He glanced at the crew, who were now whispering among themselves.

My stomach dropped. "Who's the artist?"

"Rachel Brown." He looked at me. "You know her?"

The crew erupted. "YES!" Martinez shouted from across the bay. More laughter echoed off the walls. Someone whistled.

I forced a smile but felt heat rising in my cheeks.

"Congratulations, you're the department liaison." Chief Patterson's tone was firm. "Not a request. It's part of your duty."

I swallowed hard. "Chief, I don't think—"

"You're the newest member of the team. It's yours." He clapped me on the shoulder. "First meeting is next week. Don't be late."

He walked away before I could protest.

The crew's teasing intensified. "Looks like someone's in trouble!"

Cooper cupped his hands around his mouth. "Try not to let her burn down the firehouse!"

I shot them both a glare.

Internal panic surged. Of course she was the artist. My life didn't need more complications, but here I was, tangled in the mess of it all.

I stepped outside, taking a moment to breathe. The sun warmed my skin, but a chill settled in my gut. Rachel Brown was the artist for the mural project. Great. Just what I needed.

Her smile flashed in my mind. Bright and chaotic, like splashes of paint on a canvas. I could almost hear her laughter, light and free.

But Maya's warning echoed. "She's healing from past hurts. She's not looking to complicate things."

I pressed my lips together. My ex had turned my life upside down, leaving me lost and alone. I had to protect myself this time. I had to protect Rachel too. She didn't need my baggage any more than I needed hers.

I shook my head, trying to clear it. Focus, Ryan. You're here to do a job. But the image of her paint-splattered hands and warm smile lingered.

"Hey, Ryan! Check it out!" Martinez shouted, waving me over.

I turned, brow furrowing as I spotted the scruffy puppy curled up behind the dumpster.

"Is that the little monster that ruined my pants?" Irritation bubbled up.

"Yeah, he's been hanging around for days." Martinez frowned.

"Why hasn't anyone called animal control?"

"The shelter is full," Frank chimed in.

My anger flared. How could anyone abandon a dog like this? We approached the puppy slowly. As I knelt, he lifted his head. His eyes were wide and hopeful. His tail wagged slowly, unsure but curious. My throat tightened at the sight. This poor pup had been neglected, yet he still trusted us.

It reminded me too much of my own situation. Trying to survive alone. Burned by people I'd trusted with everything.

I reached out a hand, palm open. The puppy sniffed cautiously, then took a tentative step forward. He bounded toward me, licking my fingers with enthusiasm when I stayed still. It hit me like a punch to the ribs.

"He already likes you!" Martinez grinned.

Cooper nudged my shoulder. "You need a partner."

"A fresh start needs a fresh friend."

I glanced at the puppy, tail wagging like a flag of hope. My resolve wavered as I looked into his bright eyes. He deserved a chance, just like I did.

"Come on, Ryan." Martinez's tone was light and encouraging. "What do you say?"

I hesitated. "I'm not ready for a dog." I shook my head. "I don't even have supplies, and my place is temporary at Henry's."

The crew wouldn't let up. "Henry loves dogs!"

"Firefighters stick together, and that includes rescue dogs!"

"Yeah, but—" I started, but they were already tossing out names.

"Sparkles!" Cooper shouted, eyes wide with mischief.

"Glitter!" someone else chimed in, laughter bubbling.

"Princess!"

My stomach twisted. "Absolutely not."

Frank stepped forward, a knowing look on his face. "What about Dozer? He bulldozed you over pretty good."

I paused, glancing down at the puppy wriggling on the ground, tail wagging. "Dozer." The name resonated. "Because that's what he does."

As if he understood, the puppy perked up, tail now a blur. He jumped to his feet, barking joyfully at the sound of his new name. My scowl wavered.

What am I doing? I came here for simple. This is not simple.

But as I looked at Dozer, my resolve shifted.

"Fine. But I'm taking him to the vet first thing tomorrow."

"Smart man," Frank said.

"Does he need shots?" Cooper asked.

"Probably everything." I rubbed the back of my neck. "What do I know about puppies?"

Martinez laughed. "You'll figure it out."

"He'll need to be neutered too. That'll calm him down some."

I looked at Dozer, who was now trying to eat my shoelace. "How much does all that cost?"

"A few hundred, maybe?" Martinez shrugged. "Worth it though."

A few hundred. Great. I was committed now.

"You'll need food. Bowls. A leash." Cooper started ticking items off on his fingers. "Probably a bed. Toys. Poop bags."

"Poop bags," I repeated flatly.

"Welcome to dog ownership." Martinez grinned.

I carefully loaded Dozer into the front of my truck, using a borrowed crate from the station. The puppy was worn out from all the excitement. Within seconds, his soft snores filled the cab. My phone buzzed. I pulled it out and saw a text from Henry.

> Hey, the realtor got back to me. Can show you that cottage tomorrow morning if you're interested. Think you'll like the neighborhood.

I stared at the screen, heart thudding. A permanent place. I hadn't thought much about settling down since moving here. Glancing over at Dozer, blissfully asleep, I couldn't help but think, *Guess we're both starting over.*

My fingers hovered over the screen as I typed back, "Yeah. Set it up."

I started the truck and pulled out of the firehouse lot. Warm sun streamed through the windshield. My thoughts drifted to the mural project. I would be seeing Rachel again. The idea sent a flutter through my stomach.

Keep it professional. Keep it simple. Don't get complicated.

I glanced at the gas gauge. Half full. Good enough to get home. But then I remembered. Dog food. Right. I needed dog food.

I pulled into the pet store parking lot and killed the engine. Dozer was still snoring in his crate. I'd just run in quick. Grab food and get out.

Ten minutes later, I stood in the dog food aisle, staring at seven thousand options. Puppy formula. Adult formula. Large breed. Small breed. Grain-free. Chicken. Beef. Salmon.

What did puppies even eat?

I grabbed my phone and typed "best puppy food" into the search bar. Six articles popped up, all contradicting each other.

"Can I help you find something?" A teenage employee appeared at my elbow, looking bored.

"Dog food. For a puppy."

"What breed?"

I blinked. "I don't know."

"You don't know what breed your puppy is?"

"I just got him. Today. Like an hour ago."

The kid's expression said he thought I was an idiot. He was probably right.

"How big is he?"

"Medium? Big paws though."

The kid sighed and grabbed a bag off the shelf. "This one's good for medium breeds. Puppy formula. You'll want to switch to adult food around a year."

"Great. Thanks." I took the bag.

"You'll need bowls too. And probably a real leash. That rope from the station isn't gonna cut it."

How did he know about the rope?

Forty-five minutes and two hundred dollars later, I loaded bags into the truck bed. Food. Bowls. A real leash. A collar. Chew toys because apparently, puppies destroyed everything. Poop bags. A dog bed that Dozer probably wouldn't use.

I slid back into the driver's seat. Dozer was awake now, nose pressed against the crate door, tail wagging.

"You better be worth it," I muttered.

He barked once, sharp and happy. I pulled back onto the road, heading toward Henry's place. My phone buzzed again. Another text from Henry.

Oh, and Rachel Brown lives next door to the cottage. Just FYI.

My hands tightened on the steering wheel.

Of course she did.

I glanced at Dozer in the rearview mirror. He was chewing on the edge of his crate, completely unconcerned about the chaos he'd brought into my life.

A loud CRACK echoed through the cab.

I looked back. Dozer had gotten his head through the crate door. The plastic latch hung broken, dangling uselessly. He wriggled forward, squeezing his entire body through the gap, and launched himself into the front seat.

"No! Dozer, get back—"

Too late. He landed on the center console, tail wagging, and immediately knocked my coffee into my lap.

Hot liquid soaked through my jeans. I swerved slightly, then corrected. Dozer, thrilled by the adventure, planted both paws on my shoulder and licked my face.

"Down! Sit! Stay!" I tried every command I could think of.

Dozer barked and lunged for the window, nose smearing across the glass.

I pulled into a gas station parking lot and stopped the truck. Sat there. Coffee-soaked. Dog paws on my shoulder. Slobber on my cheek.

Dozer looked at me, tongue lolling, tail still wagging like this was the best day of his life.

I looked back at him.

"What have I done?"

Chapter Three

Rachels's Cottage

Rachel

Dali YOWLED, her fur bristling as she leaped off the windowsill. I was in my zone, painting away with my favorite playlist blasting, lost in the swirl of colors on my canvas. Then a loud crash made me jump, and my paint water spilled across the palette. "What is it, Dali?"

I leaned over to peek out the window. Beyond my small front yard, I could see the ocean, gray and restless under winter clouds. The private road that dead-ended at our cluster of beach cottages was usually empty this time of year. But now a truck sat pulled up next door at the old Whitmore place.

My stomach dropped.

The cottage had been empty for months. Two men hopped out, and a massive puppy bounded after them, all floppy ears and wagging tail. Salt air drifted through my cracked window, mixing with the smell of acrylic paint.

Recognition hit me like a wave.

Maya's brother. Ryan. Again.

First the hurricane cleanup. Then my popcorn cleanup. Now here?

My throat closed. Oh no. The guy I'd embarrassingly flirted with before Maya gave me that hands-off talk about his heartbreak. Heat crept up my cheeks. Not next door. Anywhere but next door.

I couldn't look away as they walked toward the house. Ryan stood tall, his dark hair catching what little winter sunlight broke through the clouds. My pulse kicked up.

No, no, no. This was not the time for that.

Dali returned to the sill, tail flicking as she watched the newcomers. Beyond them, waves crashed against the shore, the rhythmic sound usually calming. Not today. "You're not helping!" I waved my paintbrush at her.

The puppy barked, sharp and happy. I pulled back from the window and paced in front of my easel. Maybe I could hide? Pretend I was busy? But what if he saw me? Our cottages were tiny, close together on this dead-end road. No tourists. No through traffic. Just us.

I couldn't avoid him if he moved in.

I took a deep breath. Glanced back outside. They were still there, chatting and laughing. Ryan looked relaxed, maybe even happy. I hated that I noticed.

I shook my head, trying to clear my thoughts. Too late. My art was forgotten, my focus shot. Excitement and dread tangled in my stomach as I watched them.

The puppy spotted Dali perched on my windowsill.

In an instant, he bolted from Ryan's side, his leash trailing behind like a forgotten ribbon. Dali's back arched as she hissed, fur standing on end. Then she took off, darting across the yard like a startled deer.

"Dali!" I shouted, but it was too late.

A wild chase erupted through both yards. The puppy was all enthusiasm, floppy ears bouncing, tail helicoptering with joy. Dali, dignified and offended, zigzagged through my winter pansies with the grace of a ballet dancer fleeing a monster. She darted under the bare branches of the crepe myrtle, Dozer crashing behind her.

I grabbed my fleece-lined utility jacket and rushed outside, heart hammering. The ocean breeze hit me, cold and sharp. Ryan was already sprinting after his dog, his tall frame moving fast. Henry stood off to the side, doubled over with laughter.

"Dozer, come back!" Ryan called.

The puppy, clearly thinking this was the best game ever, barked joyfully as he trampled through what used to be my carefully arranged purple and yellow pansies.

"Get her, Rachel!" Henry hollered between laughs.

"Thanks for the support!" I shot back, eyes locked on Dali as she leaped onto my garden bench, then launched herself toward the low fence separating our small yards.

The puppy bounded after her, knocking over a terracotta pot. It shattered. Soil exploded across the grass.

"Dozer, no!" Ryan lunged for the leash, missed, almost face-planted.

I bit down on a laugh despite the chaos. Watching this serious firefighter chase a rogue puppy through my yard, with the ocean crashing behind him and seagulls shrieking overhead, was not how I'd expected my afternoon to go.

Dali made her move, climbing up my leg like I was a tree. "Ouch! Dali, not the claws!" I winced but managed to catch her, cradling her against me. She squirmed, indignant, but I held tight.

Ryan caught up to the puppy, who was still bouncing around like he'd won a prize. "You little rascal." Ryan was breathless but smiling as he clipped the leash back onto the dog's collar.

We stood there, panting and mortified, our animals finally under control. The sound of waves filled the silence between us. I looked over at Ryan, who was brushing dirt off his shirt. Soil streaked across one shoulder. A leaf stuck in his hair.

"Sorry about that," I mumbled, heat rising in my cheeks.

He chuckled, shaking his head. "No, that's on me. He's still learning... everything."

Henry was practically vibrating with delight. "You two should get your pets together more often. Best entertainment I've had all week!"

I shot him a look.

Dali hissed at the puppy, who seemed entirely pleased with himself despite the destruction in his wake.

"Is he new?" I asked, trying to focus on the dog instead of the way Ryan's shirt stretched across his shoulders as he caught his breath.

"Got him yesterday," Ryan said, glancing down at the dog with a mix of exasperation and affection. "Found him behind the firehouse. Shelter was full."

"So you adopted him?" My heart did a stupid little squeeze.

"More like he adopted me." Ryan's mouth quirked. "Bulldozed me over in the parking lot. Hence the name."

"Dozer," I said, testing it out. The puppy's ears perked up at the sound. "That's perfect."

"Yeah, well, he's living up to it." Ryan gestured at my demolished pansies. "I'll replace those. And the pot. I'm really sorry."

"It's fine. They needed replanting anyway." Lie. They'd been thriving despite the winter chill. But watching this grumpy firefighter worry about my flowers squeezed at my resolve to keep a distance between us.

Henry stepped in, clearly sensing an opportunity to make things more awkward. "Rachel, this is my friend Ryan Rodriguez. Ryan, this is Rachel Brown."

Ryan looked caught off guard by the formal introduction, then smiled. "Oh, I remember."

I gestured toward Dali, who was still glaring daggers at Dozer. "This is Dali."

Ryan blinked. "Dolly?"

"What? No. Dali."

"That's what I said. Dolly."

I couldn't help but laugh. "Dal-EEE. Like Salvador Dali. The artist?"

He glanced at Dali, who was now flicking her tail in supreme annoyance. "The mustache guy? I see the resemblance. Black and white tux, black tail, white gloves."

"She has the same flair for drama."

As if on cue, Dali yowled, her voice sharp and demanding, competing with the seagulls.

Henry doubled over laughing.

Ryan's mouth twitched, fighting a smile. "Fair enough."

Dozer chose that moment to lunge forward, tail wagging, trying to make friends. Dali's back arched. I tightened my grip. "Nope. Not happening."

"Dozer, sit." Ryan's voice went firm.

The puppy sat. For two seconds. Then he was up again, wiggling with barely contained excitement.

"Still working on commands," Ryan said, ears going pink.

"How old is he?"

"No idea. Vet appointment's tomorrow." Ryan rubbed the back of his neck. "I'm kind of making this up as I go."

The vulnerability in that admission made my throat tight. This serious, professional firefighter was just as lost as the rest of us.

Henry grinned, clearly enjoying the chaos. "So, we're checking out the Whitmore cottage."

There it was. Confirmed. I kept my voice light. "Oh, that place? It's nice. Lots of character."

Inside, I was trying not to think about what daily proximity would mean. Failed. The private dead-end road meant no tourists, no buffer, no escape routes.

Ryan nodded. "Yeah, I've heard it has good beach access." He glanced toward the ocean, visible from where we stood in my small front yard.

His eyes flicked down to my overalls, then back up. Heat crawled up my neck. I brushed a hand through my messy hair, wishing I'd at least changed before running outside.

"Rachel's an artist," Henry said, like this wasn't already painfully obvious from my paint-covered state. "She knows all about the neighborhood. Right?"

"Um, yeah." I stammered. "The beach is just down there. Private access from the cottages. You'll love it."

Stop selling him on the place, Rachel.

Dozer trotted over to Dali, tail still wagging with optimism. "Come on, Dali, be nice," I said, but she hissed again, arching her back.

"Dali doesn't want to make friends," Ryan observed.

"She's shy," I lied. Dali wasn't shy. She was judging everyone and finding them lacking.

Henry chuckled. "You two should get together more often! This is entertaining!"

I shot him another look, stomach twisting. Dozer jumped toward Dali. I grabbed his collar before he could launch. "No, no! Not again!"

Ryan moved to help at the same time. Our hands collided on the dog's collar. His fingers were warm, calloused. My breath caught.

We froze. Stared at each other.

The ocean roared behind us. Salt air swirled around us. But all I could focus on was the warmth of his hand against mine.

"Sorry," I blurted, pulling back.

"No, I—" Ryan cleared his throat, straightened. "Thanks."

The air felt thick.

Henry was grinning like he'd won the lottery.

I clutched Dali tighter, needing her to ground me. "So, cottage viewing. You should probably..."

"Right. Yeah." Ryan nodded, stepping back, putting professional distance between us again. "We should go."

But he didn't move. His gaze lingered on me for a heartbeat longer, and I couldn't read his expression. Warmth? Confusion? Regret?

Then Henry clapped him on the shoulder. "Come on, let's see if this place is worth it."

Ryan and Henry headed inside, Dozer bounding after them with renewed energy. I turned away, retreating to my cottage with Dali tucked under my arm. She squirmed, clearly annoyed at being carried.

I set her down and tried to return to my painting, but my brush hovered above the canvas. Paint forgotten.

My phone buzzed with Mom's name. I silenced it. I'd call her back later—after I'd finished pretending everything was fine.

I kept sneaking glances out the window. Ryan's tall figure moved through the rooms, examining the walls. Henry gestured, probably cracking jokes. Dozer's nose pressed against the glass, sniffing. Beyond them, the ocean stretched gray and endless.

I paced. Tried to shake off the anxious energy thrumming through me.

This was fine. Totally fine. He probably wouldn't even buy the place.

But as I turned back to the window, I realized I'd been staring for five minutes straight.

"Get it together, Rachel," I muttered.

Maya's warning echoed. "He's healing from heartbreak. Don't complicate things."

Good. Because I wasn't changing for anyone. I glanced around my studio. Paint splatters on the walls. Brushes scattered everywhere. Dali glaring from her perch. This was who I was.

My ex had tried to change me. Never again.

Professional distance. Right. I could try, at least.

But my heart hammered as I watched them through the window.

Ryan stepped out of the cottage. Sunlight broke through the clouds, catching his dark hair. Beyond him, the ocean sparkled. Our eyes locked across the small yards.

Time stretched.

I couldn't look away. The world faded. Just the two of us in this charged moment, the sound of waves and seagulls disappearing into nothing.

Henry's voice broke the spell. "Hey, Ryan!" He called out, tone light and teasing.

Ryan turned back to him, nodding. Henry grinned, clapping Ryan on the back like they were celebrating a victory.

Ryan glanced back in my direction one more time. "Can't beat the view," I overheard.

He turned toward the ocean, but for half a second, his eyes had been on my cottage.

My stomach dropped. Did he mean...? No. The ocean. Obviously, the ocean.

Oh no. He's going to buy it. He's really going to live next door. On this quiet, isolated road where there's nowhere to hide.

I turned back to my easel, trying to focus on the painting. The ocean study needed another layer. Cool blues. Maybe some violet in the shadows. My hand was steady as I loaded the brush. See? Totally fine. Completely calm about my new neighbor situation.

A tremendous crash echoed from my bedroom, followed by Dali's triumphant meow.

"DALI, NO!"

Chapter Four

The Grind

Ryan

"Dozer, no! That's not—" I lunged for the sandwich board as it tipped. The massive puppy darted in, tail helicoptering with joy, and shoved his nose against the chalkboard surface, smearing today's coffee special into an abstract masterpiece. "I swear he thinks everything's a game."

Dozer executed a perfect play-bow and barked once, as if to say, "Your move, human."

"Hey! He's got personality!" Henry called from inside The Grind, coffee cup in hand, laughter bubbling up.

I shot back, tone gruff. "He's got no manners!"

The corners of my mouth threatened to betray me. It was hard to stay serious when Dozer was being so ridiculous. Finally, Dozer plopped down outside, looking like he'd just won a prize.

We stepped inside from the cold. The rich scent of coffee and fresh pastries hit me, mixing with the low hum of conversation. The Grind was small and cozy, all exposed brick and mismatched furniture. Local art covered the walls. A chalkboard menu hung behind the counter, and soft indie music played from speakers I couldn't see.

Fresh paint gleamed on the trim. New tables dotted the space. The espresso machine looked brand new, all chrome and polish.

"Place looks good," I said, glancing around. "Hard to believe it took hurricane damage."

Henry grinned. "Reopened about a week before you got to town. New equipment, refinished floors, the works. Can't keep up with orders."

"Town's bouncing back."

"Always does." Henry grinned. "Seaholly's resilient like that."

Dozer immediately turned on his charm. He trotted over to a woman at the counter, his big brown eyes shining. She bent down, and her face lit up as she scratched behind his ears.

"Look at him go," I muttered, unable to hide my grin.

We grabbed a corner table. I'd barely settled into my chair when Dozer's head popped up. His nose twitched. His eyes locked onto something.

An elderly man at the next table had just received a blueberry scone. He set it down on his plate, turned to grab his coffee, and that was all the opportunity Dozer needed.

The massive puppy lunged. Snatched the scone off the plate in one smooth motion. Crumbs exploded everywhere.

"DOZER!" I jumped up, horrified.

The man turned back to his empty plate, confusion crossing his face. Then he looked down at Dozer, who was happily demolishing the evidence, tail wagging with pure joy.

"I am so sorry," I said, rushing over. "He's new. I'm still training him. I'll pay for that. And another one. I'm really sorry."

The man stared at Dozer for a long moment. Then his face cracked into a smile. "Well, at least someone's enjoying it." He chuckled. "Don't worry about it, son. I've had dogs. They're trouble. But they're worth it."

"No, please, let me—"

"It's fine." The man waved me off.

I grabbed Dozer's collar and pulled him back to our table, mortified. Henry was trying not to laugh and failing.

"So much for having your life together," Henry said between chuckles.

I dropped into my chair, Dozer settling under the table like nothing had happened. "This was a mistake."

"The dog or the cottage?"

"Both. Maybe."

Henry leaned forward. "Speaking of which. Rachel."

"Don't." I kept my voice low but firm.

Henry's eyes sparked with mischief. "The way you two looked at each other—"

"We were wrangling animals. It was chaos."

"Chaos or not, it was chemistry." He grinned like he'd just discovered hidden treasure.

I crossed my arms. "It doesn't matter."

"Why not?"

"She's Maya's friend. Maya warned me she's dealing with her own stuff. Not looking to complicate things."

Henry studied me for a long moment. "And what about you? Are you ready for this?"

"Ready for what?"

"Whatever's happening between you two." He gestured vaguely. "I saw how you looked at her. That's not nothing."

My jaw clenched. "I came here for a fresh start. Clean slate. No complications."

"You keep saying that." Henry took a sip of his coffee. "But I think you spent so long trying to be what your ex wanted, trying to fit into that department's politics, that you forgot what you actually want."

I stayed silent. He wasn't wrong. My ex-fiancée had wanted me to play the game. Keep my head down. Choose career advancement over doing the right thing. When I couldn't be that guy anymore, everything fell apart.

"Rachel's not going to try to change you," Henry continued. "She barely has her own life together. But maybe that's exactly what you need."

I thought about her paint-splattered smile. The way she'd clutched that hissing cat. The chaos surrounding her like an aura. "It's a bad idea."

"Probably," Henry agreed. "But you're thinking about buying that cottage anyway, aren't you?"

Before I could answer, the café door burst open.

My crew spotted me right away, and a wave of teasing grins washed over their faces.

"Rodriguez! Fancy meeting you here!" Martinez shouted as they approached, their laughter filling the air.

My face heated up.

"Look who's got a puppy!" Cooper yelled, pointing under the table. "You actually kept him!"

Dozer, sensing the attention, wiggled out from beneath the table, his tail wagging like a flag. He soaked up their affection, leaning into their hands as they all bent down to pet him.

The crew shifted their focus. "So we heard about the cottage viewing..." Martinez began, eyes glinting with mischief.

"Next to a certain artist..." another chimed in, nudging his buddy.

"Small town, word travels fast." One of them laughed, glancing at me.

I glared at them. Said nothing.

"Oh, he's got it bad."

"I don't have anything," I said flatly.

"Yet," they all said in unison, voices dripping with playful mockery.

My cheeks burned. Henry was glowing with delight. They launched into every embarrassing detail they'd heard. The animal chase. The awkward moments. The mix-up between "Dolly" and "Dali." Each story made me squirm.

"You moved here for a fresh start and immediately found trouble."

"The best kind of trouble," another added, grinning wide.

Just then, Dozer spotted someone at another table with a muffin. His curiosity piqued, he stretched out, knocking my coffee cup over with his wagging tail. The hot liquid spilled across the table, and I jumped up, trying to save what I could.

The crew howled with laughter, their joy echoing in the small café. I scrambled to clean up the mess while Dozer looked pleased with himself, tail still wagging as if he'd just accomplished something grand.

Henry, leaning back in his chair, deadpanned, "You're really selling that 'I've got my life together' image."

"I came here for a fresh start. Quiet. Simple." My voice cracked a little.

One of the guys leaned forward, shaking his head. "Buddy, you're looking at a house next to a woman who sets off fire alarms, and you adopted a puppy the size of a small horse. You're doing 'simple' wrong."

Even I had to laugh at that. I looked down at Dozer, who was now sniffing around the floor as if searching for more crumbs.

"Seriously, though," Martinez said. "You signing the papers?"

"Haven't decided yet."

Cooper snorted. "Right. That's why you looked at her like that."

I shot him a glare, but it only made them laugh harder.

"Good luck with that, Rodriguez," Martinez said as they headed for the door. "Small town. Everyone's gonna know everything."

"Great," I muttered.

The café buzzed with chatter as my crew left for the station, leaving Henry and me at our table. Dozer was busy working his magic on the other customers, leaning into their legs for pets and treats. His charm was undeniable.

Henry sipped his coffee, eyes fixed on me. "You're going to buy it, aren't you?"

I pulled out my phone and opened the photos from yesterday's viewing. The cottage was small but solid. Good bones, like I'd told Henry. But it needed work. The kitchen cabinets were outdated. The bathroom tile was cracked. The deck out back looked like it might collapse if you breathed on it wrong.

I scrolled through the images. Peeling paint. Overgrown yard. A fence that leaned at an angle.

"It needs a lot of work," I said, more to myself than Henry.

"You're handy, right?"

"Yeah, but this is months of weekends. New deck. Tile work. Paint. Landscaping."

"So?" Henry raised an eyebrow. "You've got time. And it's not like you have anything better to do."

I kept scrolling. Stopped at a photo of the front porch. You could see Rachel's cottage in the background, close enough to notice the wind chimes hanging from her eaves. Close enough to see the paint-splattered tarp covering something in her yard.

Close enough.

"Good view?" Henry asked, grin spreading.

My throat tightened. I thought about Rachel standing in her yard, paint-splattered and laughing. The way her eyes had met mine across the space between the cottages.

"Yeah," I admitted quietly. "Good view."

Henry's grin widened. "So what are you waiting for?"

I stared at the realtor's contact. The screen glowed in front of me, each word heavy with possibility. I thought about Rachel next door. The complication, the risk, the thrill of it. Henry watched me silently, sipping his coffee, waiting for me to make a move.

Taking a deep breath, I made my decision. I typed a message: "I'll take it. When can we close?" My finger hovered over the send button. Doubt crept in, but I pushed it aside.

"Don't overthink it," Henry said, voice steady.

With one last moment of hesitation, I hit send before I could change my mind.

Henry raised his coffee cup. "To fresh starts and terrible decisions."

I clinked my cup against his, a grin spreading across my face. "And chaotic neighbors."

Dozer barked as if in agreement, his tail wagging like a flag.

What am I doing?

Chapter Five

The Hardware Store

Rachel

I stood on my tiptoes on the bottom shelf, one hand gripping the edge of the upper shelving unit for balance, the other reaching desperately for a package of anchors on the overstock shelf.

"Come on," I muttered, fingers brushing the package. So close. "Just a little more..."

The fluorescent lights buzzed overhead. Country music played softly from speakers I couldn't see. The smell of sawdust and paint thinner filled my nose. My broken curtain rod lay on the floor below me, abandoned in my quest for the mysterious hardware.

I stretched higher, my flannel shirt riding up, one foot leaving the shelf for extra reach. Almost there. The package was labeled "Heavy Duty Drywall Anchors," but who knew if that was what I actually needed. There were seventeen types. Seventeen. Who needed seventeen types of anchors?

A hand reached past me, effortlessly grabbed the package I'd been struggling with, and held it out.

"This what you need?"

I yelped, lost my balance, and would have fallen if a strong arm hadn't steadied me at the elbow.

Ryan Rodriguez stood there, one hand holding the anchors, the other keeping me upright, looking entirely too amused. Clean jeans. Flannel shirt. Work boots. A shopping cart full of locks and renovation supplies sat behind him.

Our eyes met.

"Oh. Hi." My voice came out higher than normal.

"Hi." He glanced at my curtain rod on the floor, then at the wall of anchors, then back at me. One corner of his mouth twitched. "Need help?"

Yes. Desperately. "I'm fine. Just... looking."

"At anchors."

"Yep. Anchors. Very interesting. So many types."

"Uh-huh." He was definitely fighting a smile now. "What happened to your curtain rod?"

I looked down at the sad, bent metal on the floor. The brackets dangled uselessly. "Dali happened."

"Your cat."

"My very dramatic cat." I sighed, climbing down from the shelf. "She decided at two in the morning that she was a lion and the curtains were prey. Climbed straight up them like she was scaling Kilimanjaro. The whole rod came crashing down."

Ryan's mouth twitched. "Does everything in your life involve destruction?"

"Pretty much, yeah."

He found it charming instead of off-putting. I could see it in the way his eyes crinkled at the corners. Derek would've rolled his eyes at the Dali story. It would've made me feel foolish for not knowing how to fix it myself. Ryan just looked... amused.

He moved past me to the anchors, pulling packages off the wall with the confidence of someone who understood exactly what each piece did. "You need drywall anchors. These. And this bracket size based on your rod diameter."

His competence shouldn't be distracting. It definitely shouldn't make my stomach flip.

I watched him explain the difference between hollow wall anchors and toggle bolts. His hands moved as he talked, gesturing at the packaging, miming the installation process. He made it sound simple. Made me feel less foolish for not knowing.

"Do you have a ladder I could borrow?" I asked when he finished.

"I don't need a ladder."

I blinked. "What do you mean? I need a ladder."

"I could install it for you. Without a ladder. I'm six-three."

"Well, I'm five-nine and I need a ladder."

His mouth curved. "Do you know how to install drywall anchors?"

"How hard can it be? I was just going to... nail it back up?"

"No. Absolutely not." He said it with genuine horror. "You'll pull the whole wall down. Then you'll have an angry landlord AND a smug cat."

I couldn't help grinning. "You said that with a lot of conviction."

"Because it's true." He grabbed a package of the right anchors and added them to my growing pile of supplies. "Let me help. I'm your neighbor now. It's what neighbors do."

The word neighbor settled between us, loaded with possibility.

"You don't have to—"

"I want to." His brown eyes were steady on mine. "Besides, I can't have you destroying the cottage next door. Property values and all."

Professional distance. That was the plan. But Ryan stood there with my broken curtain rod supplies, waiting for an answer.

"Okay," I heard myself say. "Thank you."

We moved through the store together. He pointed out useful items I didn't know existed. Explained the difference between wood screws and drywall screws. Showed me which level was the best quality for the price.

I found myself relaxing into his presence. His dry humor made the whole experience less overwhelming. When I picked up a measuring tape covered in flowers, he raised an eyebrow.

"You need a real measuring tape," he said. Not a question.

"I like flowers."

"It's three inches short of the standard length, and the lock mechanism is plastic. It'll break in a month."

I held it up anyway. "But flowers."

Ryan shook his head, but he was smiling. He grabbed a better quality tape—plain black, professional—and added it to my basket. "Get this one for actual measuring. Keep the flower one for looking pretty."

"That's ridiculous. I don't need two measuring tapes."

"You will when the pretty one breaks."

I laughed and let him add it to my pile. We moved through the store like we'd done this before—easy conversation, comfortable silences, the kind of rhythm that usually took months to build with someone.

At the paint section, I stopped to examine color samples. Couldn't help myself. Always looking, always seeing possibilities.

Ryan paused beside me. "Thinking about repainting?"

"Maybe? I don't know." I held up a sage green card, then a deeper forest shade. "My studio walls are white. Clean and practical. But sometimes I wonder if color would help me think better."

"What does your art look like?"

The question surprised me. Most people asked what I painted or if I sold anything. Ryan wanted to know what it looked like—the aesthetic, the feeling.

"Ocean scenes mostly. Seascapes. Some portraits." I waved the green samples. "Lots of blues and greens. Water colors."

"Then paint your walls." He said it like the decision was obvious. "If you spend all day with those colors, why not live in them?"

I stared at him. Derek had hated it when I talked about repainting. Said white walls were more professional, more adult. That my impulse to add color everywhere was childish.

"What?" Ryan asked, noticing my expression.

"Nothing. That's just... good advice."

We wound up at the checkout together, our separate purchases merging into adjacent spaces on the conveyor belt. The cashier rang up my items first, and I caught sight of Mrs. Henderson one aisle over, staring directly at us with undisguised interest.

My face went hot. Small towns. Everyone saw everything.

Ryan noticed me notice. He glanced over, spotted Mrs. Henderson, and waved. The older woman beamed and waved back like she'd been caught at nothing more suspicious than shopping.

"She's going to tell Maya," I muttered.

"Maya already knows I'm moving in next door. This won't be news."

"She's going to make it news."

His shoulder brushed mine as he leaned in slightly. "Let her. I've got nothing to hide."

The words sent warmth through my chest. Like this—us standing together, shopping together, making plans—wasn't something to hide. Wasn't something wrong.

Outside, we loaded purchases into my car. Ryan carried the heavier items without asking, arranging them carefully in my trunk so nothing would shift during the drive.

"When's good for the curtain rod installation?" I pulled out my phone, already scrolling through my calendar.

We compared schedules—my art classes, his shifts at the firehouse. Found a pocket of time on Thursday afternoon when we were both free.

"I should warn you," Ryan said. "I'm particular about things being level. It's going to be perfectly straight."

"Nothing in my house is perfectly straight."

His eyes crinkled at the corners. "I noticed."

My heart did something complicated. "I'll see you Thursday then."

"Thursday. Try not to destroy anything else before then."

"No promises. Dali's creative."

Ryan laughed again—that same genuine sound from earlier. It did things to me I didn't want to examine.

I drove home with my phone buzzing in the cupholder. Two texts from Maya before I even left the parking lot.

> **Heard you ran into Ryan at the hardware store.**

> **Small town, big gossip.**

I texted back at a red light.

> **How do you already know that??**

Mrs. Henderson was there. Obviously. She's already called me.

I groaned and dropped my forehead against the steering wheel. The light turned green. Someone honked behind me.

Another text came through as I pulled into my driveway.

> He's coming over Thursday to help you? That's very neighborly of him.

I sat in my parked car, staring at the bag of curtain rod supplies on my passenger seat. Hardware store supplies. From Ryan. Who was moving in next door. Who'd be in my cottage on Thursday, seeing exactly how chaotic I really was.

He was coming to my cottage. My chaotic, paint-covered, cat-destroyed cottage. It was going to be interesting.

I remembered his smile. The way his eyes warmed when he talked to me. How he'd explained the hardware patiently, without condescension.

I grabbed my supplies and headed inside, where Dali sat on the windowsill looking perfectly innocent. The cat's tail swished once, slow and deliberate.

"This is your fault," I told her.

Dali blinked, unconcerned, and began washing her paw.

My phone buzzed again.

Another text from Maya.

> Double date Friday? I promise to behave.

I typed back.

> He's just being nice. Neighbor stuff.

Maya fired back instantly.

> Keep telling yourself that. Haha.

She wasn't wrong.

I tossed my phone on the couch and looked at the empty space where my curtain rod used to be. At the paint-stained floors and the easels taking up half my living room, and the organized chaos that made sense to me but probably looked like madness to everyone else.

Dali meowed from her perch, and I could've sworn the cat was laughing at me.

Thursday was just a neighbor helping a neighbor.

It's not like we were going to share a meal together or anything.

Chapter Six

Ryan's Cottage

Ryan

Dozer galloped through the empty cottage with my work boot in his mouth. His floppy ears bounced, tail wagging like this was the best game he'd ever invented. The boot dangled like a trophy.

"Dozer. Drop it." I used my firm voice. The one that worked on recruits.

He paused, looked at me, and bolted in the opposite direction.

The movers laughed. Both of them. Standing in my half-empty living room with a couch between them, watching me get outsmarted by a puppy.

"Need help?" one of them asked, grinning.

"I've got it." I lunged for Dozer.

He dodged. Sprinted through the kitchen. Knocked over a stack of boxes labeled "KITCHEN - FRAGILE." The sound of breaking glass echoed through the cottage.

The movers weren't even pretending not to laugh anymore.

I cornered Dozer in the bedroom. He crouched low, boot still in his mouth, tail wagging. This was playtime. This was fun. This was absolutely not the organized, controlled moving day I'd planned.

"Give me the boot," I said.

Dozer's tail wagged harder.

I feinted left. He went right. I dove. He darted between my legs. I ended up sprawled on the floor, empty-handed, while Dozer trotted back to the living room victorious.

One of the movers was actually wiping tears from his eyes.

I got up, brushed myself off, and caught Dozer in the kitchen doorway. Grabbed the boot. Pulled. He pulled back. We had a brief tug-of-war before I managed to wrestle it free.

The boot was covered in slobber and had two new tooth marks.

"Great," I muttered.

I set it down and looked at its mate—still pristine, laces perfectly tied the way I'd left them this morning. Dozer immediately lunged for that one too.

"No!" I snatched it up. "You've destroyed enough for one day."

Dozer sat, tail still wagging, looking incredibly pleased with himself.

A knock on the door saved me from further humiliation.

I opened it to find Rachel holding a cardboard drink carrier with two coffee cups. Paint-splattered overalls. Oversized puffer coat. Hair in a messy bun held together by what might have been a paintbrush. Her cheeks were pink from the cold.

"Hi." She held up the coffees. "Thought you might need fuel. Moving day and all."

I stood there, sweaty and disheveled, holding my slobber-covered boot. "That's really nice of you."

"I heard the chaos from next door." Her eyes crinkled. "Figured you could use reinforcements."

Dozer bounded over, tail wagging with renewed enthusiasm. He jumped up, paws on her legs, nearly knocking the coffee carrier out of her hands.

"Dozer, down!" I grabbed his collar.

"It's okay." Rachel laughed and managed to get the coffees onto a box. Then she crouched down and let Dozer lick her face. "Hi, buddy. Are you making your dad's life difficult?"

Dozer's entire back end wagged.

"He stole my boot." I held it up as evidence. "And broke half my dishes."

"Sounds about right." She scratched behind Dozer's ears. "Dali once knocked over an entire bookshelf trying to catch a moth."

The movers appeared in the doorway, looking between us with knowing grins. "We're gonna grab the dresser from the truck," one of them said. "Take your time."

They left before I could respond.

Rachel stood, brushing dog hair off her overalls. "I can go if you're busy. I just thought—"

"No. Stay." The word came out too quick. Too eager. I tried to course-correct. "I mean, if you want. The coffee's great. Thank you."

She smiled and grabbed two cups, handing me one. "Where do you want things?"

"I have a plan." I pulled out my phone and showed her the furniture layout I'd mapped out. Every piece measured and marked. Every room plotted for maximum function and flow.

Rachel studied it, head tilted. "This won't work."

"What?"

"Your couch." She pointed at the diagram. "You have it facing the wall with the window. You'll have glare on your TV during the day."

I looked at my carefully measured plan. She was right.

"And your dining table." She gestured to another section. "You have it in the corner. But if you put it here—" She pointed to a spot I'd left empty. "—you get the morning light. Makes breakfast better."

"I measured everything."

"You measured for function." Her voice was gentle. "Not for how you'll actually live here."

I wanted to argue. Wanted to defend my precise planning. But she moved to the window, gesturing with her coffee cup.

"The light comes in here in the afternoon. See how it hits that wall?" She traced an invisible line through the air. "If you put your bookshelf there instead of where you planned, you'll actually be able to see the spines. Your plan has it in shadow."

I looked at where she was pointing. She was right. Again.

"You're kind of annoying," I said.

She laughed. "I get that a lot."

The movers returned with the dresser. Rachel immediately started directing them, explaining her vision for the space. They looked at me for confirmation. I nodded, still holding my slobber-boot.

We fell into a rhythm. Rachel seeing the space with her artist's eye. Me providing the muscle and precision. Her chaos meeting my order somewhere in the middle.

She'd suggest. I'd execute. We'd adjust together.

When we moved the couch, our hands brushed reaching for the same corner. When we hung the TV, she held the level while I drilled. When we positioned the bookshelf, she stood back critiquing while I made micro-adjustments until she was satisfied.

"Left. No, your other left. Up a hair. Perfect."

Dozer helped by stealing packing paper and running through the cottage with it streaming behind him like a cape. Every time we turned around, there was more chaos. More destruction. More mess.

Rachel thought it was hilarious.

"He's got spirit," she said, watching him attack a roll of bubble wrap.

"He's got no survival instinct." But I was smiling.

Through the window, I caught sight of Dali sitting in Rachel's yard. The cat watched the proceedings with obvious disdain, tail flicking with irritation.

Dozer spotted her. His entire body went rigid. Then he launched himself at the window, barking joyfully, tail wagging, paws scrabbling against the glass.

Dali didn't move. Just stared at him like he was the most pathetic creature she'd ever seen.

"She's judging us," Rachel said.

"She's judging him."

"She judges everyone." Rachel moved to the window. "Dali! Be nice!"

The cat yawned, showing all her teeth, then turned and stalked away.

Dozer whined, heartbroken.

"She'll come around," Rachel said. "Maybe. Possibly. Probably not."

"I'm starving," Rachel announced, pulling out her phone. "Pizza? My treat for letting me boss you around all day."

"You already brought coffee. I've got this one."

Twenty minutes later, the delivery guy handed over two large boxes at the door.

We took a break, sitting on the floor among half-unpacked boxes. Rachel bit into her slice and cheese stretched between her mouth and the pizza, refusing to break. She laughed, trying to catch it with her finger. Dozer's head popped up, nose twitching at the smell of pepperoni.

"Don't even think about it," I warned him.

He looked at me with those big puppy eyes. Rachel snuck him a piece of crust when she thought I wasn't looking.

"I saw that."

"He helped move furniture," she said, grinning. "He earned it."

"He knocked over three boxes and stole my boot."

"Exactly. Very helpful." She took another bite. "Besides, you can't resist him either. I've seen you slip him treats."

"That's different. Those are training rewards."

"Uh-huh. For what? Being cute?"

I didn't have a good answer for that. Dozer sprawled across both our laps, snoring. His paws twitched in his sleep.

"He's dreaming," Rachel said softly.

"Probably about stealing more boots."

She laughed. Her shoulder pressed against mine in the small space. Paint still under her fingernails. Hair falling out of its bun. She looked tired and happy and completely at home in my disaster of a moving day.

I wanted this. This exact chaos.

The thought hit me hard. Unexpected. Terrifying.

"What?" Rachel asked, catching my expression.

"Nothing. Just... thanks for today. I couldn't have done this without you."

"That's what neighbors are for, right?"

The word felt wrong. Insufficient. We weren't just neighbors. Couldn't be just neighbors. Not after today. Not after the hardware store. Not after she'd spent hours helping me make this cottage feel like home.

But I didn't know what we were. Didn't know what I was allowed to want.

The moment stretched. Rachel looked at her phone. "I should probably go. Let you finish unpacking."

I didn't want her to leave. Couldn't think of a reason for her to stay that didn't sound desperate or presumptuous.

"Okay," I said.

She stood, carefully extracting herself from under Dozer's paw. The puppy barely stirred.

I walked her to the door. She paused on the threshold, looking back at the cottage. "It's going to be great when you're done. I can already see it."

"You gave me a better vision than I had."

"That's what I do." She smiled. "See possibilities."

She left. I closed the door and looked around at the half-unpacked cottage.

My phone rang. Maya.

"How's the move?"

"Chaotic. Dozer destroyed half my stuff. Rachel helped."

"Of course she did." Maya's voice warmed. "She's good people."

"She is."

"Ryan..." Maya paused. "Be patient with her, okay? She's going through some stuff."

My hand tightened on the phone. "What stuff?"

"Not my story to tell. But be patient."

We hung up. I looked out the window into the gray winter dusk. Rachel's cottage lights were on. Maya's words echoed: "Be patient with her."

I could do that.

Chapter Seven

The Easel

Rachel

I shifted the seascape left. Too much. Shifted it right. Still wrong. Stepped back, tilted my head, moved it left again.

"It's perfect," Vivian called from across the gallery. "You're stalling."

I stepped back, arms crossed, staring at the painting like it might reveal some secret alignment I'd missed. Ocean waves crashed across the canvas in shades of blue and gray and white. One of my better pieces. The light hit it perfectly from this angle.

It looked fine.

I adjusted it anyway.

Vivian appeared beside me, wearing a straight, fitted, tailored A-line dress and pointed pumps. I was still in my heavy sweater from the cold drive over. She was in her late fifties, elegant in the way gallery owners always seemed to be. Honey blonde hair swept into a perfect twist. Reading glasses on a chain around her neck. The kind of woman who made style look effortless.

"What's distracting you?" she asked.

"Nothing. The mural project."

"The mural." She said it flat. Not buying it. "Or the firefighter?"

Heat crept up my neck. "How did you—"

"Small town, darling." Vivian smiled. "Also, you've been sketching hands for fifteen minutes."

I looked down at my notebook. She was right. Ryan's hands filled the page. Strong fingers. The way they'd held the hardware store bags. How they'd moved when he explained drywall anchors.

I snapped the notebook shut.

"It's not like—"

"Of course not." Vivian's smile widened. "That's why you've drawn his hands with photographic detail."

I wanted to argue. Couldn't. My cheeks burned.

"My new neighbor is complicated," I managed.

"Neighbors usually are." She gestured toward her office. "Come on. Let's talk about the show."

The show. Right. The reason I was here.

"Oh, before I forget," Vivian said, pausing before we reached her office. "Tomorrow. Galentine's lunch at The Pier House. One o'clock. You, me, and a few of the other local artists. Say yes."

I smiled. "That sounds perfect."

"Good. You need to get out more. Socialize with people who aren't covered in paint or pulling shifts at the fire station." Her eyes sparkled. "Though if you want to invite your firefighter neighbor..."

"Vivian."

She laughed. "Fine, fine. Just us girls. Wear something nice. Celebrate being single and fabulous."

"I can do that."

"Excellent. Come on." She led me toward her office.

I followed her past white walls hung with local art. The space smelled like coffee and musty paper. Vivian had owned The Easel for twenty-four years, championed local artists, connected us with collectors who actually paid.

She'd been trying to get me a solo show for months.

We sat in her office. She pulled up images on her laptop—my seascapes, the ones she wanted to feature. Each painting represented hours of work, mornings on the beach, salt air and changing light.

"Opening night is coming up soon," Vivian said. "Robert Vanderson will be there."

My stomach flipped. "The Portland collector?"

"The same." She leaned back in her chair. "He's specifically interested in your work, Rachel. This could lead to gallery representation in Portland. More commissions. Real money."

Real money. The kind I needed.

"You'd need to produce three or four more pieces," Vivian continued. "Strong pieces. And be present for installation, the opening, and the meet-and-greet after."

Not much time. But doable.

"That's ambitious," I said.

"It's perfect timing." Vivian watched me over her glasses. "This is a good thing, Rachel. Why do you look worried?"

I forced a smile. "Not worried. Processing."

She didn't look convinced but let it drop. Turned her laptop toward me, showed me the proposed layout. Where each painting would hang. The lighting plan. How the space would flow.

It was beautiful. Professional. Everything I'd worked toward.

"I also have an idea," Vivian said. "I've seen your mural sketches."

I'd brought them yesterday to show her my progress. Preliminary studies of firefighters, rough compositions, faces I was starting to know.

"They're stunning," she continued. "Raw. Emotional. They capture something real."

"Thanks. It's still early work."

"What if we did a companion series for the show? 'Everyday Heroes of Seaholly.' The firefighters, obviously. But also teachers, shopkeepers, people who make the community work." She leaned forward, excited now. "We could sell prints with proceeds going to the fire department. Perfect community connection. Great PR. Meaningful work."

My mind went immediately to Ryan. More time sketching him. Photographing him. Studying the way he moved, the expressions he didn't know he made.

Professionally brilliant.

Personally dangerous.

"That's a lot to take on," I said carefully.

"You're already doing the studies for the mural. This would expand on them." Vivian smiled. "Plus, it gives you a reason to spend more time with your firefighter neighbor."

Heat flooded my face again. "Vivian—"

"Just saying." She held up her hands, innocent. "Artistic inspiration comes in many forms."

I should've been thrilled. This was the opportunity I'd been working towards. Recognition. Validation. A real chance at making art my full career instead of something I squeezed between teaching kids and scraping by.

Instead, my phone rang. Mom's ringtone.

I grabbed it like a lifeline. "Sorry. I need to—"

"Of course." Vivian waved me toward the door. "Take your time."

I stepped outside onto the sidewalk. The cold air hit my face. Gray clouds hung low overhead. I answered before I could overthink it.

"Hi, Mom."

"Rachel, sweetheart." Mom's voice was tight, strained. "I'm sorry to bother you. Is this a bad time?"

"No, I'm at the gallery. What's wrong?"

"It's my tooth. The back molar." She paused, and I heard her wince. "It's been hurting since yesterday morning, but now it's gotten worse. I can barely chew."

My stomach tightened. "Did you call Dr. Maxwell?"

"I tried. They can't get me in until next Tuesday." Her voice wavered. "I don't know if I can wait that long. The pain keeps getting worse."

"Amy called urgent care but they said to call a dentist."

"Okay. Don't worry, Mom. Let me make some calls. I'll find someone who can see you sooner."

"Rachel, you don't have to—"

"Mom. I'm going to handle this. Can you take ibuprofen for now?"

"I took some an hour ago. It's not helping much."

"Okay. I'll call you back in a bit, alright? Just hang tight."

"Thank you, sweetheart. I'm sorry to—"

"Don't apologize. I'll figure this out. Talk soon."

"I love you."

"Love you too."

I hung up. My mind was already running through dentist offices in Mom's area.

The gallery door opened behind me. Vivian appeared with her coat, concern written across her face.

"Rachel." She touched my arm gently. "What happened?"

"Mom's tooth. Severe pain. Her regular dentist can't see her until next week." I looked at Vivian. "I need to find someone who can see her sooner. Probably tomorrow."

Vivian's expression shifted from concern to understanding. "The lunch."

"I'm so sorry. I'll have to cancel. If I can get her an appointment tomorrow, I need to drive her. She can't manage it alone."

"Of course not. Don't even think twice about it." Vivian squeezed my arm. "Come inside. You can use my office to make calls. I'll pull up dentists in her area."

Relief flooded through me. "Thank you."

"That's what friends do." She guided me back into the gallery. "Let's find your mom some help."

We went back inside. Vivian pulled up her laptop, typed quickly. "Here. Emergency dental clinics in your mom's area. Start with these."

She turned the screen toward me. Five offices listed.

I pulled out my phone and started calling.

The first office had no openings. The second was closed for the day. The third could fit her in next week—not soon enough.

On the fourth call, a receptionist with a kind voice said, "We have an opening tomorrow at eleven. Dr. Russell does emergency appointments on Fridays."

Relief washed through me. "I'll take it. Her name is Beverly Brown."

I gave them Mom's information, confirmed the address, and triple-checked the time.

When I hung up, Vivian was watching with a small smile.

"You got it?"

"Tomorrow at eleven." I texted Mom immediately.

> *Found you an appointment. Tomorrow at 11am with Dr. Russell. I'll pick you up at 9:30.*

Her response came fast.

> *Thank you, sweetheart. You're a lifesaver.*

I looked up at Vivian. "Crisis averted. For now."

"Thank you," I said. "For helping. For the office space. For understanding about tomorrow."

"That's what friends do." Vivian sat across from me. "Now. About the show. We still have time to adjust the timeline if you need it. Taking care of your mom comes first."

"No." The word came out firm. "I can do both. Tomorrow's just one day. The appointment, drive back, make sure she's settled. I'll be home by evening."

Vivian studied my face. "And the companion series? The heroes of Seaholly?"

Ryan's face flashed through my mind. His hands. The sketches I couldn't stop making.

"Yes," I said. "I want to."

"Good." Vivian pulled her laptop closer. "Then let's talk timeline."

We'd spent the next hour planning. Which pieces needed finishing. When I'd deliver them. How many studies I'd need for the companion series. Vivian walked me through each step, made it feel manageable.

Almost manageable.

Late afternoon had arrived by the time I left. The sun hung low over the ocean, washing everything in coral and rose despite the cold. Beautiful. Light I liked to chase with my camera.

I drove home past Ryan's cottage. His truck was in the driveway. Lights on inside. He was there. Right next door.

In my own driveway now, I sat there, engine running.

Tomorrow would be long. Early start, hour-plus drive, dentist appointment, making sure Mom was settled and had everything she needed. No Galentine's lunch with Vivian and the other artists. Just dentist chairs and highway traffic.

But Mom's tooth would be handled. That mattered more.

I grabbed my notebook from the passenger seat. Flipped it open to the sketches of Ryan's hands. Added another from memory—the way he'd held his coffee cup at the hardware store, fingers wrapped around the warmth.

My phone buzzed. A text from Captain Patterson.

> *Stopping by the station this week? The guys are excited to see your progress.*

I typed back quickly.

> *Tuesday work?*

> *Perfect. 10 am?*

> *See you then.*

I looked at Ryan's cottage. His truck in the driveway. Lights on inside.

The mural would take time. The show had a deadline. Mom would need me again—tooth pain today, something else next week.

I didn't know how it would all fit together. But I'd figure it out.

One thing at a time.

Chapter Eight

The Firehouse

Ryan

"Stop, drop, and roll!"

Sixteen elementary school kids hit the firehouse floor, giggling and wiggling as they practiced the safety move I'd just demonstrated. Half of them rolled into each other. One girl rolled right into Dozer, who thought this was the best game ever and started licking her face.

The kids erupted in laughter. Within seconds, the safety demonstration devolved into chaos as every kid abandoned the exercise to swarm my dog.

"Dozer!" one boy shouted, throwing his arms around the puppy's neck. Dozer promptly sat on him.

"He's so soft!" another girl squealed, burying her face in his fur. Dozer's tail wagged so hard it knocked over a traffic cone.

"Is he trying to eat my shoelaces?" a boy asked, giggling as Dozer mouthed at his sneakers.

Dozer was in heaven. His tail wagged so hard his entire back end moved. He soaked up the attention, moving from kid to kid, licking faces, accepting pets, stepping on toes, knocking small children over with his enthusiasm.

"Alright, alright." I tried to regain control. "Dozer's very friendly, but we need to finish learning about fire safety."

No one was listening. They were too busy cooing over my dog, who had tangled himself in his own leash and was now spinning in circles trying to free himself.

Martinez appeared beside me. "Very professional demonstration, Rodriguez. Really driving home the safety message."

"Shut up."

"Should we add 'attacked by friendly dog' to our list of fire hazards?" Cooper called from across the bay.

The crew was loving this.

Tommy hung back from the crowd, watching. When the chaos cleared slightly, he approached Dozer carefully, quietly. The dog turned to him immediately, sat down, and let Tommy pet him without the wiggling excitement he'd shown the others.

"He likes you," I said.

Tommy's face lit up. "Really?"

"Really. You're being gentle and calm. Dogs appreciate that."

The morning had started like most mornings at the station. Coffee. Equipment checks. My crew giving me endless grief about Rachel.

"Rodriguez, you gonna ask her out or just moon over her forever?" Martinez had called from across the bay.

"There's nothing to moon over. We're neighbors."

"Neighbors who spent four hours reorganizing your furniture," Cooper added. "Mrs. Henderson told my wife all about it. Very cozy, apparently."

"Mrs. Henderson needs a hobby."

"She has one. Watching you." Coop grinned.

The crew had laughed. I'd tried to focus on checking the hose connections.

Frank, our senior firefighter, came to stand beside me. He'd been with the department for twenty-eight years, had the kind of steady presence that made everyone listen when he talked.

"Life's short, Rodriguez," he said quietly. "Don't waste time being scared."

Before I could respond, Chief Patterson's voice boomed across the bay. "Rodriguez! My office."

The crew made kissing noises as I walked away.

Chief Patterson sat behind his desk, looking at his computer screen. He gestured for me to sit.

"The mural project. Rachel Brown starts her photography sessions next week. Tuesday, right?"

"Yes, sir. I've been coordinating with her."

"Good." He leaned back in his chair. "The town council called this morning. They're very excited about this. Want to make sure we're giving her full access."

"She'll have whatever she needs."

"I know she will. You've been handling it well." He paused, then smiled slightly. "Also got an interesting call this morning. Mrs. Henderson."

My stomach dropped. "Sir?"

"She wanted to tell me what a wonderful asset Dozer is to the community. Said the kids at her church group couldn't stop talking about him after you brought him to their fire safety presentation last month." Chief paused, mouth twitching. "Although she did mention he ate three donuts off the refreshment table and knocked over a folding chair chasing his own tail."

I winced. "That sounds accurate."

"She also said he drooled on her good shoes." Chief was definitely fighting a smile now. "But apparently the kids loved him anyway. She suggested we should consider getting a therapy dog for the department. For community outreach, helping people after traumatic calls. She specifically mentioned Dozer has potential."

Potential. Not perfection. That tracked.

"He's still a puppy, sir. He's chaotic."

"He's calm with people who need calm. I've noticed that." Chief pulled up his computer. "Think about it. There are certification programs. Could be good for the department. Good for community relations."

I thought about Dozer with the kids today. How gentle he'd been despite their enthusiasm. How he'd sat patiently for Tommy.

"I'll look into it."

"Good man." Chief closed his laptop. "Now get out of here. You've got a school group to finish educating."

When I returned to the bay, the kids had been corralled by their teacher. Dozer sat beside her, perfectly behaved, as if he hadn't just caused a minor riot.

"Alright." I drew their attention back. "Who can tell me what the most important thing to remember in a fire is?"

"Get out!" several kids shouted at once.

"Exactly. Don't try to save your toys, don't hide, don't wait. Get out and call 911."

I showed them the fire truck. Let them climb into the cab. Explained what each piece of equipment did and why it mattered. Made it fun and interactive so they'd remember.

Tommy watched everything with careful attention. When I asked for a volunteer to try on the helmet, he raised his hand. Small victory.

One little girl raised her hand. "Are you a hero?"

The question caught me off guard. "I'm just someone who helps people."

"That's what heroes do," she insisted.

"Then I guess we're all heroes." I gestured to my crew. "We show up when people need us."

When the teacher started gathering the kids to leave, Tommy hung back. He approached slowly, shyly, holding a folded piece of paper.

"I made this for you," he said, voice quiet.

I took it, unfolded it carefully. A drawing. Detailed and careful, colored with obvious concentration. A firefighter standing in front of a fire truck, gear rendered with surprising accuracy for a kid his age.

Rachel's teaching style was all over it. The way she'd shown him to observe details, to take his time, to put care into his work.

"Miss Rachel says heroes come in all kinds," Tommy said. "Not just firefighters. But... are you a hero?"

I knelt to his level. My throat went tight. "I think real heroes are people who show up when others need them. Like you calling 911 if there's an emergency. That makes you a hero too."

"Really?"

"Really. You know what to do to keep yourself and your family safe. That's important."

Tommy smiled, gap-toothed and genuine. Then he threw his arms around my neck in a quick hug before running to catch up with his class.

I stood there holding his drawing, watching them file out. The teacher waved her thanks. The kids called goodbye to Dozer, who wagged his tail at everyone.

Frank walked over, coffee in hand. "That dog's got what it takes. Saw how he was with those kids."

"Yeah?"

"Calm. Patient. Let them pet him without getting overexcited." Frank took a sip of coffee. "Chief mentioned the therapy dog idea."

"He did."

"You should do it. We've been talking about getting one for the department. Community outreach, school visits, helping people after traumatic calls." Frank gestured at Dozer. "He's got the temperament for it. And he clearly loves the attention."

I thought about it. Dozer at my side during calls. Helping comfort people who'd just lost everything in a fire. Visiting schools, hospitals, nursing homes.

"What would it take?"

"Training. Certification. A couple months of work." Frank smiled. "But I've seen a lot of dogs come through here over the years. He's got what it takes."

Dozer leaned against my leg, solid and warm. A therapy dog. My chaotic puppy who'd stolen my boot and destroyed half my moving boxes, helping people heal.

"I'll look into it."

Frank clapped me on the shoulder. "Good man. Now get back to work before Martinez starts more rumors about you and the artist."

The rest of the shift passed in routine calls. A false alarm at the grocery store. An elderly woman who'd fallen and needed help getting up, no injuries but scared and shaken. We stayed with her until her daughter arrived, made her tea, made sure she felt safe.

When my shift ended, I went home. Fed Dozer. Made dinner. Hung Tommy's drawing on my refrigerator with a magnet.

A hero.

The kid saw me as a hero.

I didn't feel like one. I felt like a guy who'd left his last post under a cloud, who'd been set up for failure by a captain who didn't like him, who'd chosen the safest option by transferring somewhere smaller and quieter.

But Tommy didn't know any of that. He just knew I'd taught him the right way to stay safe.

Maybe that was enough.

My phone buzzed.

Text from Rachel

> *Hi! Just wanted to confirm Tuesday for the photography session. 10 am still work? And we're still on for Thursday at 3:30 for the curtain rod?*

My pulse jumped. Two days this week. Tuesday at the firehouse. Thursday at her cottage.

> *Tuesday at 10 works. Thursday at 3:30 works. See you then.*

Three dots appeared. Disappeared. Appeared again.

> *Thanks for being flexible with the schedule. I know coordinating all this is extra work.*

> *It's not extra work. Happy to help.*

The dots appeared again, then disappeared. No response.

I stared at my phone. Tuesday was four days away. Thursday was six.

Six days until I'd be in her cottage, installing her curtain rod, in her space where everything was paint and chaos and exactly her.

I looked at Tommy's drawing on my fridge. At Dozer sprawled on the floor, already snoring. At my cottage which was finally starting to feel like home.

Keep it professional, I told myself. *She's the artist. You're the liaison. That's all.*

But I was already counting down the days.

Chapter Nine

The Grind

Rachel

The bell above The Grind's door chimed as I pushed inside, already spotted Maya in her camel hair coat. I needed caffeine and sympathy, preferably in that order.

Maya sat at our usual table by the window, two coffee cups already waiting. Her knowing smirk told me everything I needed to know about this ambush.

"Don't start," I said, dropping into the chair across from her.
"I didn't say anything."
"You're thinking it."
Her grin widened. "Am I?"
I grabbed the coffee. Took a long sip. Burned my tongue. Didn't care.
Behind the counter, Henry glanced over with that fond, exasperated look he always gave Maya when she was scheming. His fiancée. They were getting married in June, and I was pretty sure this entire situation was going to end

up in their wedding toasts. Dune, his lab mix, dozed in a patch of sunlight near the door.

"So," Maya said, leaning forward. "My brother."

I groaned. "Maya—"

"You bought a ladder together."

"We did NOT buy a ladder together. We ran into each other at the hardware store."

"Mrs. Henderson said you looked very cozy in the checkout line."

"Mrs. Henderson needs a hobby that isn't watching me."

Maya laughed. "She called me within five minutes. Said you two were 'absolutely adorable together.'"

I dropped my head onto the table. The wood felt cool against my forehead. Maybe I could just stay here. Paint this view.

"Also heard you helped him move in," Maya continued, mercilessly.

I lifted my head. "I brought coffee. As a neighbor. That's what neighbors do."

"Uh huh. And the four hours you spent reorganizing his furniture?"

"He had terrible furniture placement. The couch was facing the wrong wall."

"So you fixed it."

"I suggested alternatives."

"For four hours."

I took another sip of coffee. Avoided her eyes. "It was complicated furniture."

Maya's laugh was warm and familiar. We'd been friends since September. Only a few months, but it felt longer. The kind of fast, deep bond that happens when you meet someone who just gets you. She knew me too well.

Which was why I knew what was coming before she said it.

Her expression shifted. Softened. The teasing faded.

"I need to tell you something," she said. "I was wrong."

I looked up, surprised. "About what?"

"After the hurricane cleanup. I warned Ryan off. Told him you were going through stuff and he should keep his distance." She wrapped both hands around her coffee cup. "I shouldn't have done that."

My stomach flipped. "Maya—"

"You were both healing. He was dealing with his stuff, you were dealing with yours. I was trying to protect both of you." She paused. "But I've been watching you two circle each other. The way he lights up when your name comes up. The way you—" She gestured at me. "—do whatever this defensive thing is when I mention him."

"I'm not defensive."

"You're literally crossing your arms right now."

I uncrossed my arms. Picked up my coffee instead.

"He's been texting me constantly," Maya said. "Asking about you."

My heart flipped. "What kind of questions?"

"'What's her favorite coffee?' 'What does she do when she's stressed?' 'Does she really name all her pets after dead artists?'" Maya's smile was gentle. "I've never seen him like this. Not even with"—she made air quotes—"*her*."

"He's a good man, Rachel." Maya leaned forward. "I was wrong to interfere. If you want him, you have my full support."

The words hung between us. Permission. Blessing. Everything I'd been waiting for without realizing it.

And it didn't matter.

My eyes burned. I blinked hard, tried to hold it together.

"Rachel?" Maya's voice went soft with concern. "What's wrong?"

Everything came tumbling out. Mom's situation. The possibility I might have to move home. How I'd been trying to map out solutions. Ryan and whether I were setting us both up to fail when I might not even be here. Whether my chaos would eventually be too much for him, like it was for Derek. Whether I was protecting him or protecting myself.

Maya listened. Didn't interrupt. Let me get it all out.

When I finished, she reached across the table and took my hand.

"You know what I think?" she said. "I think you're the kind of person who gets resourceful when you're backed into a corner. Creative. You figure things out. You always have."

"Tell that to Ryan. He's heard me singing off-key at two in the morning. Still waves at me."

"Ryan literally laughs at your chaos. He thinks it's charming."

"For now. Derek thought it was charming too. At first."

"Derek was an insecure idiot who needed you small to feel big. Ryan's not Derek." Maya squeezed my hand. "Don't make decisions based on what might go wrong instead of what could go right."

Part of me knew she was right. I just had to figure out logistics without blowing up my life here.

My phone rang. Mom's ringtone.

I pulled my hand away from Maya's, stared at the screen. Couldn't not answer.

"I should take this," I said, already standing.

Maya nodded, understanding.

I stepped outside onto the sidewalk, wishing I'd grabbed my jacket. Cold wind whipped through my hair as I answered the call.

"Hi, Mom."

"Rachel, sweetheart. How are you?"

"Good. I'm at The Grind with Maya. What's up?"

"I talked to Dr. Bryant today about those automatic pill dispensers you've been researching."

My heart lifted. "You did?"

"You were right. She thinks it's a smart system to have in place." Mom's voice was lighter than it had been in weeks. "She's ordering one. Should arrive next week."

Relief flooded through me. "That's great, Mom."

"And I talked to Amy about the transition. She said if the dispenser works well and I'm managing okay with it, she might be able to refer me to someone in her network when she's ready to move on."

"So we can find the right fit."

"Exactly. Be thoughtful about it." She paused. "You've been working hard on this, honey. Thank you."

"Of course. That's what I'm here for."

"I know. But I'm grateful anyway."

We talked logistics. Details. Dr. Bryant's recommendations. The features on the dispenser. It wasn't a complete solution. Just forward momentum. But it was something.

When I hung up, I stared at Maya.

"What just happened?" she asked.

"Mom called her doctor. The pill dispenser I've been researching—Dr. Bryant's ordering it. And Amy might have referrals when she transitions out." The words felt lighter. "We have time to figure this out properly."

Maya's grin was immediate. "See? Something good."

"Something good," I echoed.

Maya opened her mouth to respond.

The door opened. Bell chimed.

Ryan walked in with Dozer.

He wore civilian clothes. Jeans. Flannel. Hair slightly messy. He looked good. He always looked good. That was part of the problem.

He spotted us. Froze in the doorway.

"Ryan!" Maya said, way too brightly. "Perfect timing!"

I wanted to sink through the floor.

Henry suddenly appeared from the back. "Maya, I need your help with something urgent. Wedding venue emergency."

Maya barely hid her grin. "Oh no. An emergency. Right now."

They disappeared toward the kitchen, leaving Ryan and me alone at the table.

Dozer immediately trotted over, tail wagging. He put his head in my lap, looking up at me with those trusting eyes.

"Sorry," He shifted his weight, awkward. "I didn't mean to interrupt."

"You didn't. They're as subtle as a brick."

He smiled slightly. Sat down across from me. Dozer stayed with me, begging shamelessly for my muffin.

I broke off a piece. Fed it to him. He took it gently, tail wagging harder.

"So," Ryan said. "Tomorrow. Ten o'clock. Station visit."

"Right. For the photography session."

"The crew's excited to meet you. Well, meet you officially. As the artist. Not as—" He gestured vaguely. "—the woman who sets off fire alarms."

I laughed despite everything. "That's how I'll be remembered. Fire alarm girl."

"Could be worse."

"How?"

"You could be 'ladder climbing girl.'"

"Hey. I almost reached those anchors."

"You were two feet off the ground."

"Details."

We smiled at each other. The moment stretched. Warmth passed between us. Understanding. Longing. Fear.

Dozer broke the tension by putting both paws on my lap, trying to reach my entire muffin.

"Dozer, down," Ryan said.

The dog ignored him. Looked at me hopefully.

"He's shameless," I said, feeding him another piece.

"Completely." Ryan was watching me. Not the dog. Me. "Are you okay?"

The question was gentle. Careful. Like he knew I'd been crying.

"Fine," I said too quickly. "Just... family stuff."

He didn't look convinced. Opened his mouth like he was going to say more.

His radio crackled. Dispatch calling.

He sighed, stood. "I have to go. Shift starts in ten."

"Okay."

He hesitated. "Tomorrow. Ten o'clock."

"I'll be there."

Dozer whined, reluctant to leave me.

"Come on, buddy," Ryan said, tugging gently on his leash.

They left. The bell chimed. I watched through the window as Ryan loaded Dozer into his truck and drove away.

Maya and Henry emerged from the kitchen immediately.

"Crisis averted," Maya announced, sitting down.

I gave her a look. "Wedding venue emergency?"

"Very urgent. Had to be handled immediately."

Henry at least had the decency to look sheepish. "I'm terrible at lying. The bride-to-be made me."

Maya studied my face. "You need to tell him."

"Tell him what?"

"That you might be leaving. Before you both get in too deep."

"We're not—there's nothing to get deep into. We're neighbors. The mural is work."

Maya gave me a pointed look. "Rachel. I saw how you looked at each other just now."

I couldn't deny it. The words died in my throat.

"You're already in too deep," Maya said softly. "Both of you."

I stared at my coffee cup. She was right. I knew she was right.

But I couldn't solve everything in one coffee shop conversation. Couldn't map out every contingency plan while my brain was still spinning. If I kept pushing, I'd fall apart right here in The Grind.

"I need to paint," I said suddenly.

Maya blinked. "What?"

"I need to paint. Clear my head." I stood up, already reaching for my bag. "There's this spot on Coral Pier. Perfect light in the mornings. I've been wanting to capture it for weeks, waiting for that thin, clear quality before the weather softens."

"Rachel, we're in the middle of—"

"I know." My voice cracked. "I just need to paint. Clear my head."

Maya studied my face. Saw whatever she needed to see. Nodded slowly. "Okay. When?"

"Tomorrow morning. Early." The idea was already taking shape in my mind. The angle I wanted. The way the sunrise would hit the water. The pier stretching into the distance like a path to somewhere better. "I do my best thinking when I paint."

"You do your best avoiding when you paint," Maya said, but her voice was gentle.

Maybe. Probably. I didn't argue.

"Be careful on that pier," she said. "The boards are old."

"I'm always careful."

"You climbed a shelf at the hardware store."

"That was different."

"How?"

"I really needed those anchors."

She laughed despite everything. Hugged me. "Text me when you're done painting."

"I will."

I left The Grind with my head full of colors. Sunrise ochre. Ocean blue. The silver-gray of weathered pier boards.

Tomorrow morning, for a few hours at least, I'd stand on that pier with nothing but canvas and paint and ocean.

Everything would be fine.

Chapter Ten

Coral Pier

Ryan

The radio crackled. "Artist trapped at Coral Pier, structure collapse, painting equipment on scene—"

My heart stopped.

I knew exactly who was out there at dawn with an easel.

I grabbed my gear before dispatch finished. Already moving. Already running.

"Rodriguez, you good?" Martinez called behind me.

I couldn't speak. Jaw tight. Just nodded and moved faster.

Captain caught my arm. "What's wrong?"

"I know her."

His expression shifted. Understanding. He let go.

I hit my truck before the guys could get the engine out. Threw it in reverse. Floored it. My emergency light flashing on the dash. My mind raced ahead. Please be okay. Please be okay. Please be okay.

Coral Pier came into view. Structure partially collapsed into the water. Weathered boards splintered and hanging. Waves crashing below. The entire far section sagging at an angle that made my stomach drop.

I spotted her easel. Empty. Knocked over. Canvas face down in the surf. Then I saw her.

Maybe twelve feet below pier level. Clinging to a beam. Waves crashing around her. The structure groaning with every surge. Her face pale. Determined. Holding on.

Ice flooded my veins.

The engine pulled up. Captain jumped out and took one look at the pier.

"Hold on. Structure's not stable. We need to set up safe."

I was already gearing up. "We don't have time. It could collapse further."

He looked at me. Saw my face. Made his decision.

"You're lead on this. Be careful."

"Always am."

I dropped to my stomach on the weathered boards. They groaned under my weight. Shifted slightly. I inched forward until I could see over the edge.

"Rachel! Hang on!"

She looked up. Saw me. Her grip was solid. White-knuckled but secure.

We had a minute. Maybe two.

The engine pulled up behind us. Martinez and Thompson already moving.

The crew set up the rope system. My hands moved through familiar motions. Harness. Carabiners. Double-check everything. My training overriding the panic in my throat.

This wasn't just another rescue.

This was Rachel.

I rappelled down. Wind whipping. Structure creaking beneath me. The beam she clung to shifted slightly. She made a small sound. Fear. Pain. Determination.

I reached her. Secured myself beside her. Our eyes met.

Her relief was immediate. Tears streaming down her face. Hands white-knuckled on the beam.

"You're getting really good at showing up when I set things on fire," she said. Voice shaking. Trying to joke. "Or, you know, fall off piers."

"Trying to keep me employed?" I secured the harness around her. My hands were steady. My heart was not.

"I'm sorry. I'm so sorry. Maya said the boards were old and I thought—"

"I need you to trust me." I kept my voice gentle but firm. "Can you do that?"

She nodded. Tears in her eyes.

I clipped her to my harness. "I've got you. I promise."

I signaled the crew. They started the ascent.

The beam groaned beneath us.

"Don't look down," I said. "Look at me."

She did. Her face inches from mine. Eyes wide. Scared. Trusting.

"Almost there," I told her. "You're doing great. Stay with me."

It felt like hours. Probably seconds.

Finally, we were over the edge. Solid ground. The crew pulling us both to safety.

Rachel's legs gave out. I caught her. Held her for just a moment before professionalism kicked back in.

The paramedics were already there. One wrapped an emergency blanket around her shoulders. Led her to sit on the ambulance bumper.

She was shaking. Cold, adrenaline, shock.

She tried to make a joke. Her voice broke instead.

I crouched in front of her. Checked her over. Scraped hands. Bruised ribs where she'd hit the beam. Soaking wet. But alive.

I was barely holding myself together.

One of my crew appeared beside me. "You know her?"

"She's my neighbor," I said. Not taking my eyes off Rachel.

The crew exchanged knowing looks. They could see it was more than that.

Captain clapped my shoulder. "Good work, Rodriguez."

The paramedic wanted to transport her to the hospital.

Rachel shook her head. "I'm fine. Just cold and scared."

"You could have a concussion, hypothermia, internal injuries—"

"I didn't hit my head. I just held on. I'm not going to the hospital."

The paramedic looked at me. I was EMT certified. Could make the call.

"Rachel, you need to be checked out properly."

"I'm fine, I just need my own bed and my cat."

Back and forth. Her getting more defensive. Me getting more worried.

I pulled rank with the paramedic. "I'm EMT certified. Let me check her over. If anything's concerning, we'll transport."

He agreed reluctantly.

I did a quick assessment. Pulse. Pupils. Palpated her ribs. She winced when I touched her left side.

"Bruised ribs, maybe cracked. You need monitoring."

"I'll be careful. Please, Ryan. I can't—I can't deal with a hospital right now."

The way she said it made me stop pushing. Fear. Exhaustion. Desperation.

I looked at the paramedic. "I'll stay with her. Watch for signs of shock or delayed injury. Any problems, I'll bring her in myself."

He gave instructions. Made me sign paperwork.

Captain appeared beside me. Knowing look. "Take the rest of your shift, Rodriguez. Make sure she's okay."

I nodded. Couldn't speak past the tightness in my throat.

The crew started packing up. Giving us space. Martinez caught my eye. Nodded once. Understanding.

I turned back to Rachel. "Can you stand?"

"I think so."

I helped her up. She swayed slightly. I caught her waist. Steadied her.

"My car's here somewhere," she said.

"You're not driving. I'm taking you home."

"Ryan—"

"Not negotiable." My voice came out rougher than I intended.

She didn't argue.

I got her into my truck. Dozer was waiting in the back. He whined when he saw her. Pushed his head between the seats. Tried to lick her face.

"Hi, buddy," she said softly. Let him comfort her.

I drove to her cottage. The short drive felt eternal. She was silent. Staring out the window. Still shaking.

I helped her inside. First time I'd been in her space.

The living room was her studio.

No couch. No coffee table. Just canvases everywhere. An easel positioned where furniture should be. Art supplies covering every surface. Shelves crammed with paints and brushes organized by color.

A massive seascape dominated one wall. Waves crashing in shades of blue and gray I didn't know existed. The light in the painting felt real. Like I could hear the ocean.

Smaller canvases lined the floor. Studies of the pier. The same pier she'd just fallen from. Different angles, different lights, different seasons. She'd been painting it for months. Learning it. Loving it.

A portrait leaned against the window. An elderly woman with soft wrinkles and kind eyes. Laughing. Every line told a story. This wasn't just technical skill.

Her art class materials spread across a table. Construction paper. Safety scissors. Washable paint. The contrast between her professional work and supplies for teaching kids.

In the corner, a mannequin draped with fabric swatches.

Rachel managed a weak joke. "Meet my roommate."

I took it all in. Her life laid bare. Unconventional. Passionate. Entirely devoted to her art.

There was literally nowhere for guests to sit. One chair buried under sketch pads.

The bedroom visible through an open door. Small. Simple. The only normal room.

I wouldn't change a single thing.

"Let's get you warm and dry," I said, helping her toward the bedroom.

Dali appeared. Meowing. Winding around Rachel's legs. The cat looked at me with suspicion but stayed close to Rachel.

Rachel's teeth were chattering now. Adrenaline wearing off.

"You need to get out of those wet clothes," I said.

She looked at me. Vulnerable.

"Can you manage, or do you need help?"

"I might need help."

I helped her carefully. Respectfully. Kept my eyes averted when I could. Got her into warm, dry clothes. Sat her on the bed. Did a proper medical check.

Bruised ribs. Painful but not broken. Scraped palms. Various bumps and cuts. Nothing requiring a hospital. But she needed rest and monitoring.

I found her kitchen. Navigated the chaos. Made her tea. Brought it back. Helped her drink it.

Tucked blankets around her like she was precious. Breakable.

"Thank you," she said. Voice rough.

"I'm staying until I'm sure you're okay."

She didn't argue. Too exhausted.

I stood to let Dozer in from the porch. He'd been waiting patiently. Lying down. Calm. Good dog.

He trotted straight to Rachel's bedside. Rested his head on the mattress beside her. She reached out. Stroked his ears.

Rachel was fighting to stay awake. Losing the battle.

She mumbled about the mural. About being more careful.

Then, half-asleep: "I lost the painting. It was almost finished. It was for Mom."

I went still. "For your mom?"

But Rachel was already drifting. Didn't hear me.

First real mention of her mother. A piece I'd been missing.

Her eyes fluttered. "Thank you for being there."

"Always," I said. Throat tight.

She didn't hear it. Already asleep.

I stayed seated on the edge of her bed. Watched her face relax into sleep. Breathing evening out. My hands wouldn't stop shaking. I pressed them flat against my thighs, but the tremor worked its way up my arms. Into my shoulders. I couldn't get enough air. Twelve feet below the pier. Clinging to a beam. The image wouldn't leave.

Rachel's phone lit up on her nightstand.

Caller ID: "Mom."

It rang once. Went to voicemail. Immediately lit up again.

"Mom" calling back.

I stared at it. Someone was worried about her. Needed to know she was okay.

The phone rang a third time.

Why hadn't Rachel mentioned her mom before?

Chapter Eleven

Rachel's Cottage

Rachel

Coffee.

The smell pulled me from sleep before the sunlight did. Rich, dark, exactly the way I liked it.

Someone was in my kitchen.

I opened my eyes. My bedroom ceiling. My window. Pale light filtered through the glass. Pain bloomed through my ribs when I tried to sit up—sharp, immediate, stealing my breath.

The pier. The fall. Ryan pulling me from the water.

Ryan stayed.

Panic and warmth twisted together in my stomach. I sat up too fast despite the screaming protest from my ribs. The room tilted. I gripped the mattress edge until everything steadied.

Sounds drifted from the kitchen. The soft clink of dishes. Water running. A low voice talking to someone.

He stayed the whole night.

I needed to get to the bathroom before he saw me like this.

The mirror was unforgiving. Hair matted on one side, sticking straight up on the other. Yesterday's mascara smudged into full raccoon territory. Bruises blooming purple across my arms and shoulders. The borrowed T-shirt Ryan must have helped me into hung loose and wrinkled.

Through the thin wall, I heard Ryan's voice. Soft, warm. Talking to Dozer, probably.

I couldn't make out the words. Just the steady murmur of him being present, being here, taking care of me.

I tried to make myself presentable. Gave up after thirty seconds. There was no fixing this without a shower I didn't have the energy for.

When I emerged from the bathroom, the whole domestic scene stole my breath.

Ryan stood at my stove, back to me, scrambling eggs in my ancient cast-iron pan. Morning light filled the kitchen window behind him—not quite warm enough to promise spring, but brighter than the gray weeks before. Toast already plated on my mismatched dishes. Coffee poured into my favorite mug—the chipped blue one I kept hidden in the back of the cabinet.

My sketchbook lay open on the table. Right where I'd left it last night before I went to the pier.

My stomach dropped.

The pages. Those pages.

But Ryan had his back to the table, focused on the stove. Maybe he hadn't noticed.

Dozer was curled up on my paint-stained floor pillow, completely at home. Dali watched from her shelf perch, tail flicking slowly. Still suspicious but not hissing for once.

Ryan had organized the chaos without changing it. Canvases moved carefully to create clear paths. Other sketchbooks stacked neatly. A clean space carved out of my usual creative mess.

But that one sketchbook stayed open on the table.

He turned, spatula in hand. His face transformed when he saw me—relief flooding his features, then concern, then tenderness underneath.

"How are you feeling?" he asked.

His competence in my space overwhelmed me. His presence here. Making breakfast like it was the most natural thing in the world. I didn't know whether to cry or kiss him.

I moved toward the coffee instead. "Sore."

"Pain scale?"

"Six." Closer to eight, but admitting that meant admitting I needed more help.

He plated the eggs beside the toast, set everything on the counter. Still in yesterday's clothes, rumpled and salt-stained. Exhaustion shadowed his eyes—he couldn't have slept much.

"You should eat," he said. "You didn't have dinner last night."

I picked up the coffee mug. He'd found my favorite beans, buried behind half-empty paint tubes and forgotten art supplies in the chaos of my cabinets.

"How are you feeling? Really." His eyes tracked over me, assessing. Still in firefighter mode.

"Sore. Cold."

"The water temperature was forty-eight degrees last night." His voice went quiet. "Your core temp had dropped when we got you in the truck. I was worried about hypothermia."

My stomach tightened. I'd been too focused on my ribs to think about that.

"You were shivering pretty hard for the first few hours. I stayed in your room to make sure it stopped. Make sure you kept warm enough." He gestured toward my bedroom. "Dozer camped out with me. Wouldn't leave the door."

That explained why the dog had been so clingy this morning.

"Thank you." My voice came out rough. "For staying. For all of this."

"Of course." He leaned against the counter, watching me with careful attention. Still monitoring, still making sure I was okay.

I settled for accepting the coffee, taking a long sip. Perfect.

I bit into the toast. Perfectly golden. The eggs were fluffy, seasoned just right. When was the last time someone made me breakfast? Derek used to, at the very beginning. Before I became too much work.

"These are really good," I said.

"Don't sound so surprised." But he smiled.

Dozer lifted his head, looked at me, then heaved himself up and padded over. He pressed his massive head against my leg, tail wagging slowly.

I scratched behind his ears. He leaned into my hand, making soft groaning sounds.

"Where's Dali?" I asked.

"Under your bed. She came out once around one AM, glared at me like I'd personally offended her entire species, then went back into hiding."

Despite everything, I almost smiled. "That sounds like her."

"She really hates me."

"She really hates everyone." I took another bite of eggs. "I don't take it personally anymore."

Ryan laughed, and the sound filled my small kitchen. Warm and real and easy.

For a moment, it felt normal. Like this could be my life. Like I deserved this kind of care.

Then I noticed my sketchbook open on the table.

Ice water flooded my veins.

The pages I didn't want anyone to see. Especially him.

Detailed studies of his hands. His profile. The way he stood. The curve of his jaw when he concentrated. Page after page of Ryan, drawn obsessively without me fully realizing what I was doing.

My face went hot. "You looked at my sketches."

Ryan's expression softened. "I hope you don't mind. I was looking at the mural work last night while you slept, and I found... these."

He was quiet, holding my gaze. The air between us shifted, heavier.

"Is that how you see me?" His voice was soft, wondering.

I couldn't speak. My throat closed around any possible response.

He was seeing what those drawings meant. What I'd been too afraid to say out loud.

I tried to deflect. "Those aren't for the mural. Just... practice."

"They're beautiful." He stepped closer. "You're... talented doesn't even cover it."

The way he was looking at me made my throat ache. Like I was precious. Like the sketches revealed what he'd been hoping to find.

I needed to move. Needed space. Needed to escape this intensity.

I turned toward the high shelf where I kept the pain medication. Reached up. My ribs screamed in immediate protest, sharp and vicious.

I gasped, stumbled back.

Ryan was there instantly. One hand steadying my waist, the other reaching past me for the bottle I couldn't reach.

"I've got it," he said.

But I'd already turned in the small space between him and the counter.

His hands on my waist. My hands instinctively gripping his arms for balance.

We were breathing the same air. Inches apart.

Neither of us moved away.

My heart raced—pain, attraction, terror, all of it swirling together. His eyes were so dark this close. I could see the depth in them, the concern written in every line of his face.

His eyes dropped to my lips. Back to my eyes.

The moment stretched, electric and impossible.

I broke it. Stepped sideways. "See? Can't even reach my own shelves."

His hands lingered a moment before he let go. Helped me sit on the stool. Set the pain medication on the counter beside me.

The air still crackled between us.

Ryan backed up, ran a hand through his hair. The frustration was visible now, carefully controlled but present.

"Rachel... what's going on?"

I swallowed two pills with cold coffee. "I fell off a pier. Pretty straightforward."

"That's not what I mean." His voice was gentle but firm. "You keep pulling away."

I tried to redirect. "I'm sorry I missed the station visit yesterday. For the mural sketches. We can reschedule—"

"Rachel."

"I just need to finalize the composition, and then I can start the actual painting—"

"You're doing it right now."

I stopped. Looked at him.

His expression looked frustrated but not angry. Just... tired. Like he was watching me run, and he didn't understand why.

"I can feel you holding back," he said. "A wall I can't get past. And I don't know if it's about me, or about something else, but—" He stopped. Shook his head. "I should go. Let you rest."

But he didn't move toward the door. And I didn't want him to leave. Neither of us said this.

My phone buzzed on the counter.

The sound shattered whatever fragile moment we'd been holding.

I glanced at the screen. My whole body tensed.

Text from Mom

> *Honey, the electric company called about a shut-off notice. I thought I paid that bill but I can't find the check. Can you help me figure this out?*

"Everything okay?" Ryan asked.

I forced brightness into my voice. "Yeah, just... my mom. She's fine."

But my hands were shaking slightly as I picked up the phone. Another text came through.

> *Also can't remember if I took my morning pills. Did I already call you about this?*

Ryan saw the crack in my armor. I knew he did. Saw the fear underneath the fake smile.

"I'm really tired," I said quickly. "Thank you for everything, but I should probably rest."

I was asking him to leave. We both knew it was an excuse.

Ryan moved toward the door. Dozer reluctantly followed, looking back at me with sad eyes.

"I'm right next door if you need anything," Ryan said at the door. "And I mean anything."

"I know. Thank you for—"

"Rachel, wait." He turned back. "Whatever you're dealing with... you don't have to deal with it alone."

My throat closed.

Before I could respond, Dali streaked past us out the open door.

Dozer bolted after her.

"Dozer, no!" Ryan lunged for his collar, missed.

I rushed outside despite my screaming ribs. "Dali! Get back here!"

Dali had climbed halfway up a tree in my front yard, branches still bare with tiny green buds just starting. She looked absolutely smug. Dozer circled the base, barking enthusiastically, tail wagging.

"Your cat is evil," Ryan said, grinning as he caught Dozer's collar.

"She's creative." I reached up. Dali hissed at me. "Okay, she's evil."

It took ten minutes to get Dali down. By the time we'd wrestled the animals back inside, we were both breathless and laughing.

Ryan paused at my door. Glanced back at me once, his expression unreadable.

Then he left with Dozer.

The door closed. His footsteps faded.

I slid down the door to sit on the floor. Picked up my phone.

Read Mom's texts again.

> *Can't remember if I took my morning pills.*

> *Did I already call you about this?*

The forgetting. The confusion about bills. The falling.

I needed to call the electric company. Sort out the bill confusion. Follow up with her doctor about the meds.

Another text came through.

> *Sorry to bother you, honey. I'm sure I'm just being silly. Don't worry about me.*

I opened my contacts. Found the electric company number. Tomorrow I'd start making calls.

Dali emerged from under the bed, stalked over, and headbutted my arm. Her version of comfort.

I scratched behind her ears and started making a list.

Chapter Twelve

The Firehouse

Ryan

The alarm bells rang mid-sentence.

I dropped my pen. Community outreach proposals could wait.

Dispatch crackled over the radio. "Structure fire, Watson residence, elderly occupant possibly inside."

The crew moved as one. Chairs scraping. Boots hitting concrete. Everyone racing to the trucks.

I grabbed my turnout gear, adrenaline already pumping. This is what we trained for. This is why we're here.

Captain barked orders. "Rodriguez, you're going in with Martinez. Structure's old, be careful."

"Copy that."

We hit the truck. Sirens wailing. The station bay doors already rising. I focused completely. Every detail sharp and clear.

This is the job.

The old Watson place sat on the edge of town, surrounded by overgrown yards and ancient oak trees. Smoke poured from the windows, black and thick.

Captain assessed the scene. "Possible victim inside. Rodriguez, Martinez—you're up. Primary search, west side entrance."

We geared up fast. Masks. Air tanks. Tools.

Martinez and I moved in sync, years of training taking over. The heat hit us the second we breached the door. Smoke so thick I couldn't see my hand in front of my face.

"Fire department! Call out!"

Nothing.

We moved through the house systematically. Living room. Kitchen. Hallway.

Then I heard it. A weak cough from the back bedroom.

"Martinez, this way."

We found him slumped against the bed. Elderly man, probably eighties. Overcome by smoke. Clutching photo albums to his chest like they were the most precious things in the world.

His whole life in those albums.

"Sir, we need to get you out." I knelt beside him, checked his vitals. Pulse weak but steady. Breathing labored.

He shook his head. Wouldn't let go of the albums. "Can't leave them. My wife. My kids. Everything."

The smoke grew thicker. The fire spreading. We didn't have time for this.

But I understood. These weren't photos. They were memories. They were proof he'd been loved. Proof his life had mattered.

"I've got you," I said. "We'll get them."

Martinez grabbed the albums. I lifted the man, supporting his weight. He felt light, fragile. Too light.

We moved fast. Back through the smoke. Through the heat. My lungs burning despite the mask.

Out into the fresh air and sunlight.

The paramedics took over immediately. Oxygen mask. Stretcher. They worked efficiently while I stepped back, letting them do their job.

Captain clapped my shoulder. "Good work, Rodriguez."

I nodded. Couldn't speak yet. Adrenaline still coursing through me.

Martinez handed the photo albums to the paramedics. They loaded everything into the ambulance.

One album fell open. A wedding photo. Young couple, 1950s maybe. The woman laughing, the man looking at her like she hung the moon.

The old man's whole life. Right there.

The old man reached for my hand. Squeezed it weakly. "Thank you."

Those two words made every risk worth it.

I followed the ambulance to the hospital. Standard protocol for smoke inhalation victims. Make sure they're stable, answer any medical questions.

A strange calm held the ER for a Friday afternoon. Mr. Watson went straight back. I waited in the hallway, still in my turnout gear, smelling like smoke.

Then the double doors burst open.

A kid came running through. Maybe eight years old. Tears streaming down his face.

Tommy.

From Rachel's art class.

He saw me and ran straight into my arms, sobbing.

I caught him automatically. Knelt to his level. "Hey, buddy. It's okay. You're okay."

"I remembered!" The words came out between sobs. "I smelled smoke and I called 911 like you said!"

My throat went tight.

Tommy's mother rushed in behind him. I recognized her from the school visit. She shook, tears in her eyes.

"He saved my father's life," she said to me. "I was out back in his garden and Tommy smelled the smoke. He got him out of the house, called 911. Everything you taught him."

I held Tommy tighter. This kid. This brave, smart kid who'd paid attention during a field trip most children forgot the second they left.

"You did exactly right," I told him. "You stayed calm. You got out. You called for help. You're a hero, Tommy."

He pulled back, looked at me with those wide eyes. "Really?"

"Really. You saved him. You did what I taught you, and you saved his life."

Tommy's mother cried now too. She hugged us both, this stranger and her son, united by crisis and relief.

"Thank you," she whispered to me. "Thank you for teaching him. For caring enough to make it stick."

I couldn't speak past the lump in my throat. Nodded.

When they went back to see Mr. Watson, I stood in that hospital hallway and understood the weight of what we do. What I do.

Teaching fire safety isn't checking a box. It's saving lives.

Tommy had saved his grandfather because I'd taken the time to make it real for him.

This matters.

I drove back to the station in a daze. Good daze. The kind where everything feels right with the world.

Martinez waited when I got back. "Heard about the Watson kid. Your student, right? From the school visit?"

"Yeah."

"Huge, man. Kid used what you taught him."

The rest of the crew gathered around. Everyone wanted to hear the story. I told them about Tommy remembering the safety protocols, about him staying calm, about the phone call that saved his grandfather.

Captain listened from his office doorway. When I finished, he nodded once. "That's the work, Rodriguez. That's why we do the community outreach."

I'd made the right choice coming to Seaholly. This is where I belong.

My shift ended at six. I drove home in the low evening light, windows down, still smelling faintly of smoke.

Dozer greeted me at the door with his usual enthusiasm. Tail wagging, full-body wiggles, like I'd been gone for years instead of hours.

"Hey, buddy. Good day?"

He barked once. Definitely yes.

I needed a shower. Needed food. Needed to decompress from the adrenaline high of the rescue.

But first, I sat on my porch steps with Dozer and breathed.

Through the trees, I could see Rachel's cottage. Her lights glowed warm. I wondered if she'd heard about the fire. Wondered if she knew Tommy had used what I'd taught him.

My phone buzzed. Text from Tommy's mother with a photo: Tommy and his grandfather in the hospital room, both smiling, holding those rescued photo albums.

> *Thank you for everything. Tommy wants you to know he's a hero now, like you.*

I stared at the photo until my vision blurred.

Another text came through, this one from Rachel.

> *Heard about the Watson fire. You okay?*

My thumb hovered over the keyboard. I wanted to call her. Wanted to see her. Wanted to tell her about Tommy and the rescue and how good it feels to make a difference.

Before I could type a response, I saw her. Walking across the yard between our cottages. Carrying a container.

She stopped at the bottom of my porch steps. "Hi."

"Hi."

"I brought food." She held up the container. "Figured you might be too tired to cook after the day you had."

I couldn't speak for a moment. She'd thought about me. Cared enough to bring dinner.

"You didn't have to do that."

"I know." She climbed the steps, sat beside me. Set the container between us. "But I wanted to."

Dozer immediately put his head in her lap, tail wagging.

She scratched behind his ears, and the tension I'd been carrying loosened.

"Tommy's mom called me," Rachel said. "Told me what happened. What he did."

"He saved his grandfather."

"Because you taught him how." She looked at me, eyes warm. "You're making a real difference here, Ryan. With the kids. With this town."

I didn't know what to say. The words felt too big, too important.

We sat in comfortable silence. Her presence easing the wound-tight feeling I hadn't realized I'd been carrying.

"I'm really glad you're here," she said quietly. "In Seaholly. Next door. Teaching Tommy. All of it."

"Me too."

Not enough for what I wanted to say. Sitting here with her felt like the best part of my day. Her showing up with food when I needed it made me feel seen in a way I'm not used to.

I'm falling for her.

But I didn't say any of that. We ate the dinner she'd brought as the sun set, feeling more at home than I had in years.

When she stood to leave, I caught her hand. "Thank you. For this. For being here."

"Where else would I be?"

There it was again. The strange note in her voice. Wistful. Sad, maybe. She pulled away gently. "Get some rest. You're a hero today."

I watched her walk back to her cottage. Dozer whined beside me.

"Yeah, buddy. I know."

I sat on the porch long after she disappeared inside. Processing the day. The rescue. Tommy's bravery. Rachel showing up when I needed her.

This is what I want. Her, here, every day.

Tommy had saved his grandfather because of what I'd taught him. Because I'd cared enough to make it real.

Rachel had shown up because she cares.

Everything feels right. Perfect, even.

So why can't I shake this feeling that she's pulling away when we get close?

Chapter Thirteen

Rachel's Cottage

Rachel

"That's not level."

Ryan paused on the step stool, drill in hand, and looked down at me. "The bubble says otherwise."

I squinted at the level I was holding. Or trying to hold. The little air bubble floated somewhere vaguely between the lines. "I think the level is broken."

"The level isn't broken."

"Then why doesn't it match what I'm seeing?"

"Because you're shaking it."

"I'm not—" I looked at my hands. They were trembling slightly. "Okay, maybe a little."

He gestured at the step stool. "Also, I thought you didn't need a ladder. Mr. I'm-Six-Foot-Three."

"I don't need a ladder for normal curtain rods." He looked up at the mounting point near the ceiling. "I didn't know you hung yours all the way up there."

"It makes the ceilings look higher."

"It makes my neck hurt."

"Fashion is pain."

"This isn't fashion. It's home decor."

"Same principle."

His mouth twitched. Fighting a smile.

Dali watched from the windowsill, tail flicking with supreme judgment. She'd destroyed this curtain rod at 3 am two days ago, and now she sat there looking incredibly pleased with herself.

Dozer lay on my paint-stained floor pillow, head on his paws, watching Ryan with devoted attention. Every time Ryan moved, Dozer's ears perked up.

"How's this?" Ryan adjusted the bracket from atop the step stool.

I held the level up again. The bubble was... close? "Good."

"Good or actually level?"

"Does it matter?"

"Yes." His voice held that patient tone. The one who said he was dealing with someone who didn't understand how things worked. "If it's not level, the rod will slide to one side."

"That sounds like a problem for future Rachel."

"I'm trying to help future Rachel."

"Future Rachel appreciates your concern but thinks you're being excessive."

He climbed down from the step stool. Took the level from my hands. Held it against the wall himself.

The bubble sat perfectly centered.

"See?" he said. "Level."

"Show-off."

But I was grinning. Couldn't help it.

He'd shown up exactly on time, toolbox in hand, Dozer at his heels. Taken one look at the curtain rod disaster and just... handled it. No judgment about Dali's destruction. No commentary on the fact that I'd left the broken rod on the floor for two days.

Just quiet competence.

My cottage had never seen this much organization. Ryan's tools were laid out on a towel. In order. By size. Each one placed with precision.

Meanwhile, my art supplies were scattered across every surface. Paint tubes. Brushes in jars. Sketch pads stacked on the chair that qualified as my only furniture.

The contrast was almost funny.

"Hand me the drill," Ryan said.

I looked at his tool arrangement. Picked up something that looked drill-ish.

"That's a screwdriver."

"They all look the same."

"They look nothing alike." But his eyes crinkled. "The drill. Yellow. With the trigger."

I found it. Handed it over. Our fingers brushed.

The contact sent a little spark through me.

He climbed back on the step stool. Started drilling. The sound loud in my small cottage.

Dozer's head popped up. Alert. Concerned about the noise.

"It's okay, buddy," I told him. "Just Ryan being excessive about straight lines."

"I can hear you."

"I know."

He kept drilling. I watched him work. The careful way he measured. How he double-checked everything. His forearms flexing as he drove the screws.

This was a mistake. Having him here. In my space. Watching him be competent and patient and perfect.

My phone rang.

I jumped. Nearly knocked over a jar of paint water.

Mom's ringtone.

I hesitated. Stepped into my bedroom. Closed the door partway.

"Hi, Mom."

"Rachel, sweetheart." Her voice attempted cheerful. Missed slightly. "Is this a bad time?"

"No, what's wrong?"

"Nothing's wrong. Well." She paused. "The aide didn't show up today. I called the agency and they said she called in sick. But they don't have anyone to send as backup."

My stomach tightened. "Are you okay? Do you need me to come?"

"No, no. I'm fine. I just thought you should know." She tried to sound casual. Breezy. "I'm managing perfectly well on my own."

"Mom."

"Really. I made my breakfast. Took my pills. I'm just... well, I was hoping to go to the store today. But I can do that tomorrow when she's back."

"What do you need from the store?" I asked. "I can order delivery."

"Oh, honey, you don't need to—"

"Mom. What do you need?"

She listed off items. Milk. Eggs. Bread. Vegetables. Basic things she should have had yesterday.

"Did the delivery come yesterday?" I asked carefully.

"It did, but..." She trailed off. "I didn't hear them knock. By the time I found everything on the porch this morning, the milk had spoiled. And the eggs were cracked."

My chest ached.

"I'm sorry, honey. I feel so foolish. I was in the back bedroom and I just didn't hear them."

"It's not your fault." I kept my voice steady. Calm. "The delivery people should knock louder."

Through the crack in the door, I could see Ryan. Still working. But his shoulders had tensed. Like he was listening. "I have an idea," I said to Mom. "Let me make some calls. I'll call you back in ten minutes."

"Rachel, you don't have to—"

"Ten minutes. I love you."

"Love you too, sweetheart."

I hung up. Stood there for a moment. Phone in my hand. Steadying myself.

Then I opened my laptop. Searched "grocery delivery with door service" plus Mom's zip code.

Found one. Called while pulling up their website.

A woman answered. Friendly. Professional.

"Our premium service includes knocking, waiting for an answer, bringing the groceries to the kitchen counter."

"What if she doesn't answer?"

"We call the number on file."

"How much?"

She told me. More expensive than regular delivery. But not unreasonable.

"I want to set up a standing weekly order."

I gave her everything. Mom's address. My payment information. Set up the first delivery for tomorrow.

"Your mother will receive an email confirmation. And we'll call you after every delivery to confirm completion."

"Thank you so much."

I called Mom back.

"Groceries are coming tomorrow at 2 pm. New service. They'll knock, bring everything inside, put it on your counter. And if you don't answer, they'll call me and we'll figure it out together."

"Oh, honey. That's too expensive."

"It's worth it. For my peace of mind." My voice cracked slightly. "Please. Let me do this."

She was quiet for a moment. Then: "Okay. Thank you, sweetheart."

"I'll call you tomorrow after they deliver. Make sure everything came okay."

"You're a good daughter, Rachel."

My throat tightened. "I love you, Mom."

"I love you too."

I hung up. Pressed my phone against my forehead. Breathed.

The drill had stopped.

I opened the door. Ryan was climbing down from the step stool. The curtain rod bracket was mounted. Perfectly level, I'm sure.

He looked at me. Saw my face.

"Everything okay?"

I tried to smile. "Yeah. Just... mom stuff."

He waited. Didn't push. Just stood there with his drill, patient and present.

The words came out before I could stop them.

"Her aide didn't show up today. Third one this year." I gestured vaguely with my phone. "The agencies are unreliable. They quit or don't show up or find better jobs. And Mom's an hour away. I can't be there every day."

Ryan set the drill down carefully. Gave me his full attention.

"The grocery delivery left everything on the porch. Mom didn't hear them knock." My jaw tightened. "By the time she found them, the milk had spoiled and the eggs were cracked. She felt terrible about the waste."

"What did you just do?" He gestured toward my bedroom. Toward the phone calls.

"Found a service that brings groceries inside. They knock, wait for her to answer, carry everything to the kitchen counter." I managed a small smile. "And if she doesn't answer, they call me. So I know she's okay."

Something shifted in his expression. Warm. Proud, almost.

"That's smart."

"It's one less thing." I looked at my hands. At the phone still clutched too tight. "But I'm always waiting for the next call. The next thing that goes wrong when I'm an hour away and can't help."

"What scares you most?" Ryan asked quietly.

I didn't have to think about it. "Her falling. Being alone. Not being able to get up or reach the phone." My voice went tight. "What if she's on the floor for hours? What if something happens and I don't know?"

Ryan's expression shifted. Understanding.

Ryan moved closer. Not touching but present.

"That's a lot to carry alone."

The gentleness in his voice nearly broke me.

Dozer got up from his pillow. Padded over. Pressed his massive head against my leg. Offering comfort the only way he knew how.

I reached down. Scratched behind his ears. Let the steady warmth of him ground me.

"What about a medical alert device?" Ryan asked. "One of those necklaces she can press if she falls?"

I shook my head. "I tried. Months ago. She refused."

"Why?"

"Because they require a key lockbox on the front door. You know, so EMTs can get in if she can't answer." I stared at the floor. "She hates the idea of a key just sitting there. Says it's an invitation for someone to break in."

Ryan's expression shifted. Professional. Problem-solving.

"We don't need a key."

I looked up. "What?"

"When we get to a house with a locked door and someone who needs help inside, we use non-intrusive methods first. We have tools to get the door open without breaking it down." He met my eyes. "A medical alert device would give you peace of mind. If something happens, she presses the button. They come. They get inside. No key needed."

Hope flickered in my chest. Small but real.

"She might still say no."

"Then you tell her it's non-negotiable." His voice went firm but gentle. "That you need this. That you can't function not knowing if she's okay."

He wasn't just problem-solving. He was seeing my fear. Understanding it.

"Okay," I said quietly. "I'll order one tonight. Make her wear it."

"Good." He squeezed my shoulder. Brief. Reassuring. "One problem at a time."

One problem at a time.

Ryan had just given me what I needed—practical help. Firefighter knowledge applied to my situation. He saw the problem and immediately knew how to make one piece of it better.

This is what he does. Sees the crisis. Finds the tools. Takes action.

And I wasn't drowning alone anymore.

Dali chose that moment to leap from the windowsill onto my easel. The whole thing wobbled. I lunged for it. Ryan grabbed the other side.

We steadied it together.

"Your cat is chaos," he said.

"She's creative."

"She's a menace."

Dozer barked once. Excited by the commotion.

"Don't even think about it," Ryan told him.

The puppy's tail wagged. Thinking about it anyway.

Ryan shook his head. Turned back to the curtain rod. "Let me finish this before they destroy something else."

He climbed back on the step stool. I handed him the rod.

He slid it into the brackets. Tested the weight. Adjusted slightly.

"Hand me that end," he said.

I lifted the other side. We worked together. Him securing one bracket. Me holding steady on the other side.

The rod clicked into place.

Ryan stepped back. Studied his work.

"It's level."

"Of course it is." I grinned. "You're excessive, remember?"

"Thorough."

"Same thing."

I watched him pack up his tools. This man who'd shown up with his toolbox. Who'd fixed my curtain rod. Who'd listened to my mom problems without making me feel weak or burdensome.

Who'd offered solutions instead of pity.

Dozer stood. Stretched. Ready to go home.

Ryan paused at my door. Toolbox in hand. Looked back at me.

"Thank you," I said. "For the curtain rod. For the advice. For... everything."

"Anytime." His voice was warm. Steady. "I'm right next door if you need anything."

"I know."

He held my gaze for a moment. Something passed between us. Understanding. Connection.

Then he left with Dozer.

The door closed softly behind them.

I stood in my cottage. Looking at the perfectly level curtain rod. At the space where he'd been standing.

My laptop sat open on the counter. Medical alert device websites already bookmarked from months ago when I'd first tried to convince Mom.

This time I had Ryan's voice in my head. *Non-negotiable. Tell her you need this.*

I pulled up the first website. Started reading through options.

Looked around my cottage. The perfectly installed curtain rod. The paint-stained floors. The easel Dali had knocked over. The organized chaos that was my life.

Ryan had stood in the middle of all this. And he hadn't tried to change anything. Hadn't suggested I clean up or organize or be different.

I picked up my sketchbook. Flipped to a blank page.

Started drawing his hands. The way they'd held the drill. The careful precision of his movements. The gentleness when he'd squeezed my shoulder.

Strong hands. Capable hands.

Hands that fixed things.

My phone buzzed again.

> *Ordering medical alert device tonight. Going to make her wear it. Thanks for the push.*

I sent the text to Mom before I could overthink it.

Her response came quickly.

> *About time. I'll wear it if it makes you feel better.*

Relief and love swelled in my chest.

> *It does. Love you.*

> *Love you too, honey. Thank you for the grocery service. You're taking good care of your old mom.*

I wasn't though. Not really. I was an hour away. Solving problems over the phone. Throwing money at services to fill the gaps.

But it was something. One problem at a time.

Like Ryan said.

I looked at my sketch. His hands taking shape on the page. Each line deliberate. Careful.

Tomorrow I'd order the medical alert device. Set up the monitoring. Make sure Mom understood how to use it.

Tonight I'd finish this sketch.

And try not to think about how good it felt to have someone in my corner. Someone who saw my mess and didn't run. Someone who offered tools instead of judgment.

Someone I was definitely, absolutely, completely not falling for.

Chapter Fourteen

Ryan's Cottage

Ryan

I moved the armchair six inches to the left. Checked the light again.

The afternoon sun hit the spot perfectly. Warm but not harsh. Natural light that wouldn't cast weird shadows across my face.

Dozer watched me from his spot on the floor. Head tilted. Knowing.

"Don't look at me like that," I told him.

He huffed.

I checked the mirror. Adjusted my uniform shirt. Smoothed down a wrinkle that probably didn't matter.

Rachel would be here in ten minutes. To sketch me. For the mural.

Professional. Work. Nothing more.

Except my hands kept fidgeting. My pulse kicked up every time I glanced at the clock.

This is ridiculous. I've faced down burning buildings. Rescued people from collapsed structures. But the thought of sitting still while Rachel studies my face for hours makes my stomach flip.

Dozer's ears perked up. He tilted his head toward Rachel's cottage.

I heard it, too. Her scream from next door.

My heart stopped. I ran.

Rachel stood on a chair in her cottage. Dali clutched in her arms. Both of them staring at the corner near her easel.

"There's a spider." She pointed with a shaking hand. "A big one."

Relief flooded me so fast I almost laughed. "You want me to kill a spider?"

"I want you to relocate it. Far away. Like, to another zip code."

The spider sat in the corner. Probably the size of a quarter. Not particularly threatening.

I couldn't help smiling. "You can handle paint fumes and power tools, but spiders..."

"Spiders are different. They have too many legs. And they move wrong."

"Everyone's afraid of something."

I crossed to the corner. Caught the spider gently in my cupped hands. Rachel watched with wide eyes while I carried it outside and released it in the bushes.

When I came back, she'd climbed down from the chair. Set Dali on the floor. Color high in her cheeks.

"Thank you. I know it's ridiculous. I can face down a collapsing pier, but a tiny spider makes me lose my mind."

"It's not ridiculous. I'm terrified of needles."

"Really?"

"Passed out getting blood drawn at the academy. In front of my entire class." I shrugged. "Fear doesn't make sense. It just is."

She smiled. The tension between us eased slightly. "I should probably come over. For the session."

"Right. Yeah. I've got everything set up."

We walked across the yard together. The afternoon warm. Comfortable. Almost normal.

Almost.

Inside my cottage, Rachel's professional armor snapped into place.

She spread out her supplies. Sketchpad. Pencils. Charcoal. Eraser. Everything arranged in calculated formation.

"Sit there." She gestured without looking at me. "The light's good."

I sat. She studied me from across the room. Assessing angles. Measuring proportions with her pencil held up.

The formality felt wrong. Too stiff. Too distant.

"Just... relax." She didn't meet my eyes. "Pretend I'm not here."

"That's impossible."

The words came out before I could stop them.

A beat of charged silence. She looked at me then. Really looked. Color rising in her cheeks again.

She picked up her pencil. "Talk to me. It helps. Makes your expressions more natural."

"About what?"

"Anything. Tell me about the transfer to Seaholly."

I leaned back in the chair. Tried to find a comfortable position. "Where do you want me to start?"

"Why here? Why this town?" Her hand moved across the page. Quick confident strokes.

"I needed a fresh start. My last department... it got complicated."

"How complicated?"

"Politics. Department drama. The kind that makes you question whether you want to keep doing the job." I shifted slightly. She made a small sound, adjusted her angle. "There was a lieutenant position opening up. I was next in line. Then suddenly I wasn't."

"That's not fair."

"No. But it happens." I watched her sketch. The way she bit her lip when she concentrated. How she tilted her head, studying me. "The captain suggested I might be happier somewhere else. Somewhere smaller. Less competitive."

She moved around me. Circling. Viewing me from different perspectives. Her presence made me hyperaware of every detail. The way I held my shoulders. Where my hands rested. The angle of my jaw.

"So you came here."

"When I was in Seaholly last fall, helped out after the hurricane. Met the captain. Good man. Good department." I paused. "He mentioned they had an opening, I followed up. Small town felt right. And best friend's here."

She moved closer to capture some detail. "And then you got Dozer?"

"Found him behind the station. Someone abandoned him there." I smiled. "Figured we both needed a fresh start."

Her pencil moved across the page. Confident. Skilled. She knew exactly what she wanted to capture.

"What about you?" I asked. "Why Seaholly?"

Her hand paused. Just for a second. Then continued.

"I needed a change too."

"From what?"

She stepped back. Studied her work. Stepped closer again. "From someone who wanted me smaller."

The bitterness in her voice caught me.

"My ex, Derek." She said his name like it tasted bad. "We were together three years. Engaged for six months. He had very specific ideas about what my life should look like."

"Like what?"

"Like I should have a real job. Office hours. Professional clothes. A 401k." She gestured with her pencil. "He wanted me to teach art at a private school. Stable income. Benefits. Summers off."

"But you wanted to create."

"I wanted to be an artist. Not just teach other people how to be artists." Her voice gained strength. "He said I was being impractical. Childish. That I needed to grow up and think about our future."

I watched her face. Saw the old hurt there.

"He said I was too much. Too chaotic. Too unpredictable." She moved around me again. Capturing a different angle. "He wanted me to be appropriate. Whatever that means."

"He sounds like an idiot."

She almost smiled. "He told me I'd never make it as an artist. That I was wasting my talent on a fantasy."

"You're not too much. You're exactly right."

She stopped moving. Looked up from her sketchpad. Our eyes met across the space between us.

The air shifted. Heavier. Electric.

"Turn your head slightly. To the left."

I did. She studied me. Not just my features anymore. Deeper.

"You really think that? That I'm not too much?"

"I think Derek was threatened by you. By your talent. By your passion." I held her gaze. "I think he wanted you smaller because he couldn't handle you at full size."

Her breath caught. She set down her pencil. Crossed to me.

"Your collar's crooked. Let me..."

She reached up to fix it. Her fingers brushed my neck.

The barest touch, but it burned. Warm and soft against my skin.

We both froze.

She stood between my knees. Me sitting. Her standing. Looking down at me.

So close I could see the darker ring around her irises. Brown bleeding into amber. The paint smudge on her jaw. Blue this time. Cerulean maybe. The way her pulse jumped in her throat.

Her hand still on my collar. Fingers curled into the fabric. My hand rested on the chair arm. Knuckles white from gripping it. Keeping myself from reaching for her.

The late afternoon light slanted through the window behind her. Lightened the edges of her hair. Made the air shimmer between us.

She smelled like vanilla, paint and soap. The combination shouldn't work, but it did.

Her breathing had gone shallow. Mine too. The only sound in the cottage.

Neither of us moved. The moment stretched. Endless and impossible and terrifying.

I could feel the heat of her. The space between us measured in inches. In heartbeats.

Her eyes dropped to my lips. Stayed there. Her tongue wet her own.

Back to my eyes.

I leaned forward. Just slightly. Testing.

She leaned down. Just as slight.

Her hand slid from my collar to my shoulder. My hand finally moved. Found her waist. Fingers spreading against the soft fabric of her shirt.

The distance between us closed. Millimeter by millimeter.

Her eyes fluttered closed. Mine started to follow.

Our lips almost touching. Almost—

CRASH! Tinkle-tinkle.

Dali yowled. Dozer barked with pure joy.

Rachel jumped back as the dog burst through the doorway, chasing the cat in a blur of fur and chaos. The vase lay shattered on the floor—Dali must have knocked it over. Now the cat raced across my couch. Dozer followed in hot pursuit with enthusiastic barking. Dali's claws scrabbed on the wood floor.

"Dozer!" I grabbed for his collar. Missed.

"Dali, you demon!" Rachel lunged for her cat.

The animals careened through the living room. Under the table. Over the chair. Absolute pandemonium.

I finally caught Dozer's collar. Rachel cornered Dali behind the couch.

We stood there. Both breathing hard. Animals panting between us.

Then we started laughing. Despite everything. Despite the shattered moment. Despite the frustration and disappointment.

"Your cat is evil," I said.

"She's creative." But Rachel grinned. "And your dog has terrible timing."

"The worst."

We got the animals separated. Dali back at Rachel's cottage unscathed. The spell broken, but the tension still simmering underneath.

Rachel gathered her supplies. Moving quickly. Too quickly. "I should go. I have enough sketches for now."

She avoided my eyes. Hands trembling as she packed her pencils.

"Rachel, wait—"

She paused at the door. Looked back.

I wanted to ask her to stay. To finish what almost happened. To stop running from whatever this is between us.

But I didn't know how to say it without pushing too hard.

"Thank you. For the session. I'll see you tomorrow?"

"Tomorrow." She nodded. Already backing away. Escaping.

She left fast. Dozer whined at my side. Missing her already.

I stood in my cottage. Staring at the closed door. The chair where she'd almost kissed me still sat in the perfect light.

Then I noticed her sketchbook on the table. Forgotten in her rush to leave.

I picked it up to set it by the door so I could return it later. So nothing would get damaged.

Loose pages slipped out. Fluttered to the floor around my feet.

I crouched to gather them. Saw what they were.

Apartment listings. Printed from rental websites. Addresses circled in red pen. Notes scribbled in margins.

"Too far from Mom." "Too expensive." "No natural light." "Beverly's area."

And there. In the white space beside a floor plan. A sketch of my hands. Quick lines. Confident strokes. My hands holding a coffee mug. The detail unmistakable.

Another listing. Another sketch in the margin. My profile this time. The way I stand.

Page after page. Apartment searches mixed with drawings of me. Like she'd been looking at rentals while thinking about what she'd be leaving behind.

My throat went tight.

She's planning to move.

She's leaving.

And she wasn't going to tell me.

Chapter Fifteen

The Firehouse

Rachel

"Dozer! No! That's not a toy!"

Too late.

The big ball of fur had already grabbed my brush in his mouth. Tail wagging furiously. Paint smeared across his jowls. His tongue. The scaffold platform. Everywhere.

He'd climbed the ladder. Fifteen feet up. His massive head appearing over the edge like this was completely normal.

On his way toward the ladder, he acted like this was the best game ever. His prize dripping cerulean blue with every step. Seventy pounds of puppy moving with surprising grace.

The crowd below erupted in laughter. The warm afternoon had drawn more people than usual.

"Come back here!" I scrambled across the scaffold after him, but he was too fast.

He descended the ladder like he'd done it a thousand times. Each step marked with blue droplets. His tail still wagging. More than pleased with himself.

Mrs. Henderson was beside herself with delight. "Oh my! What an adventurer! Look at him go!"

I climbed down after him. My legs shaking from the sudden movement. Caught Dozer at the bottom. Wrestled my paintbrush free while he tried to lick my face with his blue-stained tongue.

"You absolute menace." I scratched behind his massive ears anyway. Couldn't help it. He was too pleased with himself to stay mad at.

Paint everywhere. On his fawn-colored fur. On my hands. On the grass. A trail of blue chaos marking his path from scaffold to ground.

I'd been up there since dawn, when the light was still cool and soft. Fifteen feet high on the scaffold, painting the fire station wall. Threw myself into the work before my brain could catch up. Before I could think about yesterday.

The physical work had helped. Broad strokes. Color blocking. Losing myself in the process. No thinking required. Just paint and motion, and the wall taking shape beneath my hands.

Until Dozer decided to climb a ladder.

The mural was coming together. Firefighters in action. The crew I'd photographed. Ryan prominent but not centered. Part of the team. The way he'd want it.

Below, a small crowd had gathered to watch. Mrs. Henderson stood front and center with a pitcher of lemonade. Supervising. Offering commentary. Living her best life.

Mrs. Henderson appeared beside me with her pitcher. "Let me get you some lemonade, dear. You've been up there for hours without a break."

"Thank you, Mrs. Henderson." I accepted the cup gratefully. My throat was dry. I hadn't realized how thirsty I'd become.

She studied the mural wall with her hands on her hips. Head tilted. Considering. "It's coming along beautifully. Though I really do think you should add a bit more red. Right there in the corner. Needs warmth."

I took a long drink of lemonade. Let the cold sweet-tart slide down my throat. Gave myself a moment before responding. "Thank you, Mrs. Henderson."

"I'm just saying, red would really make it pop." She gestured at the upper left corner. "Don't you think? A nice bright red?"

"I appreciate the suggestion." My professional smile held firm. Warm. Patient. "I'll keep it in mind."

I had absolutely no intention of adding red. The color palette worked. Fire tones would come later in specific places. Not splashed randomly in corners.

But Mrs. Henderson meant well. She loved this project. Felt ownership in it. I could be gracious. Though this time, she was wrong.

Unlike when she'd told Ryan his writing needed work. He'd mentioned that once. How she'd been brutally honest about his fire safety pamphlets being too technical. She'd been right then. He'd told me how he'd rewritten everything to be clearer. More accessible.

"Have you seen the article in the Gazette?" she asked. "About the mural? They quoted you. Very impressive."

"I saw it." The article mentioned the community support. The town's excitement.

"They mentioned Ryan too. How he's been helping with community outreach." She watched me carefully. Her eyes too knowing. "You two make a lovely team."

My stomach tightened. The lemonade turned sour in my mouth. "We're not a team. We're just neighbors."

"Hmm." Mrs. Henderson's expression said she didn't believe that for a second. "Well, neighbor or not, he cares about you very much."

I didn't know how to respond to that. Focused on Dozer instead. Tried to wipe more paint off his jowls with the hem of my shirt.

I needed to get back to work. Back up on the scaffold, where I didn't have to think about Ryan or teams or whatever Mrs. Henderson thought she saw between us.

I was about to climb back up when I heard his voice.

"You left your sketchbook at my place. Thought you might need it."

My breath caught. Lodged somewhere in my throat. I turned slowly.

Ryan stood at the edge of the crowd. Holding my sketchbook. The one I'd forgotten in my panicked retreat yesterday. The one that probably still had drawings of him scattered through the pages.

The one that might have my studio searches visible.

Dozer bounded over to him immediately. Tail wagging. Blue paint smearing Ryan's jeans when he jumped up in greeting.

"Hey, buddy. What did you get into?" Ryan looked at the paint, then at me.

Ryan was holding my sketchbook. Looking up at me on the scaffold.

The crowd was still watching. All of them. Mrs. Henderson most of all. Her eyes bright with interest and speculation.

"Oh. Thanks." I forced casual into my voice. "You can just leave it down there."

I started climbing back up the ladder. Away from him. Away from this conversation.

"Rachel."

Something in his voice made me pause halfway up. My hands gripping the ladder rungs.

"We almost kissed yesterday."

I froze. Every muscle in my body locking up.

"Dozer interrupted, so technically—" I tried to deflect.

"Can we talk about this?"

I climbed higher. Not looking at him. "I'm kind of in the middle of something. Maybe later?"

"Hard to run away when you're fifteen feet up."

The words landed like a physical blow. He knew. He knew my pattern. Knew I'd been avoiding him.

I stopped climbing. Caught.

Mrs. Henderson was watching this exchange with great interest. Trying not to look like she was eavesdropping. Failing.

I sat down on the scaffold platform. Defeated.

"Ryan, I... it's complicated."

"So uncomplicate it. Talk to me."

But with the crowd below. Mrs. Henderson's ears perked up. This wasn't the place. Wasn't the moment.

"Not here. Not now."

"When?"

"Soon. I promise."

The awkward moment stretched between us. The crowd shifting. Uncomfortable. Waiting.

Mrs. Henderson broke the silence by approaching Ryan. Perfectly timed intervention.

"Ryan, dear, while you're here, my porch railing is loose. Keeps me up at night worrying about falling."

She'd clearly been waiting for an opportunity to mention this.

Ryan's attention shifted immediately. "I can fix that for you, Mrs. Henderson."

"Would you?" She was delighted. "That's so kind! I'd hire someone, but it's so expensive on a fixed income."

"Happy to help. When works for you?"

Ryan pulled up his calendar and they made plans. Mrs. Henderson glancing between Ryan and me. Clear matchmaking intentions. She looked pleased with herself.

I watched this from above. Seeing Mrs. Henderson's meddling, but also her genuine need. The railing probably was loose. She probably did worry about falling.

And Ryan would fix it without hesitation. Because that's who he was.

The crowd began to disperse. Mrs. Henderson left satisfied. Got her repair scheduled and her entertainment.

Ryan was still there. Looking up at me.

"I meant it. When you're ready to talk, I'm here."

He held up the sketchbook. I climbed down carefully. Took it from him. Our fingers brushed. Sent tingles up my arm. Impossible to ignore.

Ryan left with Dozer. The dog still had paint on his nose. Both of them heading toward his truck.

I stood alone in the parking lot. Sketchbook clutched to my body.

Climbed back up to the scaffold. Opened the sketchbook to see what I'd captured yesterday.

My preliminary mural sketches filled the first section. Studies of the firefighters. Ryan's hands holding equipment. The crew in action.

And there. Tucked between drawings. My studio searches. Printed pages with listings circled. Notes everywhere. Proximity to Beverly's house highlighted. Rental costs underlined. Available move-in dates starred.

Did he see them? Does he know?

But he didn't mention it. Didn't confront me about it.

Was he giving me space to tell him myself?

The guilt intensified. Crawled up my throat. Made breathing difficult.

I forced myself to paint. Loaded my brush with burnt sienna. Started working on the gear details with careful strokes. The physical work helping somewhat. Giving my hands something to do while my mind spun.

Hours passed. The sun climbed higher. Heat built up on the scaffold platform, making the metal warm under my hands. My shoulders screamed. My hands cramped. I kept working.

The mural was taking shape. Coming together exactly as I'd envisioned. The fire station wall transformed into a tribute to the people who protected Seaholly.

My phone buzzed in my pocket. I ignored it. Kept painting.

It buzzed again. Insistent. Demanding attention.

I pulled it out with my free hand. Balanced precariously on the scaffold. Read the screen.

Text from Mom

> *Honey, my internet went out. I can't get it to work. I've tried unplugging everything like you showed me but nothing's happening. I'm so frustrated.*

Another text came through immediately.

> *I was trying to shop online for a new cardigan. Now I can't do anything.*

I sat down on the scaffold platform. My legs unable to hold me. Relief flooding through me so fast it made me dizzy.

The internet. Just the internet.

Not a fall. Not the hospital. Not something terrible.

I took a breath. This wasn't a crisis. I could fix this.

Paintbrush still in my lap. Paint dripping onto my jeans. I steadied myself.

I texted Mom back.

> *I'm calling right now.*

Automated menus. Long wait times. Finally, a person on the line.

"There's an outage in your mother's area," the representative said. "Crews are working on it now. Service should be restored by 6 pm."

My shoulders relaxed. "Thank you."

I texted Mom back.

> There's an outage in your area. They're fixing it now - should be back by 6 pm. I'll call you tonight to make sure it's working.

Mom's response came quickly.

> Thank you, sweetheart. What would I do without you?

I stared at that text. The weight of it pressing down on me.

Looked at the fire station below. The bay doors where trucks rolled out to emergencies. Ryan doing the work he was meant to do. Where he belonged.

Looked at my phone. My mother over an hour away. Needing me for things like this. Small crises that would only get more frequent.

The math was impossible. I couldn't be in two places at once.

Couldn't finish the mural if I moved.

Couldn't pursue anything with Ryan if I were leaving.

Couldn't leave my mother struggling alone.

Ryan said, "When you're ready to talk." But how do you tell someone you might have to leave when you're falling in love with them?

Chapter Sixteen

Mrs. Henderson's House

Ryan

"You're doing it wrong, dear."

I looked up from my position on Mrs. Henderson's porch. She stood in the doorway, holding a pitcher of lemonade and wearing an expression of cheerful superiority.

"Is that so?" I kept my voice mild. Amused.

"My husband always loosened that bolt first." She pointed at a different bolt entirely with her free hand.

The bolt I'd been working on wouldn't budge. I'd adjusted my grip on the wrench, applied more pressure. Put my shoulder into it. The metal stayed stubbornly in place. Stripped threads or rust, maybe both.

I studied the railing structure. Saw what she meant. The whole thing was designed to work in sequence. The tension had to be released before the main bolt would turn.

I switched to the bolt she'd indicated. It gave immediately.

Then I went back to the original. Turned smoothly this time.

"Huh." I sat back on my heels. Looked up at her. "Thanks."

She smiled. Pleased with herself. Set the lemonade on the porch table.

Dozer lay in the yard below, watching me work. Patient. Calm. His massive head resting on his paws. Good dog.

Mrs. Henderson settled into her rocker. Bundled in her coat. Made herself comfortable. I suspected I was in for extended supervision.

Our dynamic was already clear. She was bossy but often right. I was patient and charmed by her.

I went back to work. Removing bolts in the proper sequence now. The railing coming apart more easily.

"How long have you been doing repairs?" she asked.

"My dad taught me young. He was a contractor."

"Harold was handy too. Always fixing something around here."

I nodded. Kept working. Let her talk.

The railing was worse than she'd described. Much worse.

I pulled at one of the support posts. It shifted in its socket. When I examined the base, I found rot. The wood crumbling under my fingers.

"Mrs. Henderson, this isn't just loose." I looked up at her. "The whole thing needs to be replaced."

"Oh my." She leaned forward in her rocker. "Is that bad?"

"It's dangerous. You could have fallen right through."

Her face paled slightly. "I've been so careful. I just stopped using the railing altogether."

Which was even more dangerous. Navigating stairs without support.

Several boards were compromised. The mounting hardware corroded. All the support posts rotted at the base. This was a full afternoon of work, minimum.

"I can do it. Just need to make a run to the hardware store for lumber and new mounting brackets."

"I can't ask you to do all that." But her voice carried hope underneath the protest.

"You're not asking. I'm offering." I stood, brushed sawdust off my jeans. "Can't have you taking a fall."

"You're such a good boy, Ryan." Her eyes went soft. "Your mother raised you right."

I thought about my mother. How she'd taught me to help neighbors. To see what needed doing and do it without being asked. To show up when people needed you.

"She tried her best."

Mrs. Henderson poured lemonade into two glasses. The ice clinking. Condensation forming on the outside.

She handed me one. "Sit with me a minute. You've been working hard."

I sat in the chair beside her rocker. Took a long drink. The lemonade cold and sweet-tart. Perfect.

Dozer trotted up the steps. Settled at my feet with a contented sigh.

"Harold built this railing," Mrs. Henderson said. She ran her hand along the weathered wood. Gentle. Like touching something precious. "Thirty-two years ago. He was so proud of it."

I heard the ache in her voice. The weight of memory.

"He did good work. It lasted a long time."

"He was a firefighter, too. Did I tell you that?"

"You mentioned it yesterday."

"Thirty years with the department." Her eyes went distant. Seeing something I couldn't. "He'd come home smelling of smoke. I never minded that smell. It meant he was safe. Home with me."

I knew that feeling. The relief of making it through a shift. Coming home intact. The smell of smoke clinging to your clothes like proof of survival.

"You must have worried every time the alarm went off."

"Every single time." She smiled softly. Sad. "But you can't love someone and cage them. He needed the work. Loved it. Couldn't imagine him doing anything else."

She looked at me. Something knowing in her expression.

"And I loved him. So I learned to live with the worry."

The words settled over me. Heavy with understanding.

She got what it meant to love a first responder. The sacrifices. The fear. The midnight wake-ups. The waiting. The choice to love anyway, despite the cost.

I didn't know what to say to that. Just nodded. Held her gaze.

She rocked slowly. Sipped her lemonade.

Then she shifted topics without warning. "I've seen you two."

I went still. "Mrs. Henderson—"

"The way you look at her when you think no one's watching."

My face went hot. Caught.

She smiled. Not unkind. "And the way she looks at you when she thinks no one's watching."

My pulse kicked up. Hope. Tentative. Fragile.

"Really?"

"Oh yes." Mrs. Henderson's voice went gentle. "She's scared though. That girl's been hurt before."

"I know. Her ex."

"Not just him." She set her glass down. "Something deeper in her life made her this way."

I wanted to ask what. Wanted to understand what kept Rachel pulling away.

But Mrs. Henderson's expression told me she'd said all she was going to say.

"Just be patient with her."

I nodded. Finished my lemonade. Set the glass down carefully.

Mrs. Henderson stood. Disappeared inside her house.

I thought she was done talking. Started to get up.

But she returned a moment later. Arms full of photo albums. The thick kind with plastic-covered pages.

"Let me show you something."

She settled back in her rocker. Opened the first album across her lap.

Pictures of Rachel. Town events. Art shows. Beach cleanups.

"She came here alone three years ago." Mrs. Henderson turned pages slowly. "Broken from that man who tried to dim her light."

I leaned closer. Studied the photos.

Rachel at a gallery opening. Wearing a dress. Her hair up. Smiling but the smile not quite reaching her eyes. Early. Before she'd settled.

Mrs. Henderson turned the page.

Rachel teaching kids. Paint everywhere. Laughing. The smile real this time.

Another page.

Rachel with Maya at the beach. Both of them soaking wet. Arms around each other. Pure joy on both faces.

"Look how she bloomed." Mrs. Henderson's voice carried pride. Affection. "Built a whole life here. Family, purpose, home."

More photos. Rachel at community gatherings. Presenting her work to the town council. Covered in paint with a classroom full of kids who adored her. Painting on the beach at sunset.

Each photo showed her more integrated. More alive. More herself.

My throat tightened. This was her home. Her life. Everything she'd built from nothing.

Everything she'd be giving up if she left.

The weight of that realization settled in my chest. Heavy. Painful.

Mrs. Henderson closed the albums. Set them aside.

"You've been hurt too." Not a question. A statement of fact.

I looked up. Surprised.

"Small town." She smiled. "People talk. I don't know the details. But I know you left your old department for a reason. That you came here looking for a fresh start."

I didn't confirm or deny. Just waited.

"My late husband used to say: you can't drive forward looking in the rearview mirror."

I laughed. Couldn't help it. "That's surprisingly good advice."

"You sound surprised, young man."

"No, I just—"

"I'm full of wisdom, dear." Mock offense in her voice. "Don't act so shocked."

"You're just full of wisdom today."

"I'm full of wisdom every day." She sniffed. "People just don't always listen."

I grinned despite myself. She was pushing me. Not to let my past stop me from pursuing Rachel. Whatever happened before was over. Time to move forward.

I stood. Stretched. My back protesting from hunching over the railing.

"I should get started on the actual repair. This is going to take a while."

The next hour passed in focused work. Removing damaged boards. Careful not to damage the house itself. Measuring for replacements. Making a list of materials I'd need.

Mrs. Henderson watched. Quiet for once. Just keeping me company.

As I was pulling the last rotted post, she spoke again. Quieter this time.

"Losing Harold was the hardest thing I've ever done."

I paused. Looked at her.

She was staring at her house. At the porch we were repairing. The windows reflecting afternoon sun.

"This house is too big for one person. Too quiet."

I heard the ache underneath. The loneliness she usually kept hidden.

"We built it together. Made our memories here. Now it echoes."

I didn't have an answer. Didn't know what to say to that kind of grief.

So I just listened. Kept my hands busy with work.

She shook off the melancholy after a moment. Sat up straighter. "Anyway. Point is..."

She paused. Let the silence stretch.

"Loneliness is harder to fix than any house, Ryan."

The words hit deeper than she probably intended.

I thought about Rachel. About myself before Seaholly. About Mrs. Henderson in this big, empty house.

All of us trying to fill the silence in different ways.

The weight of that truth settled over me. Heavy. Real.

I finished removing the last damaged piece. Started packing up my tools. The repair was as complete as I could make it today. Tomorrow I'd come back with new materials. Rebuild it properly.

Mrs. Henderson inspected my work. Nodded approval.

"You did well. Thank you, dear."

"I'll be back tomorrow afternoon. Get this finished for you."

"You're very kind."

I loaded my tools in the truck bed. Dozer already waiting by the passenger door.

Mrs. Henderson stood on her porch. Watching me.

"Sometimes the best solutions to problems come from the most unexpected places."

I paused. Wrench in hand. Looked at her.

"What do you mean?"

She smiled. Mysterious. Knowing. "Time will tell."

I waited for more. Some clarification. Some hint.

But she just stood there. Smiling that enigmatic smile.

"Mrs. Henderson—" I started.

"Hmm?"

"You can't just say cryptic things and walk away."

Her smile widened. "I absolutely can. I'm old. It's my privilege."

She turned. Headed for her door.

"Wait—"

"See you tomorrow, dear. Same time."

She disappeared inside. The door closing behind her with gentle finality.

I stood there in her driveway. Tools in hand. Completely confused.

Dozer whined from the truck. Ready to go home.

"Yeah, buddy. I know."

I finished loading my tools. Closed the truck bed. Dozer already waiting by the passenger door.

"Don't give up on her, Ryan!" Mrs. Henderson called from the porch.

I looked back. She stood there with her arms crossed. That knowing smile on her face.

"I won't," I called back.

She nodded. Satisfied. Then disappeared inside.

I got in my truck. Sat there. Engine off. Just thinking.

Thought about Rachel on the scaffold yesterday. Avoiding me. Climbing higher to escape the conversation. "It's complicated."

Thought about the photo albums. Rachel's life here in Seaholly. Three years of building community. Finding home. Blooming.

Thought about her sketchbook. The studio searches I'd glimpsed. Notes about proximity to her mother. Rental costs. Move-in dates.

I started the truck. Sat there idling.

Dozer put his massive head on my thigh. Patient. Supportive.

The pieces were right there. I could feel the answer hovering. Almost visible.

But I couldn't quite connect them. Couldn't see the full picture.

Mrs. Henderson said unexpected solutions.

Rachel's pulling away.

What am I missing?

Chapter Seventeen

Beverly's House

Rachel

"Mom!" I rushed through the kitchen and turned off the burner.

A pot boiling over, water hissing onto the burner. Steam everywhere. The smoke alarm shrieking.

Mom was attempting to climb on a chair to reach the alarm. Wincing. One hand pressed against her lower back.

She froze when she saw me. Stepped back from the chair.

I grabbed a dish towel, waved it under the smoke detector until it stopped screaming. Opened the window over the sink. Cold air rushed in.

"I had it under control."

I turned to look at her. Really look.

She was pale. Holding herself carefully. Like movement hurt.

"When did this start?"

"Just a few minutes ago. I was making spaghetti and I forgot—" She waved a hand. Dismissive. "It's fine. I'm fine."

But she wasn't fine.

"Come sit down." I took her arm gently. Guided her to the kitchen table.

She sank into the chair with a small sound. Relief mixed with pain.

"Mom, no more climbing on chairs. Ever." I held her gaze. "If there's smoke and the alarm goes off, you get out of the house first. Then you call 911. Promise me."

"I will."

I pulled out the chair across from her. Sat down. Looked around the kitchen with new eyes.

The sink was full of dirty dishes. Stacked precariously. Some with dried food crusted on them.

The trash overflowed. Clearly hadn't been taken out in days.

Unopened mail was stacked on the counter. Bills. Notices. The pile at least six inches tall.

"You usually call first." Mom's voice was quiet. Almost apologetic. "I would've tidied up."

My throat tightened. She'd been hiding this. Making everything look fine when I called ahead. Only showing me what she wanted me to see.

How long had she been struggling like this?

"Mom, I'm going to help you with the mail."

"Rachel, you don't need to—"

"I do." I kept my voice firm but gentle. "Keep everything in this basket and when I come for Wednesday dinners, we'll go through it together. Most of this I can set up online. We'll come up with a new system" She nodded.

The bruise on her left arm was darker than last time I'd seen it. Purple-black. Spreading from wrist to elbow.

"Mom. What happened to your arm?"

"Just clumsy lately." She pulled her sleeve down. Covered it. "Getting old."

"When did you fall?"

"I didn't fall. I just bumped it on the—" She stopped. Caught. "It's nothing."

It wasn't nothing.

I closed my eyes. Took a breath. Tried to keep my voice steady.

"Let me order us something, Mom."

She started to protest. To insist she could make dinner.

"Thai food?" I pulled out my phone. "From that place you like?"

"That would be nice."

I ordered while she sat quietly. Hands folded on the table. Looking smaller than I remembered.

When had she gotten so small?

The food arrived half hour later. I paid. Brought it to the table. Got plates and forks.

We sat with the white containers between us. Both pretending this was fine. Just a normal dinner. Nothing wrong.

Mom tried to keep the conversation light. Asked about the mural. About my students. About the gallery show coming up.

I answered. Kept my voice upbeat. Smiled when appropriate.

But the unspoken weight between us was heavier than any words.

We both knew everything had changed.

Neither of us wanted to say it out loud.

Mom's phone sat on the table between the cartons of pad thai and spring rolls. The screen lit up with a notification.

She picked it up. Scrolled. Her face brightened.

"I saw the article about your mural. The sketches look beautiful."

I paused mid-bite. "You saw that?"

"Mrs. Kowalski showed me. Very proud of her neighbor's daughter." She turned the phone so I could see. The local news website. Photos of my preliminary sketches. The fire station wall half-painted.

My stomach dropped.

Because there, in almost every sketch, was Ryan.

His hands holding equipment. His profile as he demonstrated something to kids. His face among the crew. Over and over.

Mom scrolled through the photos slowly. Studying each one.

"That firefighter. He's in almost every sketch."

My face went hot. Caught.

"Tell me about him."

"Mom—"

"Rachel." She set the phone down. Looked at me with those eyes that had always seen through my deflections. "Tell me about him."

I wanted to change the subject. To redirect. To protect this fragile thing that might not even exist.

But I found myself talking instead.

About Ryan showing up at the community center that first day. About the hardware store and my ridiculous shelf-climbing. About the pier rescue and him staying all night to make sure I was okay.

About the spider in my cottage. His patient amusement. The way he'd carried it outside so carefully.

About the almost-kiss in his cottage. Dozer interrupting. The way my heart had hammered afterward.

About how he looked at me. Like I was exactly right. Not too much. Not too chaotic. Just... right.

Mom listened. Really listened. Her face softening as I talked.

Recognition dawning.

"You're in love with him."

"I— it's not— we haven't even—" I stumbled over the words. Panic rising.

"Honey." Her voice went impossibly gentle. Sad, almost. Like she already knew what was coming.

We finished eating in quieter tones. The conversation shifting to safer topics. The weather. Mrs. Kowalski's garden. Small things that didn't matter.

I helped Mom get ready for bed.

She moved slowly. Each step careful. I steadied her arm when she stood. Waited outside the bathroom door in case she needed help.

When she emerged in her nightgown, I walked her to her bedroom. Made sure she had water on the nightstand. Her phone plugged in and charging.

"I'm fine, honey. You don't need to fuss."

"I know." But I fussed anyway.

"Mom, you added photos." I looked at her nightstand.

It was covered with them. Framed pictures arranged carefully. A gallery of moments.

Me as a child. Paint-covered and grinning. Holding up a finger painting of our old house.

"I remember this!" I picked up the frame. "I was so proud of that painting."

Me at my high school art show. Standing beside my first real canvas. Nervous and proud.

But there were recent ones too.

Me at a gallery opening in Seaholly. Wearing that blue dress Maya had insisted I buy. Laughing at something off-camera.

Me teaching kids. Paint everywhere. Surrounded by chaos and color.

Me at the beach with Maya. Both of us windblown and happy. Arms around each other.

Mom had been following my life from afar. Collecting these moments. Keeping track.

I picked up the one of me and Maya at the farmers market. We were both holding canvas bags overflowing with vegetables. Laughing. Pure joy on both our faces.

I didn't even know this photo existed. Maya must have sent it to her.

"We'd just realized we both bought the same giant zucchini." I smiled at the memory. "Maya said we could start a zucchini bread empire."

"You're so happy there." Mom's voice came from the bed. Soft. "I see it in every picture."

My throat went tight. I set the frame down carefully. "I'm happy with you too, Mom."

"Not the same kind of happy, honey. And that's okay. That's good."

"Don't say that."

"I'm saying it because it's true." She settled against her pillows. Looked at me with those knowing eyes. "You bloomed there. In Seaholly. I've watched it happen."

I shook my head. Couldn't speak past the lump building.

"I won't let myself be the frost that kills that."

"Mom—"

"I mean it, Rachel. Whatever you're planning, whatever you think you need to do, I want you to hear me." She reached for my hand. Held it tight. "I see you. I'm grateful. But I don't want you to give up your life for me."

She was giving me permission.

Permission I didn't want. Couldn't accept.

Because the math didn't change just because she released me from obligation.

She still needed help. Still couldn't manage alone.

But Mom planted the seed anyway. Let it sit between us in the quiet bedroom.

I kissed her forehead. Turned off the lamp. Left her door cracked open in case she needed me.

I tackled the kitchen.

Washed dishes. Took out the trash. Wiped down counters. Sorted through the mail pile, separating bills from junk.

I could fix a messy kitchen. I couldn't fix everything else.

I drove home alone with my thoughts and the darkness pressing against my windshield.

Replayed the evening in my head. Mom struggling with the stove. The bruises. The fear underneath her brave face.

The kitchen in disarray. Expired food. Forgotten bills. Small disasters piling up.

Thought about my mural. Half-finished on the fire station wall.

Thought about my gallery show. Robert Vanderson coming to see it. My breakthrough moment.

Thought about Tommy and his drawings. My Tuesday art class. Sixteen kids who looked forward to creating with me every week.

Thought about Ryan.

Him teaching me how to install curtain rods properly after Dali had nearly brought down half my wall. Running into him at the taco joint and sharing a quick meal. Small chats in our yards while Dozer and Dali chased each other. How he looked at me like I mattered.

Thought about Mrs. Henderson's knowing smiles. Maya giving me her blessing. Henry's quiet approval.

The life I'd built in Seaholly. Brick by brick. Canvas by canvas. Friend by friend.

Three years of becoming myself.

I pulled into my driveway. I could see Ryan's cottage. His lights were on.

So close. Just thirty seconds away.

I looked at my own cottage. My studio visible through the window. The life I'd built here.

The life I had to leave.

I have to tell him.

Chapter Eighteen

The Firehouse

Ryan

"Okay, everyone laugh like Ryan just told a terrible dad joke!"

The crew erupted. Genuine, loud, the kind of laughter that echoed off the bay doors and bounced around the engine bays. Afternoon sun slanted through the high windows, warm and bright. The smell of cut grass drifted in from the park across the street.

Rachel stood behind her camera. Professional. In control. Except for the slight curve of her mouth as she pressed the shutter.

"My jokes aren't terrible," I said.

More laughter. Rachel's smile widened behind her viewfinder.

"That's exactly what someone with terrible jokes would say," Cooper called out.

"Remember the one about the ladder?" Martinez grinned. "We're still recovering from that one."

"It was a good joke."

"It was painful," Jenkins said. "Physically painful."

Rachel lowered her camera. "Okay, that's perfect. The natural banter is exactly what we need."

She checked the screen on her camera. Nodded. Satisfied.

But she wouldn't look at me. Not directly. Not the way she looked at everyone else.

Martinez elbowed Cooper. They exchanged glances. The whole crew noticed. The tension sat heavy in the air like smoke after a fire.

Rachel moved through the group. Adjusting positions. Making suggestions. Coaxing out personalities with ease that made it look effortless.

"Jenkins, tilt your head. Yeah, like that. Perfect."

"Cooper, stop trying so hard. You look constipated."

Cooper straightened immediately. "I was going for intense."

"You were going for gas pains." Rachel grinned. "Relax. You're a firefighter, not a fashion model."

The crew laughed. Relaxed. She had this gift for putting people at ease. Making them forget about the camera. Making them just be themselves.

I should've been part of this group shot. Should've been standing with my crew.

Instead I hung back. Watching her work.

The way she tilted her head when composing a shot. How she tucked hair behind her ear when concentrating. The gentle way she directed even the shyest guys, making them comfortable in front of the lens.

She belonged here. With them. With me.

Except she wouldn't meet my eyes.

When she did glance my direction, her expression went carefully blank. Neutral. Professional.

Like I was a stranger.

"That's a wrap on the group shots." Rachel packed her camera. "Thanks, everyone. These are going to be great."

The crew dispersed. Heading back to their tasks. Throwing congratulations at Rachel as they passed.

"You're a miracle worker," Martinez said. "Making us look good."

"I work with what I've got."

But the warmth in her voice disappeared when her eyes accidentally met mine across the bay.

She looked away quickly. Started organizing her equipment with focused intensity.

"Ryan, you're up." Her voice went clinical. Professional mask locked firmly in place. "Let's do some individual shots."

She gestured toward the equipment area. All business.

I walked over. Hyperaware of her nearness. The vanilla scent of her shampoo. The paint stain on her left thumb. A smudge of something purple near her wrist.

She'd been painting this morning. Before coming here.

"Hold the axe." She moved around me with the camera. A barrier between us. "No, more natural. Like you're actually using it."

I adjusted my grip. The axe familiar in my hands.

"Turn slightly left. Chin up. Good."

Click. Click. Click.

"Relax your shoulders. You're too tense."

Hard to relax when she was this close. When I could see the exact shade of brown in her eyes. When I wanted to reach out and wipe away the smudge of paint on her wrist.

"Let's try one more. By the truck."

I moved where she pointed. She circled me. Viewing angles. Checking light. Using the camera to keep space between us.

I wanted to talk. Wanted to ask what was wrong. What had changed.

She kept redirecting to the shoot.

"Lean against the door. No, the other way. Yeah."

Click. Click. Click.

"Look toward the window. Natural. Like you're checking something."

I did. She moved closer. Adjusted the angle.

Our eyes met for half a second.

I saw it. The same thing I'd seen at my cottage. At the coffee shop. At the mural wall.

She felt this too. Whatever this was between us.

But she looked away immediately. Stepped back.

"Perfect. That's good."

The crew watched from across the bay. Quiet now. Whatever they were thinking, they were smart enough to stay out of it.

Jenkins caught my eye. Raised an eyebrow. A silent question.

I shook my head. Not now.

Rachel lowered her camera. Studied the screen. Scrolled through images.

"I think we're good."

Her voice cracked on the last word. Just slightly. Just enough for me to hear.

I opened my mouth. She turned away before I could speak.

Started packing her equipment with quick, efficient movements.

Running again.

Chief Patterson gathered everyone in the bay. His voice boomed across the space.

"Great work today, folks. Calendar sales are going strong. All proceeds to hurricane relief."

The crew murmured appreciation. Good cause. Good community project.

"We've already pre-sold two hundred copies. Town council is thrilled. This is exactly the kind of community engagement they want to see."

Martinez whooped. Cooper clapped.

"Town council's stopping by next week to check progress on the mural." He looked directly at Rachel and me. "They want to see how it's coming along. Talk about the dedication. You two have been partners on this from the start. Great team."

Silence stretched. Awkward. Heavy.

Rachel forced a smile. "Sure. That's fine."

Her voice came out strained. Tight. Wrong.

Partners. The word hung between us like an accusation.

The Chief didn't seem to notice. "They're excited about this project. Rachel, you've done incredible work. Ryan, you've been a solid liaison. Whole thing reflects well on the department."

Rachel nodded. Murmured thanks. Went back to packing her equipment.

The irony tasted bitter in my mouth.

We were partners on paper. For the town. For the project.

But the distance between us felt insurmountable.

The shoot wrapped. Rachel moved immediately to her equipment. Packing with quick, efficient movements. Clearly trying to avoid lingering.

The crew wanted to chat. Thank her. Tell her how much they appreciated her work.

"These photos are amazing," Jenkins said, looking over her shoulder at her camera screen. "You made us look like actual professionals."

"You are actual professionals." Rachel smiled. But it didn't reach her eyes.

"You know what I mean." Jenkins grinned. "Calendar-worthy professionals."

"That's the goal." Rachel coiled a cable. Tucked it into her bag.

Cooper approached. "You should stop by more often. The guys love having you around."

"I'll be back to work on the mural." She kept packing. "That'll take a few more weeks at least."

"I meant just to hang out. Grab coffee with the crew."

"Oh. You mean voluntarily? Without a professional reason?" She almost laughed. "That's dangerous. I might bring my chaos with me."

"That's kind of the point."

"We'll see."

We'll see. The words landed like a punch.

Like she wasn't planning to come back.

Not after the mural was done.

Martinez joined the conversation. "You should do more work with us. Community events. Fundraisers. You've got a good eye."

"Thanks." Rachel kept packing. Moving constantly. "I appreciate that."

She stayed friendly but brief. Smiling. Nodding. Moving constantly toward her car.

The crew couldn't see it. They just saw professional Rachel wrapping up a job.

But I saw the way her hands shook slightly coiling cables. How she wouldn't look toward where I stood. The tremor in her laugh when Jenkins made a joke.

She was bolting.

And I'd had enough.

Outside in the parking lot, Rachel loaded equipment into her trunk. Moving fast. Focused. Avoiding eye contact with the station doors.

Avoiding me.

"Rachel, wait."

She stopped. Shoulders tensing. She didn't turn around.
Closed her eyes. Took a breath. Like she'd been expecting this.
Dreading this.
"We can't keep doing this."
"Doing what?" Her voice came out small.
"Pretending. Avoiding. Whatever this is where we act like strangers."
She finally turned around.
Mascara smudged. Eyes red. Cheeks blotchy.
She'd been crying.
My heart cracked open.
"Hey." I stepped closer. Softer. "What's wrong?"
She shook her head. Wouldn't answer.
"Rachel, please."
"I'm fine." The lie was obvious. "Just tired."
"You're not fine." I kept my voice gentle. "You've been crying. You won't look at me. You packed up like the building was on fire."
A bitter laugh escaped her. "Appropriate metaphor."
"Talk to me. Please. What's going on?"
Rachel tried to deflect. Shook her head. Started to turn away.
I didn't let her.
"I know you're scared. I'm scared too. But we can—"
"You should be scared." The words tumbled out. Breaking. Raw. "You should run. I'm chaos, Ryan. My life is a mess. My cat is a literal demon, my studio is where normal people have living rooms, I burn popcorn and set off fire alarms, I can barely take care of myself—"
"I know." I stepped closer. "I love all of it."
She stopped mid-sentence. Stared at me.
"I don't want you any other way." Another step. Close enough to see every shade of brown in her eyes. "I don't want some neat, organized life. I want you. Paint-stained and chaotic and setting off alarms and exactly as you are."
She was crying harder now. Shaking her head like she could deny what I was saying.
"Whatever Derek made you feel, whatever he said about you being too much—he was wrong." I held her gaze. "You're not too much. You're everything."

My words landed. Breaking something open in her.

Her face crumpled. She covered her mouth with one hand. Tears streaming down her face.

For a second, I thought she might step forward. Might let me hold her. Instead, she stepped back.

"That's not the problem." Her voice broke on the words.

I went still. Confused. Desperate. "Then what is? Tell me. Whatever it is, we can figure it out."

"I..." She looked at me. Such heartbreak in her eyes it stopped my breath. "I can't do this. Not right now. I'm sorry."

She turned to get in her car. Hands fumbling with her keys. Dropping them once before managing to unlock the door.

"Rachel, please." I reached for her. Didn't touch her. Wouldn't cross that line without permission. "Just tell me what's wrong. Let me help."

She turned back. Tears streaming down her face. Mascara running. Hair falling out of her ponytail.

Beautiful and breaking and so far out of my reach.

"You can't help with this. Nobody can."

She got in her car before I could respond.

"Rachel—"

The door closed. The engine started.

She drove away. Didn't look back. Didn't hesitate.

Just left.

I stood alone in the parking lot. Watching her taillights disappear down the street. Past the corner store. Past the intersection.

Gone.

Footsteps behind me. Frank appeared at my shoulder.

"You okay, Rodriguez?"

I kept staring after her car. Even after it turned the corner. Even after I couldn't see it anymore.

"I don't know."

Frank waited. Didn't push. Just stood there in solidarity.

I ran my hands through my hair. Pressure building in my throat. Behind my eyes.

She loved me. I knew she did. Saw it in her eyes. In the way she looked at me. In how she couldn't look at me.

But something was wrong. Something she wouldn't tell me.
Something that made her cry like her heart was breaking.
"Want to talk about it?" Frank asked.
"Nothing to talk about. She made her choice."
"Did she though?" Frank tilted his head. "Because from where I was standing, that didn't look like a choice. That looked like someone running scared."
I didn't answer.
Frank clapped me on the shoulder once. "Give her time. Whatever she's dealing with, she'll figure it out."
He headed back inside. Left me alone in the parking lot.
The sun hung low. Still hours from dark.
I stood there until my hands stopped shaking. Until I could breathe normally again. Until the ache in my chest dulled to something manageable.
She's in love with me too.
So why does it feel like she's saying goodbye?

Chapter Nineteen

Rachel's Cottage

Rachel

The charcoal smudged under my thumb. Wrong angle. Wrong shadow. I erased the line for the third time.

Midnight pushed toward one am. My cottage-studio felt too quiet. Too still. The window was cracked open—warm night air drifting in, carrying salt and the distant sound of waves. Just me and Dali and the mural studies spread across my worktable.

I'd been trying to lose myself in work since getting home. Since driving away from Ryan in that parking lot. Since seeing his face in my rearview mirror.

Heartbroken. Confused.

I want YOU. Paint-stained and chaotic and exactly as you are.

His words kept playing on repeat. Wouldn't let me concentrate.

I pressed harder with the charcoal. The firefighter's face took shape on the page. Strong jawline. Determined eyes.

Ryan's face.

I threw the charcoal down. Scrubbed my hands over my eyes.

Useless. I couldn't focus. Couldn't think about anything except how he'd looked at me. How his voice cracked when he said I was everything.

My phone buzzed on the table.

I grabbed it without thinking. Probably Maya checking in. She'd texted earlier asking if I was okay.

Ryan's name lit up the screen.

My heart stopped.

The message loaded.

> Dozer's sick. Ate something bad. At emergency vet. He's really sick.

No.

I read it again. The words didn't change.

Dozer. His dog. The mastiff who'd interrupted our almost-kiss. Who loved Ryan with everything. Who was his family.

Really sick.

I was out the door in seconds. Didn't grab a jacket. Didn't think. Just ran.

Keys. Car. Go.

I drove too fast. Hands shaking on the wheel. Heart pounding in my throat. The roads were empty, streetlights cutting through humid darkness.

The emergency vet was twenty minutes away. I made it in fifteen.

The parking lot was half empty. Late night. Early morning. Whatever this hour was called.

I parked crooked. Didn't care. Ran for the doors.

The waiting room hit me with fluorescent lights and antiseptic smell. Too bright. Too clean. The quiet anxiety of people with sick pets pressed down on everything.

Ryan was pacing.

Still in his uniform from shift. Navy pants. Department shirt. Hair disheveled like he'd been running his hands through it. Face pale under the harsh lights.

Devastated.

When he saw me, relief washed over his face. His whole body sagged.

"You came."

"Of course I came." I took his hands. They were freezing. "What happened?"

"I don't know. He was fine when I got home from shift. Then he started throwing up. Wouldn't stop." Ryan's words tumbled out fast. "He was shaking. Couldn't stand. I brought him straight here."

I pulled him toward the plastic chairs. Made him sit.

His leg bounced immediately. Nervous energy with nowhere to go.

I kept hold of his hand. Started rubbing circles with my thumb like my mom used to when I was scared.

"They'll figure it out. He's strong."

Ryan nodded. Didn't look convinced.

We sat in silence. His grip on my hand almost painful. Like he was afraid I'd disappear if he let go.

An older couple sat across from us. Their cat carrier between them. A college kid paced by the vending machines. Phone pressed to his ear. Explaining to someone who wasn't here.

The clock on the wall ticked. Loud. Relentless.

Five minutes felt like an hour.

Ryan's leg kept bouncing. I put my other hand on his knee. Gentle pressure.

"He's going to be okay."

"You don't know that."

"I know. But I believe it anyway."

He looked at me then. Really looked. Vulnerable.

"I'm glad you're here."

"Where else would I be?"

The question came out before I could stop it. Loaded with too much meaning.

Where else would I be except right here. Right beside him. Where I belonged.

Even though I'd run from him hours ago. Even though I'd left him in that parking lot. Even though everything was complicated and impossible.

He needed me. So I came.

Simple as that.

Forty minutes later, a vet in blue scrubs emerged from the back. Clipboard in hand. Face carefully neutral.

Ryan shot to his feet. I stood with him. Still holding his hand.

"Rodriguez?"

"That's me. Dozer. How is he?"

"He's stable." The vet smiled. Actual warmth now. "We think he ingested rat poison or spoiled food. But you got him here fast. That's what saved him."

Ryan's relief was immediate. Physical. Like strings cut.

"He's okay?"

"He's going to be fine. We've got him on IV fluids and activated charcoal to absorb the toxins. We'll monitor him for a few more hours, but he should be able to go home tonight."

"Tonight? Not tomorrow?"

"Tonight. He's a strong dog. Young. Healthy. He'll recover quickly."

Ryan made a sound. Half laugh, half sob. He turned to me.

I wrapped my arms around him right there in the waiting room.

He held me back. Face buried in my shoulder. Shaking.

The vet gave us privacy. Disappeared back through the doors.

I held him. Let him fall apart. Let him breathe.

"He's okay."

Ryan nodded against my shoulder. Arms tight around my waist.

We stood there under fluorescent lights. In a waiting room that smelled like fear and antiseptic. Holding each other while strangers looked away.

Eventually, he pulled back. Wiped his eyes. Embarrassed.

"Sorry. I just—"

"Don't." I touched his face. Made him look at me. "Don't apologize."

He nodded. Took a shaky breath.

We sat back down. Still close. Still touching.

Waiting for Dozer.

Ryan's hand found mine on the armrest. Our fingers laced together naturally.

"I know it's stupid. He's just a dog."

"It's not stupid." The words came out fierce. "Don't say that."

He looked at me. Surprised.

"He's not just a dog. He's your family. He matters."

Ryan's throat worked. "Yeah. He does."

Silence stretched. Comfortable despite everything.

"I found him behind the station. The day I transferred here. Someone just left him there."

My stomach twisted.

"He was so small. Skinny. Scared of everything." Ryan's thumb traced patterns on my hand. "I took him home that day. Couldn't leave him there. Second chances for both of us."

His voice broke. "He's the first thing that felt like home in a long time."

My throat went tight. "He was lucky you found him."

"I was lucky he found me."

I couldn't speak.

I understood. Completely.

"Dali saved me too. After Derek. After the engagement ended."

Ryan looked at me. Waiting.

"I felt like I'd never be enough for anyone. Like there was something fundamentally wrong with me." The words hurt coming out. Old wounds. "Dali just showed up one day. A stray. Sat on my doorstep. Chose me."

"And you kept her."

"I kept her." I smiled despite the tears threatening. "Even though she's a demon. Even though she destroys everything. She chose me when I needed to be chosen."

Ryan's hand tightened on mine. "Wounded and healing. Both of us."

I nodded. Couldn't speak.

Two hours later, the vet brought Dozer out.

The mastiff looked groggy but stable. Tail giving weak wags when he saw Ryan.

Ryan dropped to his knees. Buried his face in Dozer's neck. The dog leaned into him. Patient. Loving.

I watched. Throat tight.

The vet ran through discharge instructions. Follow-up appointment in five days. Watch for lethargy, vomiting, loss of appetite. Call immediately if anything seems wrong.

Ryan nodded. Took the paperwork. Helped Dozer walk slowly to my car.

We'd driven separately. Ryan had ridden in the ambulance with Dozer. Left his truck at the cottage.

Dozer sprawled across my back seat. Taking up every inch of space. Ryan kept turning around to check on him.

I drove carefully. Protectively. Like I was carrying precious cargo.

Because I was.

At Ryan's cottage, we settled Dozer on the couch. Blankets underneath. More blankets on top.

The dog fell asleep immediately. Exhausted.

Ryan sat beside him. Hand on Dozer's side. Feeling him breathe. Rise and fall. Rise and fall.

I stood in the doorway. Watching.

The tenderness in Ryan's face. The relief. The love.

This was who he was at his core. Protector. Caretaker. Devoted.

This was the man I was falling for.

"I'll make tea." Quiet. Trying to give him space.

I went to his kitchen. Knew where everything was now. Had been here enough times. Helped him unpack. Reorganized his furniture. Brought him coffee.

Left pieces of myself in his space without meaning to.

Mugs in the cabinet. Tea bags in the drawer by the stove. Honey in the pantry.

I filled the kettle. Set it on the burner. Waited for the water to boil.

His cottage felt lived-in now. Not the empty space it had been when he first moved in.

Traces of both of us here.

My jacket on his coat hook. His coffee mug with my lipstick stain from yesterday morning. Still in the sink. Unwashed.

Like we belonged together.

I wanted this. All of it.

The kettle whistled. I poured water over tea bags. Added honey to both mugs.

Carried them back to the living room.

Ryan was still with Dozer. Hand on the dog's side. Monitoring his breathing.

I sat on the floor by the couch. Handed him a mug.

"Thank you for coming. I know things are complicated between us."

"Where else would I be?"

The question hung between us. Loaded.

Both remembering yesterday. His declaration in the parking lot. My running.

But tonight was different. Stripped down. Honest.

Tonight we were just two people who cared about each other. Who showed up when it mattered.

"Stay. Just until he's settled. Just to make sure he's okay through the night."

I knew I should leave.

This was dangerous. Getting closer when I had to pull away.

But I couldn't leave him. Not tonight.

"Okay. Just for a while."

We talked quietly. Sharing stories about our pets.

Dali's reign of terror over my cottage. The time she knocked over an entire bookshelf chasing a moth.

Dozer's puppy days. How he'd eaten Ryan's favorite boots. Twice.

Both of us exhausted. From fear to relief to this strange peaceful space between.

Somewhere in the conversation, we shifted closer.

Ryan's hand moved from Dozer. Reached toward me.

Our faces close now. Eyes locked.

The moment stretched. Charged. Inevitable.

Both leaning in. Breath mingling.

Just as our lips were about to touch—

Dozer lifted his massive head. Gave me a big, gross, slobbery lick right across my face.

I yelped. Jerked back. Wiping dog drool.

Ryan laughed. The sound surprised out of him despite everything.

"Your dog has terrible timing."

"He really does." Ryan's eyes were warm. Full of affection.

We settled back. Smiling at each other across Dozer.

The almost-kiss hung in the air between us. The tension didn't dissipate. Just shifted.

Changed into something quieter. Sweeter.

Eventually, exhaustion won.

I curled up at one end of the couch. Ryan at the other. Dozer peaceful between us.

The best worst chaperone.

My eyes drifted closed. Just for a minute. Just to rest.

I woke to sunlight.

Bright morning light filled Ryan's windows. Warm. Birds already singing outside.

Disoriented for a second. Where was I?

Ryan's cottage. His couch. Dozer between us.

I'd fallen asleep.

Ryan was awake. Watching me with an expression that broke my heart.

Tender. Yearning. Hopeful. Loving.

Sleep-rumbled. Exhausted. Vulnerable. Beautiful.

He'd never looked more appealing.

"Hi."

"Hi." I sat up. Stretched. "How's he doing?"

Ryan checked Dozer over. Gentle hands running over the mastiff's sides. Checking his breathing. His temperature.

"Better. Much better." Relief clear in his voice. "Crisis averted."

Dozer stirred. Tail wagging. Feeling better.

Comfortable silence settled over us. Morning light. The three of us together.

The moment was perfect.

And impossible.

Ryan looked at me. Hopeful.

"Stay for breakfast?"

My heart cracked.

I wanted to say yes more than anything.

Wanted to stay for breakfast and lunch and dinner and every meal after. Wanted mornings like this. Emergencies like this. All of it.

But I couldn't keep doing this when I might be leaving.

"I should go. Let you both rest."

I stood. Gathered my things. Phone. Keys. Jacket from his coat hook.

Ryan watched. Confusion flickering across his face. Then hurt.

"Rachel—"

"I'm glad Dozer's okay."

I left before he could respond.
Before I said yes to something I couldn't keep.
I have to tell him.

Chapter Twenty

The Boardwalk

Ryan

Figured I'd find you here."

Nothing. She kept painting, oblivious.

The ocean roared between us. Waves crashing loud enough to drown out everything else.

She stood at her easel, working the canvas with frantic strokes. Her movements were desperate, her whole body behind each one. Paint streaked her arms. Her hair fell loose from its bun, wild in the ocean breeze.

Even from the parking lot, I could see she'd been crying.

I'd checked the firehouse first. Then the gallery. Both empty. I knew where she'd be.

The same place she always ran when she needed to think, to paint, to avoid. Her spot on the boardwalk, where the light hit perfect at sunset.

I was done waiting.

I approached slowly. Sand crunched under my boots. The ocean roared to my left. The distance closed between us.

She'd looked at me this morning like I'd hung the moon. Like she wanted to kiss me as badly as I wanted to kiss her. Then she'd bolted. Left me standing in my own kitchen, coffee getting cold, wondering what the hell I'd done wrong.

Nothing. I hadn't done anything wrong. We both knew it.

Rachel was scared. I got that. But running wouldn't fix scared. Running just made everything worse.

Up close, the painting looked like chaos. Blues drowning reds. Colors bleeding into each other, muddy and unfocused. No composition, no planning. Just grief bleeding onto canvas.

Her hands shook. Paint dripped from her brush onto the sand.

"You left without breakfast."

Rachel froze. Her paintbrush hovered midair. She didn't turn around.

"I had to get home. Feed Dali."

The lie hung between us. Obvious. Weak.

"Rachel." I kept my voice gentle. "Look at me."

She turned. Finally. The paintbrush clutched in her hand like a weapon. Her eyes were swollen, red-rimmed. Every defense she owned locked into place.

"We need to talk about this."

"There's nothing to talk about."

"I think there's everything to talk about."

The sunset faded behind us. Rachel's jaw worked like she wanted to say something, wanted to bolt, wanted to scream. She did none of those things. She turned back to her canvas.

Her shoulders hunched forward. Protective. Like if she made herself small enough, I'd give up and leave.

Not a chance.

I stepped closer. Close enough to see the paint splattered across her collarbone. Close enough to smell turpentine and salt air and her lavender soap.

"Have dinner with me." The words came out steady. Sure. "A real date. Not for the mural, not as neighbors. Just us."

"Ryan—"

"I'm asking you out. On a date." I took another step. "Because I'm in love with you and I think you love me too."

The words landed heavy in the quiet evening. Rachel backed up. Her heel hit the easel leg. She gripped the paintbrush tighter, knuckles white.

"I can't."

"Can't or won't?"

"Both. Neither. I don't know." Her voice cracked.

"Then help me understand. Tell me why."

Rachel stared at me. Her face crumpled. All those walls she'd been holding up came crashing down.

"Because I'm moving."

The words hit me like a physical blow. Knocked the air from my lungs.

"What?"

"I'm moving." Her voice broke on the words. "Away from Seaholly. Away from here. That's why I've been avoiding you. That's why I keep running."

I couldn't speak. Couldn't process.

Rachel set down her paintbrush. Wiped at her face with paint-stained hands, leaving streaks of blue and red across her cheeks.

"My mom needs me." The words came out quiet. Defeated. "She can't live alone anymore. She's forgetting things. Falling. The insurance ran out for home health aide and Mom can't afford it otherwise."

She wrapped her arms around herself. "I have to go take care of her. There's no one else."

The ocean crashed behind us. The wind picked up. Rachel shivered in just her paint-stained shirt.

"When did you find out?"

"A while ago." She looked at the sand. "I've been trying to figure something out. Some way to make it work. But I can't."

My mind raced. Problem-solving mode kicking in despite the hurt.

"Bring her here."

"My cottage is too small. I can't afford in-home care." Her voice stayed flat. Exhausted. "She needs more help than I can give her alone."

"Then we'll find another solution. Together."

Rachel looked at me. Something breaking in her expression.

"I've looked, Ryan. I've researched every option I can think of. Studios near her. Apartments. Care facilities. The numbers don't work. I haven't found a way to make it work."

"Have you asked for help? From friends? The community?"

She flinched. Like the suggestion hurt.
"This isn't anyone else's problem."
"It is if you're leaving. It is if I'm losing you."
"You can't lose something you never had."
The words hit like a punch. I flinched. Couldn't hide it.
Pain flashed across her face immediately. She realized what she'd said.
"I didn't mean—"
"Is that what you think?" My voice came out rough. "That this isn't real?"
"No. I just meant—" She stopped. Started again. "We're not together. We haven't—"
"We haven't what?" The hurt sharpened to something else. Frustration. Fear. "Haven't spent every day together? Haven't almost kissed more times than I can count? Haven't fallen asleep on my couch with our dog and cat between us?"
Rachel's face crumpled. "I'm sorry."
The apology took the wind from my anger.
"I'm sorry," she said again. Tears streaming down her face now. "For shutting you out. For running. I was scared of this. Of telling you and watching you realize I'm leaving."
She wiped at her face. Smearing more paint. "I thought if I kept you at a distance, it wouldn't hurt so much when I had to go."
The honesty broke something open in me.
I closed the distance between us and pulled her into my arms.
She came willingly. Collapsed against me like she'd been holding herself up for too long. Her face pressed into my chest. Her hands fisted in my shirt. Paint-stained fingers gripping like I was the only solid thing in her world.
I wrapped my arms around her. One hand spanning her back, the other cradling her head. She felt small against me. Fragile in a way I'd never noticed before. Like all those walls she built made her seem bigger than she was.
She shook with silent sobs. Her whole body trembling.
I held her tighter. Let her break. Let her pour out everything she'd been holding in.
Her breathing was ragged against my chest. Warm through my shirt. I could feel her heartbeat. Fast and frightened.
"It's okay," I murmured into her hair. "I've got you."
She made a sound. Half sob, half laugh. "You shouldn't. I'm a mess."

"You're my mess."

That made her cry harder.

We stood there while the sun disappeared completely. The beach emptying around us. The temperature dropping. I didn't care. Didn't move.

Just held her.

Eventually, her breathing steadied. The shaking stopped. She stayed pressed against me. Like she was gathering strength from the contact.

I could smell her. Lavender soap under the salt air. Paint in her hair. The ocean on her skin.

She pulled back slightly. Just enough to look up at me.

Her eyes were red. Swollen. Paint smudged across her cheeks. Hair wild and falling out of its bun.

She'd never looked more beautiful.

I touched her face. Gently wiped paint from her cheek with my thumb. Blue and red and orange smeared across her skin.

She went still under my touch.

I held her face with both hands. Tilted her chin up. Her skin was soft. Warm. I could feel her pulse under my thumbs.

"I don't want to lose you," she whispered.

"Then don't leave."

"I don't know how not to."

My hands stayed on her face. Her hands still gripped my shirt. We stood so close I could feel her breath on my throat.

Every instinct I had screamed to close the distance. Kiss her. Make promises. Tell her we'd figure it out.

But I couldn't. Not yet.

Rachel's eyes searched mine. So much want in them. So much fear.

She leaned forward slightly. Testing. Her gaze dropped to my mouth.

My heartbeat increased.

I wanted this. Wanted her. Had wanted her for so long I couldn't remember not wanting her.

But she pulled back. Just an inch. Just enough.

"We can't start something we might have to end." Her voice was barely above a whisper. "It'll hurt too much."

The words settled between us. True. Painful. Smart.

I wanted to argue. Wanted to say we'd figure it out. Wanted to kiss her anyway and deal with the consequences later.

But she was right. Starting something now, when she might leave, when there was no solution yet—it would destroy us both.

I let my hands slide from her face. Down her arms. Caught her hands in mine.

Paint-stained fingers. Shaking slightly. Small in my grip.

I squeezed gently. "Okay. We fix this first. Then we talk about us."

Relief and disappointment warred across her face.

"Okay." The word came out rough. "We fix this first. Then we talk about us."

Relief and disappointment warred across her face.

"Let me help," I said. "Let me look for options. You don't have to do this alone."

"Ryan—"

"I'm not asking you to promise anything. I'm just asking you to let me try."

She looked at me for a long moment. Something shifting in her expression.

"Okay."

The word was quiet. But it was everything.

She was letting me in. Finally. Not running. Not shutting me out.

Just letting me help.

We stood there as darkness settled over the beach. The temperature dropped. Rachel shivered.

I didn't want to let go of her hands. But we'd set the boundary. Fix this first. Then us.

"Go home," I whispered. "Get some rest. We'll figure this out."

Rachel nodded. Started gathering her supplies with shaking hands.

I helped her pack up. Carried her easel to her car. Loaded the wet canvas carefully in the back.

She climbed into the driver's seat. Looked up at me through the open window.

"Thank you. For not giving up on me."

"I'm not going anywhere."

She drove away. Tail lights disappearing down the coast road.

I stood in the empty parking lot. Breathing hard. Thinking.

She won't fight for us. Not because she doesn't want to. Because she's too overwhelmed to see past the impossible.

So I'll fight for both of us.

I pulled out my phone. Called Henry.

"Henry? I need to talk to you. About Rachel. About her mom. Can I come by?"

Chapter Twenty-One

The Grind

Mrs. Henderson

My knitting needles maintained their steady rhythm. Click-click-click.
I counted stitches under my breath. "Knit two, purl one."
Excellent cover for eavesdropping.
The corner booth possessed remarkable acoustics—empty shop, high ceilings, sound carrying beautifully. I'd tested every table three weeks ago. This one won by a considerable margin.
Ryan's voice cracked across the silence. "She told me. Finally told me."
I added another stitch. Casual enough. My head stayed down.
"About her mom?" Henry's voice was soft. Kind. Good quality in a man.
"Beverly can't live alone anymore." The words came fast. Desperate. Poor dear. "Needs help with everything. The home health aide insurance ran out last month."
My needles stopped entirely.
Beverly Brown.

Of course. Rachel had seemed distracted lately. Now it made perfect sense.

"Rachel's looked at every option." Ryan's voice grew thick. "Studios near her mom. Apartments. In-home care. Nothing works. She can't afford to keep the cottage and pay for care there."

"So she's leaving," Henry said quietly.

"Yeah." A pause. "Leaving me."

The pain in those two words could have split wood.

I set down my knitting. Picked up my tea. Cold. Dreadful. I drank it anyway. Henry had more important matters than fetching me a fresh cup.

Ryan's voice stayed rough. Catching on words. "That's why I'm here. There has to be something we're missing. Some option we haven't thought of."

"There has to be," Henry said quietly.

"I can't lose her." Ryan's voice was determined despite the rough edges. "I'm still new to Seaholly—you know everyone here. Is there anything local we might not have thought of? Any resources?"

"Let me put some feelers out," Henry said. "I know pretty much everyone in town. Someone might have ideas we haven't considered."

Under the counter, Dozer lifted his massive head. The puppy watched Ryan with worried brown eyes.

Smart dog.

Dozer stood, shook himself, and trotted directly to my table.

He sat. Stared at my yarn.

"Don't even think about it," I told him.

His tail wagged.

"I mean it."

He lunged, grabbed my yarn ball, and took off running.

"For heaven's sake." I stood. "You incorrigible beast."

Gray yarn unspooled across the floor. Dozer pranced toward the counter like he'd won a prize.

Dune lifted his head, watched Dozer approach with the stolen yarn, and thumped his tail once.

"Henry." I kept my voice sharp. "Your establishment has been overrun by thieves."

Henry looked up, saw Dozer with my yarn trailing behind him. "I'm so sorry, Mrs. Henderson. Dozer, drop it."

Dozer dropped it immediately and sat, looking inordinately proud.

Ryan appeared beside the counter, eyes red-rimmed, face blotchy. He grabbed Dozer's collar. "I'm sorry. He's been—I haven't been walking him enough."

"He's a puppy." I retrieved my yarn and began winding it back. "Puppies are restless. It's their fundamental nature."

Ryan nodded, apparently unable to manage words.

Poor dear. He looked devastated.

I softened my voice. Slightly.

"Sit down before you fall down."

"I should go—"

"You're a mess." I pointed at the chair across from me. "Sit."

He sat.

I continued winding yarn, letting the silence stretch.

"Beverly's a good woman," I said finally.

Ryan's head snapped up. "You know her?"

"She visited last spring. We knitted together." I met his eyes directly. "Liked her immediately. Practical woman. Sensible."

"How do you—were you listening?" Ryan's eyes widened.

"I may be old, but I'm not deaf." I met his gaze directly. "And the acoustics in this establishment are excellent."

I finished winding my yarn and set it on the counter.

My mind worked. Beverly needed care. Rachel needed to stay. Ryan needed Rachel. Simple problem. Complex variables. But solvable, I suspected, with proper planning.

But I couldn't simply announce a solution. Not yet. These things required research and careful consideration. And truth be told, these young people needed to sit with their feelings rather than rushing toward panic.

"You love her," I said. Not a question.

Ryan nodded.

"And she loves you."

"I—yeah. I'm certain."

"Good." I picked up my knitting bag. "Then trust her. Trust that she's capable of handling difficult situations."

"But—"

"And trust that sometimes solutions emerge from unexpected quarters."

I headed toward the door.

"Mrs. Henderson?" Ryan's voice stopped me.

I turned.

He stood now, desperate hope on his face. "Is there—do you know something? Some way to help?"

I smiled. Small. Mysterious.

"I know a great many things, dear. The question is whether I choose to share them."

Henry's eyes narrowed. He knew that smile.

"Mrs. Henderson," he started cautiously. "Are you scheming?"

"I prefer the term 'problem-solving.'" I adjusted my cardigan. "Give me a few days to make some inquiries."

"For what?" Ryan stepped forward. "Please. If there's anything—"

"Patience." I looked at him over my reading glasses. "These matters require proper attention. Rushing helps no one."

"But Rachel—"

"Rachel isn't departing tomorrow." My voice remained firm but not unkind. "You have time. Use it wisely. Take that dog for a proper walk. Get some sleep. Eat a respectable meal."

Ryan's jaw clenched, frustration and hope warring across his features.

"Sometimes," I said, "the best mysteries have the simplest solutions."

I walked out.

The afternoon sun felt warm. Pleasant.

I pulled out my phone and scrolled to Beverly's number. We'd exchanged them last spring, called twice since. Once in June to recommend a mystery novel. Once after Harold died in December.

She'd sent a proper handwritten card. No platitudes.

I pressed call.

Three rings.

"Hello?"

"Beverly. It's Margaret Henderson."

"Margaret!" Genuine pleasure in her voice. "How wonderful to hear from you. How are you managing?"

"Well enough." I turned toward home. Three blocks. "And you? How are you truly?"

A pause. Too long.

"I'm fine."

Liar.

"Beverly."

"Really, I'm—"

"I've known you for one afternoon and two phone calls. That's sufficient to recognize when you're disguising the truth."

She sighed. "Not particularly well, if I'm being honest."

"Then be honest."

She told me. Memory problems. Started about six months ago. Forgetting things, getting confused. Left the stove on twice.

"The doctor says I'm isolated. Depressed. That if I had more people around, more things to do, the memory issues would improve." Her voice sharpened with frustration. "Easy enough to say. Rather harder to accomplish when you live alone. I haven't told Rachel what the doctor said—didn't want to worry her more."

I climbed my front steps. My hip protested. Getting old was dreadful.

"Do you still knit?" I asked.

"Every day. Working on a blanket currently."

"I'm making scarves. Gray merino." I unlocked my door and stepped inside. "Keeps my hands busy while I listen to audiobooks."

"Audiobooks! What do you listen to?"

"Mysteries, primarily. Dorothy Sayers at the moment. Rereading."

"Oh, I love mysteries!" Beverly's voice brightened considerably. "Agatha Christie, Louise Penny, Ruth Rendell. I used to have a whole book club dedicated to them."

I paused mid-step. "You read Louise Penny?"

"Every single book. Inspector Gamache is—" She stopped. "Well. I used to read them constantly. Now I can't keep the plots straight anymore. Forget which characters are which. I've been rereading the same Agatha Christie over and over. At least when I forget whodunit, it's still exciting."

"Which Christie?"

"Murder on the Orient Express."

"One of her finest." I smiled despite myself. A fellow mystery enthusiast. How delightful. "The new Louise Penny came out in September. Classic Gamache."

"There's a new one?" Genuine longing in her voice. "I didn't know."

I settled into Harold's chair by the window. Pulled out my notebook. Made a few quick notes.

"I'm so glad you called," Beverly said. "What made you think of me today?"

"Can't a woman be curious about an old friend's situation?"

"We've known each other for one afternoon and two phone calls."

"And yet here we are, discussing mystery novels like old book club companions." I tapped my pen against the notebook. "Sometimes friendships don't require extensive timelines."

Beverly went quiet for a moment. "You're scheming something."

"I prefer 'problem-solving.'"

"That's exactly what Rachel says about you." Warmth filled her voice. "She mentions you frequently. Says you're the sharpest person in Seaholly."

"She's correct."

"She also says you meddle comprehensively."

"Also accurate. Someone must. Young people are spectacularly terrible at solving their own problems."

"That's exactly what Rachel says about you." Warmth in her voice. "She mentions you frequently. Says you're the sharpest person in Seaholly."

"She's correct."

"She also says you meddle comprehensively."

"Also accurate. Someone must."

"She loves him, you know. That firefighter. Ryan."

"I'm aware."

"She's heartbroken about leaving. They're looking at options together, but nothing's working out." Beverly's voice thickened. "She's built such a beautiful life there."

"I'm bringing her blueberry muffins tomorrow," I said. "She mentioned loving them."

"You bake?" Beverly's voice lifted. "I used to bake constantly. There's something satisfying about following a recipe precisely."

"Baking is an exact science. Not a guesswork game."

"Exactly. Measure twice, bake once."

"Which is precisely why I'm telling you this." I paused deliberately. "Don't make any irrevocable decisions yet." "About Rachel relocating. About selling your home. Not yet."

"Why not?"

"Because sometimes solutions emerge from unexpected quarters. Give it a week. Perhaps two."

"Margaret—"

"Trust me. Please."

She laughed uncertainly. "Everyone in Seaholly says when you use that tone, miracles occur."

"Not miracles. Simply careful planning and creative problem-solving."

"All right. I'll wait."

"Good woman. I'll speak with you soon."

I ended the call and set my phone on Harold's desk.

Looked at my notebook. Beverly's situation documented in quick shorthand.

I pulled out a fresh legal pad and began making lists. Medical. Legal. Financial. Each category spawning questions requiring answers.

My reading glasses slipped. I pushed them up, kept working.

Harold's pocket watch sat on the desk—the one I'd given him for our thirtieth anniversary. I picked it up, turned it over.

He would have enjoyed this puzzle. Would have sat beside me offering suggestions.

I set it down and returned to my lists.

I smiled.

The house was still, but my mind was active. Organizing. Planning. Solving.

Chapter Twenty-Two

The Firehouse

Ryan

"Rodriguez, you okay?" Martinez called from across the bay. "You're gonna burn yourself out, man."

I grabbed my water bottle, drained half of it. "I'm fine. Again from the top."

"Ryan—"

"From the top."

Martinez exchanged a look with Coop. They knew I wasn't fine. The whole crew knew. But they also knew better than to push.

Five AM had come too early. Always did.

I'd been at the station since before sunrise, running training drills with the crew. My third extra shift this week. Maybe my fourth. I'd lost count.

My muscles burned. My lungs ached. Sweat soaked through my shirt. Good. The exhaustion helped.

We ran the drill again. Ladder deployment, rooftop access, simulated rescue. I pushed harder than necessary. Faster than the exercise required.

Dozer watched from the sidelines, head on his paws. His brown eyes tracked my every move with concern a dog shouldn't be capable of showing.

The physical exhaustion helped. Barely.

Because when I stopped moving, I thought about her. About Rachel on that boardwalk, wind whipping her hair, telling me she had to leave. About the look on her face when she said there was no solution.

About how I couldn't find one either, no matter how hard I tried.

So I kept moving.

Frank caught me during the water break. The senior firefighter had a presence that made everyone listen when he talked.

"You're pushing too hard, kid." He kept his voice low. Private. "What's going on?"

"I'm fine."

"That's the third time you've said that this morning. Still not true."

I took another drink. Didn't answer.

Frank didn't push. Just stood there. Patient. The way he always was.

"Life's short, Rodriguez," he said finally. "Don't waste time being scared."

My jaw tightened. "I'm not scared."

"Then what are you?"

Heartbroken. Desperate. Helpless.

I didn't say any of that. Just shook my head.

Frank clapped my shoulder. "Whatever it is, running yourself into the ground won't fix it."

He walked away before I could respond.

My mind drifted back to yesterday afternoon.

Henry had said, "Don't underestimate Mrs. Henderson."

I took another drink. Pushed the thoughts away.

Back to work. Back to drills. Back to not thinking.

After morning drills, Chief Patterson pulled me aside.

"Rodriguez. My office."

His tone gave nothing away. Serious but not angry. Pleased but not excited.

I followed him through the bay, Dozer trotting behind us.

Chief's office smelled like coffee and old leather. He closed the door, gestured to the chair across from his desk.

I sat. Dozer settled at my feet.

"I'll get right to it." Chief leaned back in his chair. "Your community outreach proposal. Budget's approved."

My head snapped up.

"Full funding. You'll manage the allocation. Supplies, printing, overtime if you need it. Whatever it takes to make the program work."

I stared at him. Processing.

The community outreach program. I'd been running it on my own time, with whatever scraps I could scrounge. Teaching fire safety at schools. Leading station tours. Building relationships with families who'd never trusted firefighters before.

At my last station, they'd called it a waste of resources. Said I should focus on the job, not playing community organizer. Made it clear my priorities were wrong.

Here, Chief Patterson was giving me a budget. Official support. Validation that this mattered.

This was huge.

"You've proven the value," Chief continued. "Community response has been excellent. Council wants to expand it. Make it permanent."

I should've been thrilled. Should've thanked him immediately.

Instead, I just nodded. "That's great. Thank you."

Chief's eyebrows rose slightly. "You don't seem excited."

"I am. It's just—" I stopped. Didn't know how to explain.

What was the point of building a program here if Rachel was leaving? What was the point of putting down roots in Seaholly if she wouldn't be here?

Chief watched me carefully. "Everything alright, Rodriguez?"

"Yeah. Fine."

"You've been running extra shifts all week. Frank says you're pushing too hard." His tone stayed professional. Not prying, just observing. "Something going on?"

I could've deflected. Should've deflected.

But I was too tired. Too worn down.

"Personal stuff. I'll handle it."

Chief nodded slowly. Didn't push for details. "Take care of whatever it is. Can't have you running yourself into the ground."

"Yes, sir."

"Good work on the outreach program. You should be proud."

I left his office, the approval sitting heavy on my shoulders instead of light.

Good news I couldn't celebrate. Another piece of the life I was building here. Another reason to stay.

Another thing that wouldn't matter if Rachel left.

The alarm bells shattered my thoughts.

"Structure fire, residential, possible occupants inside!"

Adrenaline kicked in like a switch flipping. I was in the zone instantly. Muscle memory taking over.

We suited up. Moved fast. Dozer retreated to his corner, ears flat, hating the sirens but understanding they meant I had to go.

The small house poured smoke into the afternoon sky. Neighbors clustered on the sidewalk, shouting about the elderly couple inside.

Martinez and I went in together. Visibility poor, heat building. We moved through the layout methodically.

Found them in the back bedroom.

Elderly man trying to help his wife, who sat on the floor near their bed. She couldn't walk well, needed assistance. The smoke was getting thicker.

"Sir, we need to go now!" I moved toward them.

The husband positioned himself between us and his wife. Protective. Stubborn.

"I'm not going without Helen!"

The smoke was getting worse. Time was running out.

I knelt down, met his eyes through my mask. "Sir, she needs you alive. Let us help you both."

Something in my tone got through.

I lifted Helen carefully. Martinez helped the husband. We moved fast, navigating back through smoke and heat.

Got them both outside. Paramedics waiting. Neighbors cheering.

Afterwards, while paramedics treated them for smoke inhalation, the couple wouldn't let go of each other's hands.

Helen coughed but smiled at her husband. "Fifty-eight years together. Couldn't bear being apart."

The old man squeezed her fingers. "Where else would I be?"

The simple certainty in his voice hit me like a physical blow.

I watched them from a few feet away, something cracking open in my chest.

That's what I wanted. That certainty. That partnership. That forever.

Fifty-eight years of choosing each other. Even in a fire. Even when it would've been easier to run alone. Even when fear said otherwise.

I wanted that with Rachel.

Back at the station, my mind was still on the elderly couple. Their hands intertwined. That unshakable devotion.

We parked the truck in the bay. I climbed out, still processing. Still feeling the weight of what I'd witnessed.

Then I stopped short.

The mural wall had been completely transformed.

What were preliminary outlines yesterday were now filled with vibrant color. Taking real shape. Coming alive.

Rachel must have been working all day while we ran drills. While we responded to the call. Hours of work I hadn't noticed until now.

My portrait anchored the center of the composition.

Stunning.

Not just accurate. Captured with care. With attention. With something that made my throat tight.

The way she'd painted me: strong but gentle. Determined but kind. Serious but with warmth in my eyes.

She saw me as a hero. Saw the best version of me.

Around my portrait, the crew in action. The community we served. The connections we'd built. Kids learning safety, families feeling protected, a town coming together.

This wasn't just a mural about firefighters. It was about belonging. Purpose. Home.

My chest physically ached looking at it.

She'd been here. Standing where I stood now. Painting me. Thinking about me while creating this.

I couldn't look away.

"Damn, Rodriguez." Martinez whistled low, walking up beside me. "She's got you looking good."

Cooper joined us, arms crossed, studying the mural. "That's the 'I'm in love' face right there. Can't fake that."

"You gonna tell her how you feel?" Martinez asked. "Or just keep moping around here?"

I forced myself to look away from the painting. "There's nothing to tell."

"Come on, man." Cooper shook his head. "You've been miserable for days. Everyone can see it."

Martinez gestured at the mural. "She painted you like that and you think there's nothing to tell?"

Frank appeared beside us. The senior firefighter had been quiet, listening. Now he spoke.

"Life's too short." His voice went serious. "We see that every day on calls. Don't waste time being scared."

The truth of that settled over me.

"What if being there isn't enough?" The question came out quiet.

Frank studied me for a long moment. "Sometimes the fight isn't about winning. It's about showing up. Being there. Not giving up even when it looks impossible."

He clapped my shoulder. "You don't strike me as someone who gives up easy, Rodriguez."

The crew dispersed. Back to work. Back to routine.

That evening, as I was about to leave for the day, Tommy arrived with his grandfather.

The kid carried something carefully. Construction paper, careful coloring, his best effort showing in every line.

"Mr. Ryan!" Tommy's face lit up when he saw me.

I knelt down to his level. "Hey, Tommy. What've you got there?"

He handed me the card, pride radiating off him.

Inside: a detailed drawing of me in my firefighter gear. Helmet, coat, the whole uniform rendered in careful crayon.

His best printing underneath: "MY HERO - Thank you for teaching us."

My throat went tight.

Tommy's grandfather put a hand on the kid's shoulder. "Tommy's friend from school had a kitchen fire last week. Used what you taught them at Safety Day. Stayed calm, got his little sister out, called 911. Everyone's fine because of what you taught these kids."

Tommy bounced on his toes. "You're teaching everyone to be heroes, Mr. Ryan!"

I looked at this kid. This bright, brave kid who saw good in the world. Who believed in heroes and safety and doing the right thing.

"You're the hero, Tommy." My voice came out rough. "You and your friend both."

I thanked him. Treasured the card. Told him how proud I was.

After they left, I stood alone in front of the mural. Dozer came over, leaned his weight against my leg. Sensing my mood the way he always did.

I scratched behind his ears.

Tommy's card was still in my hands. I looked up at the mural.

This mattered. This job. This community. These kids learning to save lives. Making a real difference here in Seaholly.

But it felt hollow without her to share it with.

My gaze drifted back to the mural. To Rachel's portrait of me. To how she'd captured something I didn't even know was visible.

She'd been here earlier today. Standing where I stood now. Hours of careful work transforming the wall.

Creating this tribute to me and my crew. Painting me like I was someone worth painting. Someone worth staying for.

The elderly couple's words echoed through my mind. "Where else would I be?"

That kind of certainty. That kind of love. I wanted it with Rachel.

Chapter Twenty-Three

The Easel

Rachel

"Ouch!"

The mat cutter slipped. Blood welled up on my thumb.

I dropped the blade. Grabbed a paper towel from Vivian's supply cabinet. Pressed it against the cut.

Not deep. Just enough to sting. Just enough to prove I had no business handling sharp objects today.

The ruined mat board sat on the worktable. Fourth one this morning. Each cut crooked, angled wrong, useless.

I'd been at The Easel since dawn. Throwing myself into show preparation. Matting sketches. Framing studies. Organizing. Anything.

Anything to avoid thinking about the boardwalk. About Ryan. About how I'd been so sure there was no solution. About how he wanted to help. And I let him.

My eyes burned. I blinked hard. Focused on the paper towel slowly turning red.

The door opened behind me. Footsteps on the hardwood floor.

"Rachel?" Vivian's voice, concerned.

I turned. She stood in the doorway wearing a fuchsia A-line dress with matching heels. Hair swept into a perfect twist. Her gaze landed on the paper towel, the blood, the pile of ruined mat boards.

"What happened?"

"Nothing. Just clumsy." I held up my thumb. "It's fine."

Vivian crossed to me. "Let me see."

She examined the cut without hesitation. "Small, but we need to bandage it properly. Can't have you bleeding on the artwork."

Of course. Vivian wouldn't risk the pieces. Very her.

"Sit." She pointed to the stool by the worktable.

I sat.

She disappeared into her office. Returned with a white plastic box. Nearly full. Didn't look like she used it much.

She cleaned the cut with an antiseptic wipe. Applied antibiotic ointment. Wrapped a bandage around my thumb with careful attention.

"There. Now you won't ruin anything." She studied me. "How long have you been here?"

"A while."

"Since dawn?"

I didn't answer.

Vivian gestured at the ruined mat boards. "You're distracted. What's going on?"

"Nothing. Just focused on the show."

"Speaking of which." She moved to the paintings spread around the gallery. "We have work to do. I need your artist statement by Monday. And don't underprice your work this time - I'm not letting you undersell yourself again. We need to finalize which pieces anchor the show. The title for the exhibition. Your bio for the catalog. What you're wearing opening night." She paused. "Are you even listening?"

"Yes. Statement. Pricing. Title. Bio. Outfit."

"Good." She stopped in front of my seascapes. "These are beautiful. Your ocean work is always strong."

"Thank you."

"But I think we should lead with the firefighter studies." She turned to look at me. "They're your most powerful work right now."

My stomach dropped. "I don't think—"

"Rachel. These sketches are remarkable." She gestured at the firefighter portraits leaning against the wall. "Raw. Emotional. They capture something real."

I wanted to argue. Wanted to insist the seascapes were safer. Better. Less revealing.

But Vivian was already moving through the sketches. Picking them up one by one. Studying each with her gallery owner's eye.

She stopped at one. Ryan during training. Concentrated. Focused.

Then another. Ryan with Dozer. That soft expression he didn't know he wore.

Another. Ryan laughing. Guard completely down.

Vivian arranged them side by side. Stood back. Studied them.

Then she picked up a sketch of Martinez. Another of Cooper. Laid them beside Ryan's portraits.

"Look at these," she said quietly.

I didn't want to look. Already knew what she'd see.

"The other firefighters are well-drawn. Competent work. Good composition." She touched Ryan's sketches. "But these? The line work is different. More careful. More detailed. Look at his hands."

She was right. I'd spent hours on his hands. The way his fingers curved. The calluses on his palms. The gentle strength in them.

"You draw him differently," Vivian said. "Not just technically. Emotionally. There's intimacy in these. Like you're not just observing him. You're seeing him."

My throat went tight.

She picked up another sketch. Ryan's profile. The one I'd drawn from memory after Safety Day. The moment I realized I was falling for him.

Vivian turned to look at me. Gentle.

"Does he know you see him this way?"

My throat went tight. "What way?"

"Like you're in love with him."

The words hit like a punch.

I tried to deny it. Opened my mouth to say she was wrong, she didn't understand, these were just studies for the mural.

Nothing came out.

I started crying. Really crying.

Vivian sat beside me on the stool. Patient. Kind. Not rushing me. Just holding space.

The whole story came out between sobs.

Mom. Ryan. The boardwalk. Leaving. All of it.

Vivian listened. Didn't interrupt. Didn't offer solutions. Just let me talk until the words ran out.

She was quiet for a moment. Her hands folded in her lap.

"My mother had dementia."

I looked up. Surprised. Vivian had never mentioned this.

"Started small. She'd forget appointments. Repeat questions. Then it got worse. She couldn't live alone anymore."

"What did you do?"

"I was terrified." Vivian's smile was sad. "I had the gallery. My life here. Moving to care for her meant losing everything. My business. My community. My independence."

I waited. Holding my breath.

"I thought there was no solution. I thought I had to choose. Either abandon my mother or abandon myself."

"But you didn't move." I gestured at the gallery around us. "You've been here for decades."

"I found in-home care." Vivian met my eyes. "It wasn't perfect. Wasn't cheap. But it worked. She stayed in her home with support. I stayed in mine. We made it work until she needed specialized care."

She paused. "The point is—I thought it was impossible. Black and white. Move or abandon her."

"But there were other options. Creative solutions I hadn't considered. I just couldn't see them through my fear."

I wanted to believe her. Desperately wanted to believe there was a way forward I hadn't seen.

"My mom can't afford full-time care." My voice came out flat. "I've checked. The numbers don't work."

"Sometimes the solutions aren't what we imagined." Vivian squeezed my hand. "But they exist, Rachel. You just have to be open to finding them."

She stood. Walked to her office. Returned with a business card and pen.

"This is the agency I used. The social worker who helped me navigate options." She wrote names and numbers on the back of the card. "Call them. Explain the situation. See what they suggest."

I took the card. "Thank you."

My voice broke on the words. Vivian squeezed my hand.

"Take the weekend," Vivian said. "Call the agency. Talk to your mom. Figure out your next steps. Then come back Monday and we'll finalize everything for the show."

"Okay."

"And Rachel?" She touched my shoulder. "That firefighter? The one you're in love with?"

My face went hot.

"He's not going anywhere. Not if he's half the man I think he is." Vivian smiled. "Sometimes the hardest part is letting people help. Letting them in."

I left the gallery with the card clutched in my hand. The names and numbers felt like a way forward.

I sat in my car in the parking lot. Stared at the information Vivian had given me.

Called the first number.

Got voicemail. Left a message. My voice shaking through the whole thing.

Called the second number.

A woman answered. Kind voice. Professional. She listened while I explained. Mom's situation. The expired insurance. My lack of options.

"Let me pull up some information," she said. "Can you hold?"

I held. Waiting felt like forever.

"Okay," the woman came back. "There are a few programs that might help. State assistance for in-home care. Some nonprofits that provide services on a sliding scale. Let me send you information."

"Really?"

"Really. I can't promise anything will work. But there are options to explore." She paused. "The most important thing is not to make any major decisions until you've looked at everything available."

We talked for ten minutes. She sent me links. Forms to fill out. People to contact.

When I hung up, I sat in my car. Crying. But different tears now.

Not hopeless tears.

Just overwhelmed ones.

I drove home. Dali greeted me at the door with her usual disdain. Meowed once. Demanded food.

I fed her. Made tea. Sat at my worktable.

Pulled out my sketchbook. The one I'd been avoiding.

Opened to a blank page.

Started drawing.

Ryan's hands. The way they'd held mine on the boardwalk before I pulled away. Strong fingers. Calloused palms. Gentle despite their size.

I drew until the light faded. Until my hand cramped. Until Dali jumped on the table and knocked over my tea.

Then I just sat there. Looking at what I'd created.

His hands reaching toward mine.

Not quite touching. Not yet.

But close. So close.

Chapter Twenty-Four

Ryan's Cottage

Ryan

"Chief, I'd like to request a transfer."

I stood in front of Chief Patterson's desk, Dozer at my feet.

Chief looked up from his paperwork. Set down his pen. His expression stayed neutral.

"You just got here, Rodriguez."

"I know."

"Sit down."

I sat. Dozer settled at my feet with a soft huff.

Chief leaned back in his chair. "You've built something here. Community outreach program. The crew respects you. Town trusts you."

"I know, sir."

"So why would you want to leave?"

"Personal situation."

Chief studied me for a long moment. "The artist?"

My face went cold.

Chief was quiet for a moment. Then he leaned forward. "Don't make a rash decision based on crisis, Rodriguez. You deal with them from a position of strength. Not by running."

"Yes, sir."

"Give it time. See how things shake out. Then make a decision with a clear head." His expression stayed professional. "That's my advice. Take it or leave it."

"I'll take it. Thank you, sir."

"Good. Now get some rest. You look like hell."

I left his office with the warning sitting heavy on my shoulders. Don't make rash decisions. Give it time.

But waiting felt impossible when every day brought Rachel closer to leaving.

My cottage smelled like garlic and saffron by the time I got home from shift.

I'd stopped at the market. Grabbed chicken, rice, peppers, tomatoes, olives. All the ingredients for arroz con pollo. Mom's recipe.

Cooking calmed me. Always had. The methodical process, the familiar motions, the tangible results.

I browned the chicken in olive oil. The sizzle filled the kitchen. Dozer watched from his bed, nose twitching.

"Not for you, buddy."

He huffed. Disappointed.

I called Maya. Put her on speaker while I worked.

"Hey, what's up?"

"Making arroz con pollo. When do the spices go in? Beginning or end?"

"Beginning. After you brown the chicken." I could hear her smile through the phone. "You stress-cooking again?"

"Maybe."

She laughed. "Don't forget the saffron. That's what makes it taste like home."

"I remember."

I heard dishes clanking in the background. Her kids shouting something.

"Hold on." Maya's voice went muffled. "Sofia, honey, I'm on the phone with Uncle Ryan." Then back to me. "Sorry. Sofia's making friendship bracelets. She's made seventeen today and wants to make one for Dozer."

"For Dozer?"

"She found a tutorial with little dog charms."

"That's sweet."

"Hold on, she wants to ask you something."

There was shuffling. Then Sofia's voice came through, bright and excited. "Uncle Ryan! Do you think Dozer will like a green bracelet or an orange one?"

"Orange. Definitely orange."

"Good! It's gonna have a bone charm too. Okay, here's Mom again. Love you!"

"Love you too, kiddo."

Maya came back on. "See? You're her favorite uncle."

"I'm her only uncle."

"Details."

We talked for another minute. Henry's latest mystery novel. A catering job she had coming up. Normal stuff that felt strange when my own life was falling apart.

"Call me if you need anything, okay?"

"I will."

After we hung up, I stared at my phone.

At Rachel's contact.

At the arroz con pollo simmering on the stove.

I typed: *Come have dinner. Not a date. Just food.*

Hit send before I could second-guess myself.

Stared at my phone. Willing it to buzz.

Five long minutes passed.

Nothing.

My heart sank, but I tried again.

I'm in this kitchen we renovated together. Feels wrong eating alone in it.

Sent. Waited.

Still nothing.

I should stop. Leave her alone. Respect her space.

I made too much chicken. My mom's recipe. It's going to go to waste.

Sent. Waited.

Nothing.

Dozer lifted his head. Whined softly.

"I know, buddy. I'm being pathetic."
He licked my hand.
One more. Just one more try.
Please?
One word. Vulnerable. Raw.
Sent. Waited.
Nothing.
I was about to give up when I looked out the window.
Saw Dali in Rachel's window. The tuxedo cat pressing against the glass, tail swishing.
Dozer whined at my door. Staring toward Rachel's cottage, tail drooping.
The two of them had become inseparable. Every time Rachel visited, Dali came along. Every time I went over, Dozer trotted beside me.
Our pets had figured out what we were still dancing around.
One last attempt.
Dozer keeps whining at your door. I think he misses Dali.
Sent. Didn't expect a response.
My phone buzzed immediately.
I stared at the crying cat emoji.
Not a yes. Not words. But not a no either.
My heart lifted with warmth.
I turned down the heat. Set the table for two. Put out the good plates, not the everyday ones.
If she was coming, I wanted it to feel special. Even if we were pretending it was just about the pets.
Shortly after, a knock on my door.
I opened it.
Rachel stood on my porch with Dali in her arms. She looked exhausted. Eyes red from crying. Hair pulled back in a messy bun. Wearing leggings and an oversized sweatshirt with paint stains on the sleeves.
But she was here.
"She wouldn't stop yowling." Rachel's voice was quiet.
"Dozer's the same."
Both of us pretending this was just about the pets. Safe excuse. Easier than admitting we needed each other.

Rachel stepped inside. Set Dali down.

The cat immediately made a beeline for my bookshelves. Leaped up, tail swishing.

She spotted a framed photo on the middle shelf. My crew at the station, all of us grinning after a rescue.

Dali eyed it. Batted at it with her paw.

The frame teetered. Tipped. Crashed to the floor.

Rachel and I both lunged. Nearly collided.

Rachel caught it, clutching it to her chest. Not broken. Just knocked loose.

"Dali! I'm so sorry—"

I almost laughed. "It's fine. She's just marking her territory."

I took the frame from Rachel's hands. Our fingers brushed.

Set it on a higher shelf, out of cat reach.

Dali, satisfied, jumped down. Strutted over to the couch where Dozer had been watching with patient amusement.

The cat and dog immediately curled up together. Dali tucking herself against Dozer's side, purring loud enough to hear across the room.

Rachel and I looked at each other. Both almost smiling despite the weight between us.

The absurdity of our pets being more functional than we were.

"So." Rachel's voice held a hint of her old warmth. "Is that what I smell? Chicken?"

"Arroz con pollo."

"It smells amazing. I can't believe you made this."

Rachel sat at my kitchen counter while I plated the food.

I could get used to this. It felt so right. That was the problem.

She pulled out her sketchbook from her bag. Always with her.

Started sketching Dozer and Dali curled together on the couch. Her charcoal moving across the page in quick strokes.

I watched her hands move while I stirred the rice one more time. Those artist's hands I'd become so familiar with. Paint-stained. Graceful. Always creating.

We talked carefully around the big things. The impossible things.

Small talk about the mural progress. "The firefighters look incredible," she said. "I finished the background details today. Community members watching, kids learning. It's really coming together."

Her gallery show coming up. "Vivian thinks we'll get a good turnout. She invited some collectors from Portland."

"What about you? Busy at the station?"

"Double shift tomorrow."

A funny call we'd had yesterday involving a cat stuck in a drainpipe. "The owner kept saying 'he's never done this before' while we're literally pulling him out of a pipe."

She made me laugh with a story about her art class. A kid who'd painted his dog blue because "dogs should get to choose their own colors."

"What did you say to that?"

"I told him it was the best reason I'd ever heard for creative license." Her smile was genuine. "Then five other kids painted their pets rainbow colors. It was chaos."

I told her about Tommy's latest visit. How the kid had asked if Ryan and Miss Rachel were getting married.

"What did you tell him?"

"I said adults were complicated." I set her plate in front of her. "He said that was a dumb answer."

The awkwardness of that hung for a moment before we both laughed. Uncomfortable but not unkind.

The kitchen smelled like garlic and saffron and home.

Rachel took her first bite. Paused. Looked up at me.

"This is really good." Surprise in her voice. "Really good. What's in it?"

"Chicken, rice, saffron, peppers, olives. My favorite recipe."

"Tell me about it." Rachel took another bite. "How you learned."

I leaned against the counter. "Saturday mornings. Mom would make arroz con pollo for the family. I'd watch her. She said the key was patience. Not rushing the browning. Letting each step take its time."

"Did you always cook with her?"

"Yeah. Every weekend. It was our time together." I paused. "She'd tell me stories about growing up while we cooked."

Rachel's expression softened. "You miss her."

"Every day."

We ate in comfortable silence for a moment.

"This tastes like home," Rachel said quietly. "Like family."

I set down my fork.

She looked up. Met my eyes.

"This is nice," she said. Almost to herself. "The kind of evening I could get used to."

She pressed her lips together like she'd said more than she meant to.

The moment shifted. Got heavier.

I leaned forward slightly. About to respond. About to say something important.

About to tell her I wanted this too. Every evening. Every morning. Every quiet moment in between.

Rachel's phone rang.

Loud in the quiet kitchen. Shattering the moment.

Rachel glanced at the screen. Her whole body tensed.

"Mom" displayed clearly.

Her face went pale. Dread instant and visible.

She answered, voice tight with fear. "Mom? What's wrong?"

I could hear Beverly's voice through the phone. Shaking. Crying.

"I fell, honey. I'm at Jasonville Hospital."

Rachel was already standing. Grabbing her keys from the counter. Her hands shook.

"I'm coming. Right now. Mom, I'll be there as soon as I can. I'm leaving now—"

She hung up. Looked at me with devastated eyes.

"I have to go. I'm sorry. I—"

She was halfway through the living room. Her sketchbook still on the counter.

I stood. "Rachel, wait. Let me come with you—"

But she was at the door, keys in hand. "I'm sorry. I have to—she's alone—"

She was gone before I could say anything else. Door closing behind her. Footsteps running down my porch.

I stood in my kitchen. Dinner half-eaten on the counter.

The warmth that had filled the space moments ago completely gone.

I rushed to the front porch. Watched Rachel's car pull out too fast, tires squealing slightly on the gravel.

The brake lights disappeared down the street.

I wanted to be there when she needed someone. But I stood there like an idiot, trying to figure out the right move. Follow her? Call? Wait? I didn't know.

I cleaned up dinner. Put away leftovers. Washed dishes.

Tried not to think about Rachel driving through the dark. Tried not to worry about Beverly. Tried not to imagine all the ways this could go wrong.

Dozer whined from the couch. Missing Rachel already.

"I know, buddy. Me too."

I sat on the floor next to him. Dali immediately climbed into my lap, purring. Claiming me in Rachel's absence.

I pulled out my phone.

Stared at it for a long time.

Chief's warning played on repeat. *Don't make rash decisions. Give it time.*

But time was running out. Rachel was planning to leave. Beverly needed help. Mrs. Henderson's solution might not work.

And I couldn't just sit here doing nothing.

I scrolled through my contacts. Found the number I needed.

My finger hovered over it.

Then I pressed call.

The line rang once. Twice.

"Jasonville Fire Department, Station Nine. How can I help you?"

Chapter Twenty-Five

Seaholly Beach

Rachel

Massive paws hit my back.

I stumbled forward, nearly dropping my camera as Dozer crashed into me. Wet sand spraying everywhere. Tail going wild.

He spun in circles. Barked with pure joy. Jumped up and planted both paws on my shoulders.

"Dozer!" I laughed and dropped to my knees. Let him tackle me properly.

He licked my face, my neck, my hands. Like I'd been gone for years.

"I missed you too, buddy."

"Dozer! I'm sorry—"

Ryan's voice carried down the beach.

I looked up.

He'd stopped several yards away. Staring.

My stomach flipped.

He looked good. Rumpled and tired but good. Running clothes. Faded Navy shirt that showed off his shoulders. Hair messy like he'd just rolled out of bed.

"Rachel." Relief flooded his face. "Hi."

"Hi."

Dozer bounded between us. Tail still going. Confused why we weren't moving toward each other.

Ryan closed the distance first. Stopped a few feet away.

Dark circles shadowed his eyes. But he was smiling.

Actually smiling.

"How's your mom?"

The question came fast. Urgent.

"She's okay." I stood, brushed sand off my knees. "Really. Bruised and sore but okay."

His whole body relaxed. "Thank god."

"The emergency necklace worked exactly like it was supposed to. She pushed the button, ambulance came in minutes." I smiled. "You were right about that."

"I'm glad."

We stood there. Morning light spill across everything. The tension between us felt different now. Not heavy. Just... charged.

"Walk?" he asked.

"Yeah."

We started along the beach. Dozer trotted ahead, nose to the sand, investigating every smell.

"So what happened?" Ryan's voice was lighter now. Easier. "After you left?"

"The drive was terrible. My brain went to worst-case scenarios the whole way." I kicked at the sand. "But when I got to the hospital, she was sitting up in bed. Talking to the nurse. Alert."

"That's great."

"They'd already done x-rays, checked everything. Nothing broken. Just bruised ribs and her hip. Some scrapes from the fall." I pulled out my phone. "Actually, I took a picture this morning when I called her. Look."

I showed him the screen. Mom sitting at her kitchen table with her breakfast. Smiling. A little pale but clearly on the mend.

"She looks good," Ryan said.

"Right? She was embarrassed more than anything. Kept apologizing for worrying me." I pocketed my phone. "The aide comes twice a day now. Mom's moving slower but she's getting around. Even made herself tea yesterday without help. Fortunately, the doctor said she could bounce back from this with the right care."

Ryan nodded. "That's really good progress."

"The hospital documented everything, so the aide was able to get insurance to extend coverage. Buys us time." I glanced at him. "And Vivian gave me leads. Care facilities near Mom's house. Companion programs. Adult communities with medical support built in."

"You made calls?"

"Left messages everywhere. Sent emails. Just waiting to hear back." I felt lighter saying it out loud. "It feels good to be doing something instead of just panicking."

His eyes held mine. Warm. Proud even.

"What about you?" I asked. "You said you had ideas."

Something flickered across his face. "Yeah. Made some calls. Still waiting to hear back."

"What kind of calls?"

"Just exploring options." He wouldn't quite meet my eyes. "Don't want to jinx it by talking about it too soon."

I wanted to push. But the look on his face stopped me.

"Okay."

We walked in silence for a moment. Comfortable this time.

Dozer barked ahead. We looked up to see him sniffing at a dark lump in the seaweed.

"Dozer, no—" Ryan started jogging toward him.

I followed.

The puppy had found a dead fish. A big one. And he was trying to roll in it.

"Dozer, stop!" Ryan grabbed his collar just as the dog flopped sideways. "No. Bad. We are not doing this."

Dozer looked offended. Tail still wagging. Like rolling in dead fish was a perfectly reasonable life choice.

I couldn't help it. I laughed.

Ryan shot me a look. "This isn't funny."

"It's a little funny."

"He's going to smell like death."

"Probably." I grinned. "But look how happy he is."

Dozer's tail blurred. Pure joy plastered across his doggy face.

Ryan sighed. Kept a firm grip on the collar. "Come on, buddy. Let's get you away from the fish corpse."

He steered Dozer down the beach. The puppy looked back at his prize like Ryan had just stolen Christmas.

"Does he do this often?" I asked.

"More than I'd like." Ryan shook his head. "Last week it was a dead crab. Week before that, seaweed that had been rotting for god knows how long."

"The joys of dog ownership."

"This wasn't in any of the training videos." But he smiled when he said it.

We kept walking. Dozer finally gave up on the fish and bounded ahead again.

"The mural's almost done," I said. "Just details left."

"Can't wait to see it finished."

"You nervous about the dedication?"

"Terrified. You?"

He laughed. "I run into fires. This shouldn't scare me."

"But?"

"But standing in front of the whole town with my face on a wall?" He grinned. "That's different."

"Your face looks good on that wall."

"Yeah?"

"Very good." I was flirting now. Couldn't help it. "Extremely paintable."

His eyes crinkled at the corners. "Paintable."

"It's a compliment."

"I'll take it."

We smiled at each other. The moment stretching.

A brown pelican swooped low over the water. Dove. Came up with a fish in its beak.

"Show-off," I said.

Ryan laughed. "Better technique than Dozer."

"Lower smell factor too."

The pelican landed on a piling nearby. Swallowed its catch whole.

We watched it for a moment. The bird preening its feathers. The ocean rolling behind it.

"I started running here in the mornings." He glanced at me. "After I moved in. Something about the ocean. The space."

"We were probably here at the same time. Different hours."

"Probably." His voice went quieter. "I used to hope I'd run into you."

My breath caught.

"Did you?"

"Every morning."

The admission hung between us.

The beach stretched ahead. Empty except for seagulls and the pelican watching us from its perch.

"Want to sit?" Ryan gestured toward a stretch of dry sand near the dunes.

"Yeah."

We sat. Close but not touching. Dozer immediately flopped between us.

I pulled my camera from around my neck. Started fiddling with the settings.

"What were you shooting before Dozer attacked you?" Ryan asked.

"Sunrise. Trying to capture the light on the water." I gestured at the ocean. "It's perfect right now.

"Did you get good shots?"

"Not really. Couldn't focus." I glanced at him. "Too distracted."

His eyes met mine. Heat and understanding passed between us.

I lifted my camera. Looked through the viewfinder at him.

Everything narrowed to just his face. Close enough to count his eyelashes.

"What are you doing?" His voice dropped lower than usual.

"You're in good light." My pulse kicked up. Something about having him in my lens. Studied. Trapped there.

"Rachel—"

"Hold still." I adjusted the focus. His jaw sharpened in the frame. The curve of his mouth.

He shifted his weight. Uncomfortable under my attention.

Heat crawled up my neck. I was staring at him. Really staring. Noticing things I shouldn't notice. The small scar near his temple. The way his throat moved when he swallowed.

"Relax," I said. "Just pretend I'm not here."

"Kind of hard when you're pointing a camera at me."

My voice came out quieter than I meant it to. "Then pretend I'm looking at something else."

"Are you?"

No. Not even close.

"Tilt your chin up slightly."

He did. The morning light caught the line of his neck. I forgot to breathe for a second.

"Now look at the ocean."

He turned his head. Profile sharp against the sky.

I clicked the shutter. My hands weren't quite steady.

"This feels weird," he said.

"You're doing great." I shifted closer. Close enough to smell salt and whatever soap he used. "Very photogenic."

"You're just saying that."

"I'm not." I zoomed in. His eyes filled the frame. "The camera loves you."

"Are you flirting with me?" he asked.

"Maybe." I grinned behind the camera. "Is it working?"

A pause. His gaze slid to me. Away from the ocean. Right at me.

He closed his eyes. Took a slow breath in. "You smell like coconut."

My heart thumped. I forgot how to think.

"Are you flirting with me?" I asked.

His smile came slow. The kind that made my pulse skip.

"Maybe," he said. "Is it working?"

"Yeah." My voice came out breathless. "It's working."

He smiled wider.

I lifted the camera again. Clicked once more. Caught him looking at me like that. Like he was thinking things he wasn't saying out loud.

My throat went dry.

"Got it," I managed.

"Can I see?"

"No." I lowered the camera. Held his stare. "Artist privilege."

"That's not fair."

"Life's not fair." Neither of us looked away. "But you'll see them eventually."

"When?"

"When I'm ready."

His eyes dropped to my mouth. Just for a second. Then back up.

"And when will that be?"

I smiled. "When I'm done torturing you."

The air between us shifted. Got heavier. Charged.

We were sitting close now. Knees almost touching. Dozer had wandered off to chase seagulls again.

I reached into my bag. Pulled out a protein bar I'd grabbed this morning.

"Want half?" I asked. "I haven't eaten yet."

"Sure."

I broke it in half. Handed him a piece.

Our fingers brushed. Just for a second.

The contact felt electric.

We ate in comfortable silence. The protein bar was chocolate and peanut butter. Not great but not terrible.

"Thanks," he said.

"Anytime."

"It hit me how normal this felt. Sharing food on a beach. Our dog— *his* dog playing nearby. The easy comfort of just being together."

This is what it could be like. If we figured everything out.

"Can I ask you something?" I said.

"Yeah."

"Why firefighting? Why did you choose it?"

He was quiet for a moment. Thinking.

"I like the work," he said. "The physical part of it. Using my hands. Problem solving in real time."

"You could've done construction. Your dad was a carpenter."

"Yeah." He nodded. "I thought about it. But firefighting has something construction doesn't."

"What's that?"

"Purpose. Community." He looked at the ocean. "Every call matters. Every shift, I'm doing something that helps people. And the team—" He paused. "It's different. You trust these guys with your life. They trust you with theirs."

"That must be intense."

"It is. But it's good." His voice was sure. "I'm good at it. And I like knowing I make a difference."

There was a simplicity to it. No grand story. Just honest work he believed in.

"Did you always want to follow this path?"

"Not always. I thought about other things. Engineering. Architecture." He shrugged. "But I kept coming back to it. The idea of showing up when people need help. Making a difference in the worst moments of their lives."

"What do you want?" I asked. "Long term?"

He turned to look at me. Eyes dark and serious.

"I want this. The job. The community. Making a difference." He paused. "And I want someone to come home to. Someone who gets it. Who understands why I do what I do."

The words settled between us. Heavy with meaning.

"Rachel." His voice went quieter.

"Yeah?"

"This is really hard."

"What is?"

"Not kissing you right now."

My breath caught.

His eyes were on my mouth. Dark. Intense.

"We agreed," I said. Voice barely above a whisper. "Fix everything first."

"I know."

"Then us."

"I know."

Neither of us moved.

The space between us felt electric. Charged with everything we weren't doing.

I wanted to close the distance. Wanted it so badly my fingers ached.

But we'd made a promise. To ourselves. To each other.

Do this right.

"We should probably—" I started.

"Yeah."

But we still didn't move.

Ryan's hand was in the sand next to mine. Close enough that I could feel the heat of him.

I shifted slightly. Let my pinky touch his.

Just that. Nothing more.

His breath hitched.

We sat there. Pinkies touching in the sand. Staring at the ocean like it held all the answers.

"Tell me about the mural," he said finally. "What details are left?"

Safe ground. I could do safe ground.

"Faces mostly. Making sure everyone's features are right. The light on the gear. Shadows." I pulled my hand back. Needed space. "And your portrait. Making sure I captured you properly."

"How do you know if you did?"

"When I look at it and see you. Not just what you look like. But who you are."

He turned to face me. "And who am I?"

The question felt bigger than painting.

"Someone who shows up," I said quietly. "Every time. Someone who cares. Who makes a difference. Who fixes things." I met his eyes. "Someone worth staying for."

The last words slipped out before I could stop them.

His expression shifted. Something fierce and tender at once.

"Rachel—"

Dozer barked. Running back toward us with a piece of driftwood in his mouth.

The moment broke.

Ryan stood. Called Dozer over. The puppy dropped the wood at his feet. "Subtle, buddy." He threw it down the beach. Dozer bounded after it.

I stood too. Brushed sand off my jeans.

"I should get going," Ryan said. "Morning shift soon."

"Right."

We walked back toward the parking lot. Slower than necessary.

At his truck, he hesitated. "Thank you. For this. For talking."

"Thank you for showing up."

"Always."

The word felt like a promise.

He climbed in. Dozer jumping into the passenger seat. The puppy pressed his nose against the window. Fogging the glass.

I waved.

Ryan waved back.

Then he was gone.

I stood there for a moment. Watching his truck disappear down the coast road.

My phone rang.

I pulled it out. Glanced at the screen.

Mrs. Henderson.

Why is she calling?

Chapter Twenty-Six

Mrs. Henderson's House

Ryan

"Wahoo!!! WHAT???"

Rachel's whoop shook Mrs. Henderson's formal living room. She bounced on her feet, hands covering her mouth, tears streaming down her face.

Mrs. Henderson beamed with satisfaction. Arms crossed. Looking like a detective who'd just solved the case of the century.

I watched Rachel with relief flooding through me. My heart starting to beat normally again.

"Are you sure?" Rachel's voice broke on the words. "Are you absolutely sure you mean it?"

"I've never been more certain of anything, dear."

Rachel laughed through tears. The sound was relief and disbelief tangled together.

Earlier, I'd walked outside to my truck.

Rachel was walking to her car. Keys in hand.

We saw each other. Waved.

Both headed to our vehicles.

I paused. Hand on the door handle.

Something felt off.

I turned back. "Wait. Where are you going?"

She stopped. Turned around. "Mrs. Henderson's. She called me for tea."

My stomach dropped. "She called you too?"

"Yeah. Two o'clock. Said it was important." Rachel's eyes narrowed slightly. "Why? Did she call you?"

"Yes. Same time. Same message."

We stared at each other across our driveways.

"Do you think..." Rachel started.

"Has to be." Hope flared in my chest. "What she was working on."

Rachel's face changed. Understanding dawning. "Her plan."

"Get in." I gestured to my truck. "We'll go together."

She didn't hesitate. Crossed the driveway and climbed into the passenger seat.

Now we sat side by side on Mrs. Henderson's settee. Her good china laid out with ceremony. The delicate kind with flowers painted on it.

Dozer had caused chaos on our arrival. Bounded out of my truck and immediately trampled through Mrs. Henderson's flower beds. Crushed her pansies. Dug up what might have been tulip bulbs.

"Dozer, no! Come here!" I'd lunged for his collar. Missed.

Mrs. Henderson approached, wagging her finger. "That dog needs proper training, Ryan. Obedience classes. Structure and discipline." Her tone was firm. Lecturing. "A dog that size can't be allowed to run amok. It's a matter of safety and respect."

"Yes, ma'am. I'm working on it."

"Work harder." She'd given Dozer a stern look. "He's perfectly capable of learning. You simply must be consistent."

Inside, Dozer curled up at our feet. Mrs. Henderson had apparently forgiven him. She even reached down to pat his head once before settling into her chair.

She poured tea with deliberate slowness. Clearly enjoying the suspense.

My knee bounced. I forced it still.

Rachel's hand found mine on the settee between us. Squeezed.

I squeezed back.

Mrs. Henderson set down the teapot with purpose.

Looked between us with those sharp, knowing eyes.

"I've been doing some detective work."

Rachel and I exchanged glances.

Mrs. Henderson continued. "I overheard you at The Grind. Ryan was quite upset. Henry trying to help."

My face went hot.

"I've been thinking about your mother ever since."

Rachel's hand tightened on mine.

Mrs. Henderson settled into her chair. Arranged her cardigan with precision.

"I've been lonely since Harold died."

Her voice stayed matter-of-fact. Just stating facts.

"The house is too big. Too quiet. Too much for one person to maintain." She gestured at the room around us. "Extra bedrooms I don't even go into anymore. A kitchen built for family dinners I eat alone. A garden Harold planted that I can't keep up with by myself."

Rachel leaned forward. Listening.

"Just me and the memories and too much silence."

Mrs. Henderson's gaze shifted to Rachel. "Your mom needs help. Can't live alone safely. Requires supervision, assistance, companionship."

Rachel's hand gripped mine harder.

I squeezed back. A silent promise.

"You're torn between your mother and the life you've built in Seaholly. Forced to choose. Both options meaning loss."

Rachel's face showed the accuracy hitting hard.

Mrs. Henderson leaned forward. "I'd like to propose a solution. Your mom moves in here. With me."

Rachel's teacup rattled against the saucer. She set it down quickly.

I stopped breathing.

My hand tightened on Rachel's. This was it. The answer we'd been looking for.

Mrs. Henderson laid out the logic like she was presenting evidence in court.

"Two lonely women. One big house with empty bedrooms. Mutual companionship. Shared responsibilities. Neither of us alone."

She ticked off points on her fingers. "Split costs. Share the space. Keep each other company."

"I need a housemate. Your mom needs support. It's quite simple, really."

The elegant obviousness of it hung in the air.

Rachel's brain visibly tried to process.

"You want Mom to live here? With you?"

Mrs. Henderson nodded. Patient.

"The guest room is ready. Just needs her furniture and personal things to make it feel like home." Mrs. Henderson's voice was practical. Confident. "We'll split utilities and groceries. Establish routines together. Companion care without the clinical coldness of hired help."

Rachel's eyes went wide.

"Your mom would be close by. Close enough for weekly dinners, emergency visits, daily check-ins."

Mrs. Henderson's expression softened. "You wouldn't have to leave Seaholly. Your cottage. Your students."

I watched her face change as she processed it.

Her hands shook. She blinked rapidly.

"But what about you?" Rachel's voice cracked. "This is your home. Your space. Your privacy."

Mrs. Henderson tilted her head. "I think I articulated that quite clearly, dear. Weren't you listening?" Her tone was patient but pointed. "Which is too big for one person and too quiet. I want the company, Rachel."

She leaned forward. "This isn't charity. This is a mutual benefit. Your mother helps me as much as I help her."

She paused. Adjusted her cardigan with precise fingers. "Did you know your mom does scrapbooking? I just started after Harold died, and Beverly has been collecting her memories for years. She told me so herself at The Grind last year when she visited. She can teach me a thing or two." Mrs. Henderson's lips pursed slightly. "Don't want to admit it, but since you're pushing, scrapbooking is out of my league."

Rachel's face softened. A small smile breaking through.

"Mom would love that," she said quietly. "Teaching someone. Sharing her hobby."

"Exactly." Mrs. Henderson nodded with satisfaction. "We'd be good for each other."

Rachel looked at our joined hands. Processing everything.

This solved everything.

Beverly would be safe. Cared for. Happy with a friend instead of alone.

Rachel wouldn't have to leave. Wouldn't have to choose between her mother and her life.

She could stay.

Rachel's face changed. Focused.

"What about Mom's house? Her things?"

"I could contact a real estate person," Rachel said, more to herself than to us. "Figure out the best options. Selling or renting."

Mrs. Henderson nodded. "And as for her belongings, she can bring whatever she wants. My house has plenty of storage. We can take our time making her room feel like home."

"But I need to talk to her first." Rachel's voice was urgent. "Make sure she wants this. She's so independent. She might feel like a burden."

"Then you tell her she'd be doing me a favor." Mrs. Henderson's tone was firm. "Because she would be. I'm tired of rattling around here alone."

Rachel nodded slowly. "I need to think through all the details before I call her. Her belongings. Her routines. Her doctors. Whether she'd even want to leave her neighborhood."

"Take your time." Mrs. Henderson's voice went gentle. Kind. "But I think you'll find she's been lonely too."

She looked between Rachel and me. "Sometimes we're so busy being strong, we forget to admit we need people."

The wisdom hung in the air.

Mrs. Henderson started to stand. Paused.

"Off my foot, please," she said primly to Dozer. "There's a good boy."

Dozer huffed. Shifted his head.

She stood. Smoothed her cardigan. "I'll just check on the kettle. See if there are any of those cookies left."

Obvious excuse to give us privacy.

She left. Footsteps fading toward the kitchen.

Rachel and I sat on the settee. Still holding hands.

The silence stretched between us.

Rachel stood. Walked to the window. Arms wrapped around herself.

Looking out at Mrs. Henderson's garden. The late afternoon light catching on new green shoots.

I watched her. Hardly daring to breathe.

"If Mom says yes..." Rachel's voice was quiet.

Long pause. My heart pounded.

"I won't have to leave. I can stay here."

She turned to face me. Slowly.

Her eyes were bright with unshed tears. Hopeful and terrified at once.

"I can keep teaching my classes. Keep my cottage."

She took a step closer to me.

"Keep my neighbor."

My throat went tight.

She was standing right in front of me now.

All her walls crumbling. Vulnerability written across every feature.

She was quiet for a moment. Processing. Her eyes searching mine.

"You said you made calls," she said finally. "What was the other option you were working on?"

I swallowed. "Not exactly an option."

"What do you mean?"

"I called Jasonville Fire Department. Asked about a transfer."

Her eyes went wide. "What?"

"If you had to move. To take care of your mom. I was going to transfer there. Be close by."

"Ryan—"

"I wasn't going to let you do it alone." I stood. Faced her. "Even if we couldn't be together. I was going to be there. As a friend. As whatever you'd let me be."

Tears spilled down her cheeks.

"You were going to leave Seaholly? For me?"

"I would have left anywhere for you."

She made a sound. Half laugh, half sob.

Then she was in my arms. I pulled her close. She buried her face in my chest. Her whole body shaking with silent sobs.

I held her. One hand spanning her back, the other cradling her head.

"I can't believe you would do that," she whispered against my shirt.

"I'd do anything for you."
She pulled back slightly. Looked up at me.
Her eyes were red. Swollen. Makeup smudged.
She'd never looked more beautiful.
Rachel's voice came softly. Barely a whisper.
"About that date..."

Chapter Twenty-Seven

The Community Center

Rachel

"Now watch how the brush moves." I demonstrated the stroke across my canvas. "See how the paint flows?"

The students watched with varying degrees of attention.

I demonstrated the same stroke again. My hand moving on autopilot while my brain replayed Ryan's words at Mrs. Henderson's house.

I'd do anything for you.

"Miss Rachel, you did the same stroke three times." Sarah's voice cut through my thoughts.

I blinked down at my canvas. She was right.

"Good observation, Sarah. Sometimes we repeat strokes for emphasis."

The kids went back to their hero portraits. Chattering about parents, teachers, firefighters, siblings.

My mind stayed elsewhere. Replaying that moment in Mrs. Henderson's living room on an endless loop.

His transfer. To Jasonville. For me.

The way he'd looked at me when I said "About that date..."
My phone buzzed. I pulled it out.
Text from Mom.

> *Still thinking about Margaret's offer. It's a big decision. Give me a few more days?*

My stomach flipped. She hadn't said no. Hadn't said yes.
Still thinking. Still possible.
I typed back.

> *Take all the time you need. No pressure.*

And I meant it. For the first time in weeks, I wasn't spiraling about worst-case scenarios. Mrs. Henderson had found a solution. Mom was considering it. That was enough for now.
The door opened.
Ryan walked in with Dozer.
My heart kicked hard.
Our eyes met across the room full of seven-year-olds.
He wore his uniform. On duty but taking his lunch break for this prearranged demonstration.
He smiled. Small. Just for me.
I smiled back.
"Mr. Ryan! Dozer!"
The kids abandoned their paintings. A mob scene of small bodies swarming toward the door.
Ryan laughed. "Whoa, guys. Give us some space here."
Dozer's tail wagged so hard his whole body moved. The massive puppy loved kids almost as much as he loved Ryan.
Ryan set up his demonstration in the cleared space near the windows.
The kids settled on the floor in a semicircle. Eager and attentive.
"Today we're talking about what to do if you see smoke in your house." Ryan's voice went clear. Patient. "Who knows the first thing you should do?"
Several hands shot up.
"Get out!" Tommy called without waiting.

"Exactly. Get out fast. Don't try to save your toys, don't hide, don't wait. Get out and call 911." Ryan demonstrated. "Can everyone practice with me?"

The kids stood. Repeated the motions.

I watched from my easel. Seeing Ryan through their eyes. Protector. Teacher. Hero.

Patient with their questions. Gentle with their excitement. Taking time from his shift to teach them how to be safe.

Something expanded in my chest.

This was who he was. Not just with me, but with everyone. Kind by nature, not by effort.

Ryan finished his demonstration. "Any questions?"

Emma's hand shot up. "Are you dating Miss Rachel now?"

My face went hot.

Small faces turned to stare at us expectantly from every direction.

How did you explain this to seven-year-olds?

We'd said things. Made promises. But we were waiting on Mom's decision before we could move forward.

The silence stretched too long. Kids starting to fidget. Emma still waiting for an answer.

I looked at Ryan.

He looked at me.

His eyes warm. Patient. Letting me answer.

"We're..." I started. Met Ryan's eyes. Saw the hope there. "We're working on it together."

Emma's nose wrinkled. "What does that mean?"

"It means good things take time," I said. "And sometimes the best things are worth waiting for."

"That's boring," Jayden announced.

Ryan laughed. "You're not wrong, buddy."

He looked at me. Something soft in his expression.

Like he appreciated what I'd said. Like we were on the same page.

The moment stretched between us. Understanding passing without words.

Then Ryan smoothly redirected. "Who wants to see inside the fire truck?"

The kids exploded with enthusiasm.

They followed Ryan and Dozer outside in a chaotic parade. Small bodies chattering about sirens and hoses and whether they could turn on the lights.

I stayed in the classroom.

Started cleaning up paint supplies. Stacking papers. Organizing the chaos.

Through the window, I watched Ryan lifting kids into the fire truck cab. Patient. Careful. Making sure each one got a turn.

Dozer sat beside him. Perfectly behaved. Letting the kids pet him without getting overexcited.

My phone buzzed again.

Text from Ryan.

> That was harder than any fire I've fought.

I smiled. Typed back.

> You handled it well.

His response came immediately.

> Can we talk later? After your class?

My pulse jumped.

> Yes. My place? 6?

> I'll be there.

I set my phone down. Pressed my hand against my stomach where butterflies had taken flight.

The kids filed back inside. Faces flushed. Voices loud with excitement about what they'd seen.

"Miss Rachel, Mr. Ryan let me turn on the lights!" Tommy bounced on his toes.

"That's wonderful, Tommy."

"And Dozer gave me a high five!"

I helped them settle back into their seats. Handed out fresh paper.

"Let's finish our hero portraits. Think about what makes your person a hero. What do they do? How do they help?"

The kids bent over their work. Markers and crayons moving across paper.

Sarah painted her mom. "She makes dinner every night even when she's tired."

Jayden drew his older brother. "He helps me with homework."

Tommy worked on his portrait of Ryan. Careful strokes. Detailed uniform. A fire truck in the background.

I moved between tables. Offering encouragement. Helping with colors. Watching their faces light up as they talked about their heroes.

This was why I taught. These moments of connection. Of creativity. Of kids learning to see the good in people.

The class ended at five.

Parents arrived for pickup. Kids showed off their paintings. Proud of their work.

Tommy's mom paused at my easel. "Thank you for having Ryan come in. Tommy hasn't stopped talking about fire safety since his last visit."

"He's great with the kids."

"And great with you, I think." She winked. "The way he looks at you."

My face went hot again.

She laughed. "Good luck with whatever you're figuring out."

After everyone left, I cleaned the room. Put away supplies. Stacked chairs. Swept up paint chips and glitter.

My phone said 5:47.

Thirteen minutes until Ryan arrived.

I drove home. Parked. Stared at my cottage.

Everything felt suspended. Hanging between what was and what could be.

Mom hadn't decided yet. Everything waited on her answer.

But Ryan had been willing to transfer. To follow me if I had to leave.

That meant something.

I went inside. Fed Dali. Changed out of my paint-stained clothes into clean jeans and a sweater.

Tried to calm my racing heart.

At exactly six, a knock sounded at my door.

I opened it.

Ryan stood on my porch. Out of uniform now. Jeans and a gray henley. Hair still damp from a shower. Oh no. Casual Ryan was a problem.

Dozer sat beside him. Tail wagging.

"Hi."

"Hi." I stepped back. "Come in."

They came inside. Dozer immediately made himself at home on my couch. Dali hissed from her perch on the bookshelf.

Ryan and I stood in my living room. A few feet apart.

The air between us felt electric.

"So," he said.

"So."

"Your mom hasn't decided yet."

"No. She's thinking about it."

He nodded slowly. "And you're waiting on her answer before we..."

"Before we move forward. Yeah." I wrapped my arms around myself. "I don't know what happens if she says no. If I still have to leave."

"Then we figure it out." Ryan's voice went firm. "Together."

"You can't just transfer for me. Your life is here. Your job. Your community. The outreach program you built."

"And you're here." He took a step closer. "That matters more."

My throat went tight. "I used to think I had to have all the answers before taking a step forward. But maybe that's not how it works."

"What do you mean?"

"Maybe we just... trust the process. See what Mom says. Trust that Mrs. Henderson's solution is as good as it seems." I looked up at him. "Instead of looking for all the ways it could go wrong."

Something shifted in his expression. Relief. Pride.

"Yeah?"

"Yeah." I squeezed his hand. "I'm tired of being scared all the time. Of assuming the worst. Mom's thinking about it. That's good."

"That's really good."

"And even if—" I stopped. Shook my head. "No. I'm not doing that anymore. Not making up problems that don't exist yet."

Ryan smiled. Pulled me closer. "Who are you and what did you do with Rachel?"

I laughed. "I don't know. She's still here somewhere. Just trying something new."

"I like it."

"Me too." And I meant it. The constant spiral of worry had been exhausting. "It feels better. Lighter."

"Good." He brushed a strand of hair behind my ear. "You deserve to feel light."

I let myself lean into him. His arms came around me. Solid. Steady.

This was what I wanted. This feeling of being held. Of not facing everything alone.

Of choosing hope instead of fear.

I pulled back. Looked up at him. "We should still wait. Until Mom decides."

He nodded. "Okay."

"But I'm not catastrophizing anymore. I'm just... waiting. Trusting."

"That's all we can do."

We stood there. Connected. Waiting.

My phone buzzed.

I pulled it out with my free hand.

Text from Mom.

> *Can we talk tomorrow? I have some questions about Margaret's offer.*

My heart kicked.

Questions. Not a no. Not a yes.

Progress.

I showed Ryan the text.

His face lit up. "That's really good. Questions mean she's seriously considering it."

"Yeah." I smiled. Actually smiled. "It is good."

"Look at you. Being optimistic."

"Don't get used to it," I said, but there was no bite in it. "I'm still learning."

"You're doing great."

He stayed for another hour. We sat on the couch. Dozer between us. Dali eventually joining from her perch.

We talked about small things. His shift. My class. The mural progress.

Anything but the big question hanging over us.

When he left, he paused at the door.
"I'm proud of you."
"For what?"
"For choosing hope." He squeezed my hand. "It looks good on you."
I smiled. "It feels good."
Then he was gone.
I closed the door. Leaned against it.
Pulled out my phone. Stared at Mom's text.

> *Can we talk tomorrow?*

Tomorrow didn't feel scary anymore. Just… next.

> *Yes. Call me whenever you're ready.*

Then I sat on my couch. Dali curled in my lap.
And for the first time in weeks, I wasn't afraid of what came next.

Chapter Twenty-Eight

The Firehouse

Ryan

Water sprayed across the truck's chrome, washing away the day's grime.

I worked the hose in steady sweeps. Left to right. Top to bottom. The methodical task kept my hands busy and my mind from spinning.

The mural dedication was coming. Soon, Rachel and I would stand in front of the whole town as partners. Soon, I'd find out if Beverly said yes to Mrs. Henderson's offer.

Soon, everything would either fall into place or fall apart.

"Hey."

Rachel's voice startled me. I shut off the water, set the hose down.

She stood in the bay entrance with her art supplies bag slung over one shoulder. Hair pulled back in a messy bun. Paint-stained jeans and an oversized flannel.

Beautiful.

"Hey." I wiped my hands on my pants. "Didn't know you were coming by."

"Final seal coat on the mural." She lifted her bag slightly. "Want to protect it before the dedication. Make sure it lasts."

"Need help?"

"I need your eyes." She set down her bag near the mural wall. "Come look at it with me?"

Dozer bounded over from his corner. Tail wagging, greeting Rachel like she'd been gone for years instead of hours.

She scratched behind his ears, laughing when he leaned his full weight against her legs.

I left the hose where it lay. Crossed the bay to stand beside her.

The mural spread across the wall. Finished now. Complete.

Firefighters in action. Community members watching. Kids learning. The pier in the background, stronger than before. And at the center, my portrait anchoring the composition.

"It's incredible," I said.

"Look closer." She stepped toward the wall. "There are details most people won't notice. But I want you to see them."

She pointed to the background. "See how the light hits the pier supports? That's early morning light. Warm. Soft. The same light from when the pier collapsed. When you pulled me out."

I leaned in. She was right. The quality of light felt specific. Hopeful.

"And here." She moved to a section showing the crew. "Each firefighter has their own light source. See? Martinez here is backlit, which makes him look heroic. But Frank has side lighting that shows the texture of his gear, the wear and tear. The different angles help move your eye through the painting. They tell the story of experience."

I studied the painting with new eyes. Seeing what she saw. Understanding the intention behind every choice.

"Why did you do it that way?"

"Because you're not all the same kind of hero." She traced the air near the painting without touching it. "Martinez is young, eager, all forward momentum. Frank has been doing this for decades. His heroism is different. Steadier. I wanted to show that."

The care she'd taken with each detail hit me. This wasn't just a pretty picture. She'd studied my crew. Understood them. Captured something true.

"What about the colors?" I asked.

Her face lit up. "Okay, so fire imagery is mostly reds and oranges. Expected. But look."

She pointed to different sections. "I used reds, yes, but also blues and greens. Cool tones to balance the heat. Because firefighting isn't just about fire. It's about water, air, the science of it. The balance."

I listened to her explain brush techniques. How she layered paint to create depth. Why she chose certain compositions over others.

This was her expertise. Her world. And she was letting me in.

"It almost feels like movement," I said, studying the wall. "Like the figures are actually doing something instead of just standing there."

Her face lit up. "Yes! That's exactly what I wanted." She moved closer to the wall. "See here? I used gloss medium in some of my paint mixes. Makes it catch the light. And here—" She pointed to shadowed areas. "—matte finish. Absorbs light instead of reflecting it."

I leaned in. She was right. The difference was subtle but striking.

"And the texture matters too." She traced the air near a firefighter's coat. "Thick paint over thin. Builds up the surface. Makes the gear look heavy, real. But the sky in the background? Thin layers. Smooth. Creates distance."

"How do you know where to do which?"

"Practice. And mistakes." She smiled. "Lots of mistakes. But also understanding light. Where it hits, where it doesn't. That's what creates the illusion of three dimensions on a flat surface."

She paused. Looked at me. "That's why I'm always outside. At the pier, the beach, anywhere I can watch the light change. People probably think I'm spacing out, but I'm studying it. How morning light differs from afternoon. How shadows move. How colors shift."

Her voice went softer. "I see everything like it could be a painting. Impressionist strokes. Broken color. It makes the world richer somehow. More alive."

The way she said it—like she was sharing a secret. Like she was letting me see how her mind worked.

She pointed to the highlights on my portrait. "These tiny spots of pure white? Placed exactly right, they make the whole figure pop forward. Get them wrong, and everything looks flat."

I studied her work with new appreciation. Every choice deliberate. Every stroke intentional.

"How long did it take you to learn all this?"

"Years. And I'm still learning." She stepped back to view the full mural. "Every painting teaches me something new."

We moved to my portrait.

My portrait. Larger than the others but not dominating the wall.

"This one took the longest," she said quietly.

"Why?"

"Because I kept getting it wrong." She studied the painting. "I'd paint your expression too serious. Then too soft. I couldn't find the balance."

"What changed?"

"I stopped trying to paint what I thought a hero should look like." She looked at me. "Started painting what I actually saw."

"Which is?"

"Someone strong but gentle. Serious but warm." Her eyes held mine. "Someone who shows up. Does the work. Doesn't need to be at the center of attention. So I didn't put you there. You're prominent, but you're giving space to everyone else. The way you actually are."

Her words landed in my throat. Made it tight.

"You painted me like I matter."

"You do matter." She said it simply. Like it was obvious.

We stood close. Shoulders nearly touching. Both looking at the mural but aware of each other in every cell.

A crash behind us shattered the moment.

Dozer had found the hose.

The massive puppy grabbed it in his mouth, tail wagging with pride at his discovery. Started walking across the bay, dragging it behind him.

"Dozer, no—" I started toward him.

Too late.

He walked between Rachel and me. The hose wrapped around our ankles as he passed, looping and tangling with each step.

We were bound together. Literally.

"Dozer!" Rachel laughed despite the situation. "What are you doing?"

The puppy just wagged harder. Kept walking. The hose pulled tighter.

I grabbed Rachel's waist to steady us both. "Don't move or we'll fall."

"Kind of hard not to move when we're tied together."

We tried to step out of the loops. Made it worse. The hose cinched tighter around our legs.

Dozer dropped his end and trotted away. Mission accomplished.

"This is ridiculous." Rachel was laughing now. Really laughing.

"Hold still." I crouched down, tried to unwrap the hose from her ankles first.

She wobbled. Her hands landed on my shoulders for balance.

I looked up at her. She looked down at me.

"If you move, we'll both go down."

"I'm not moving. You're pulling."

"I'm not pulling. The hose is pulling."

"That doesn't even make sense."

I unwound one loop. Two. The third one tightened when I tried to loosen it.

"Okay, lift your left foot."

She lifted her right.

"Your other left."

"I know which foot is left." But she was laughing. "You're confusing me."

"Step back. No, forward. Wait—"

Her foot caught on another loop. She stumbled. I caught her waist with both hands.

We froze. Her hands still on my shoulders. My hands on her waist. Close enough that I could see paint flecks on her jawline.

"This is ridiculous," she said softly.

"Completely ridiculous."

Neither of us moved.

Then Dozer barked once. Proud of his handiwork.

The spell broke. Rachel laughed. Really laughed.

I finally got us untangled. Stood. We were closer than before. Neither of us stepped back.

"Come on." I gestured to the truck. "Let's sit before he finds something else to destroy."

We sat on the clean bumper. Dry enough.

Dozer sprawled at our feet. Pleased with his chaos.

Rachel caught her breath. She ran her thumb along her fingernails in a slow, absent rhythm. I'd noticed her do it before when she was working through something.

Comfortable silence settled. But charged. Full of things unsaid.

"The dedication's coming," Rachel said finally.

"Yeah."

"Chief called us partners. From the start."

The word hung between us. Loaded with meaning.

"We are partners." I turned slightly to look at her. "On this project. This mural. We built it together."

"We did." She picked at paint on her jeans. "I couldn't have done it without you. The scaffolding, the community outreach, getting the crew to trust me."

"You earned their trust. I just opened the door."

She smiled. Small but genuine. "Still. We make a good team." She took a breath. "Even if I should warn you—I'm not a very conventional type of woman."

Her tone was almost casual. But her voice carried an edge. Vulnerability masked as humor.

"Define conventional."

"You know. Normal. Predictable." She gestured at herself. "I set microwaves on fire. My cat destroys things. I have paint in my hair more often than not. Nothing in my life goes according to plan."

Sounded like she was giving me an out. Expecting me to take it.

"I've been with someone who didn't accept that." Her voice dropped. "Who made me feel like I was too much."

I watched her profile. The way she held herself. Braced for rejection.

"I don't want conventional." My voice came out rougher than intended. "I want you."

She turned to look at me. Eyes wide. Uncertain.

"The whole package," I continued. "The chaos and the paint stains and the crying cat and the fire alarms. The passion for your art and the way you see beauty everywhere. The way you teach kids and make my crew laugh and challenge me to be better."

Her breath caught.

"I don't want you to be less. I want all of it. All of you."

"Ryan—"

"I'm not Derek." I held her gaze. "I'm not going to tolerate your passion. I'm going to celebrate it. Because that's what makes you you."

She blinked rapidly. Eyes bright.

"Tonight you taught me to see your art differently," I said. "Not just pretty pictures. The intention. The meaning. The skill behind every choice."

I gestured to the mural. "That matters. Your work matters. You matter."

She looked down at her hands. Paint-stained fingers twisted together.

"I'm usually the strong one. The capable one." She looked up at me. "I handle things. I figure stuff out. I don't wait around for other people to save me."

Something shifted in her expression. Recognition.

"But somewhere along the way, I lost that." Her voice went softer. "With Derek. With Mom getting older. I started second-guessing everything. Waiting for things to fall apart instead of believing I could handle whatever came."

"You're still that person," I said. "The capable one. You're handling this. You found solutions. You asked for help when you needed it."

"Maybe." She was quiet for a moment. "I can't control what Mom decides. But I can control what I do. And I choose to believe this will work out."

We sat in silence. Dozer's tail thumped once against the concrete.

Rachel looked at the mural. Her eyes scanning the colors, the composition, the details she'd labored over.

"When I was spiraling," she said slowly, "my colors turned to mud. Everything I painted looked wrong. Dull. Lifeless."

We sat in silence. Dozer's tail thumped once against the concrete.

Rachel looked at the mural. Her eyes scanning the colors, the composition, the details she'd labored over.

"When I was spiraling," she said slowly, "my colors turned to mud. Everything I painted looked wrong. Dull. Lifeless."

I remembered. The stress in her shoulders. The tension in her jaw. The way she'd pulled away.

"But look at this." She gestured to the mural. "The colors are vivid. They show depth. Meaning. They work together the way they're supposed to."

She turned to look at me. Really look at me.

"As an artist, I've learned to read it. When colors work. When composition clicks. When all the elements are finally in place."

Her expression shifted. Something like wonder crossing her features.

"You understanding my art," she said quietly. "Mrs. Henderson's solution. Mom thinking about it. The mural nearly complete. You, right here, saying you want all of me."

She looked at the painting. Then back at me.

"This feels like that. Like when all the brushstrokes finally align."

Hope bloomed in my throat. Cautious but real.

"Sometimes you can feel it before you see it," she said. "When all the elements are finally in place."

She smiled. Small but genuine. The first real smile I'd seen from her in too long.

"Something good is coming."

Chapter Twenty-Nine

Rachel's Cottage

Rachel

Three easels stood arranged in my living room. Ocean scene on the left. Portrait study in the middle. Abstract piece on the right.

I'd been moving between them since I got home from the firehouse. Not systematically—just wherever my instinct pulled me next. Add a layer here, soften a shadow there, back to the first when the color called to me.

Ryan's words kept playing on repeat. *I don't want conventional. I want you.*

The door opened without a knock.

Maya walked in carrying two bottles of champagne and a container from her catering supplies.

"Celebration time."

I set down my brush. "What are we celebrating?"

"Life. Art. My brother finding someone who makes him smile like an idiot." She set everything on my kitchen counter. Opened the container to reveal fancy cheese, crackers, and some kind of spread with herbs. "Leftover from a wedding tasting. Bride chose the other option. Her loss, our gain."

"Maya—"

"Also, you look like you've been painting for twelve hours straight and need actual food." She grabbed two mugs from my cabinet. We were out of wine glasses. "When's the last time you ate?"

I paused. "Lunch?"

"Try again."

"I don't know. A while."

She popped the first champagne bottle with practiced ease. "That's what I thought."

She poured generous amounts into both mugs. Handed me one.

I took it. Drank. Champagne from a mug felt absurd and perfect.

Maya studied the paintings around us. All different subjects. The pier. The ocean. The firehouse. Ryan's hands in various sketches.

His hands kept appearing. I couldn't seem to stop drawing them.

"So." Maya sat on my couch. Dali immediately claimed her lap. "My brother."

"Maya—"

"He's never brought anyone to meet the family before."

I froze with my mug halfway to my mouth.

"Not once," she continued. "Not even when he was dating seriously before he moved here. He keeps his personal life separate. Private."

"We're not—"

"He's never looked at anyone the way he looks at you."

My throat went tight.

Maya scratched behind Dali's ears. The cat purred, oblivious to the tension. "He's been stress-cooking at midnight. Made three different kinds of sauces yesterday. Dozer keeps bringing him your scarf. The one you left at the firehouse. Carries it around like a security blanket."

Heat crept up my neck. "I didn't mean for that."

"I know." Her eyes met mine. Warm. Understanding. "He's completely gone for you. Everyone can see it."

I drank more champagne. Looked down at my paint-stained hands.

"Derek spent three years making you feel like you were too much," Maya said gently. "But Ryan? He thinks your chaos is perfect. He told me so. Used the word 'perfect.'"

Tears burned behind my eyes.

"I was wrong," Maya continued. "When Ryan first moved here. I warned him off. Told him you were recovering from Derek. That you weren't ready. That he should keep his distance."

"Maya—"

"I thought I was protecting you both." She met my eyes. "But I see now how good you are together. His stability grounds your chaos. Your creativity brightens his ordered world. You balance each other."

Tears spilled down my cheeks.

"So I'm here to celebrate," Maya said. "Because you're choosing happiness. Because Mom might say yes. Because something good is coming. I can feel it."

My phone rang.

Beverly's name lit up the screen.

My stomach flipped. This was it.

"Answer it," Maya said gently.

I pressed accept. "Mom?"

"Honey!" Beverly's tone came through bright. Excited. "I talked to Dr. Bryant."

I sat up straighter. Waited.

"She thinks Margaret's offer is wonderful for me."

My heart kicked. "Yeah?"

"I'm saying yes." Beverly sounded lighter than she had in months. "I want to move in with Margaret."

The room tilted. Everything in me went still. "You're sure?"

"Completely sure." Beverly was almost laughing. "Margaret and I spent hours on the phone. We talked about everything. Our late husbands. Knitting patterns. Books we've read. She's delightful, Rachel. I forgot how nice it is to have a friend."

I couldn't speak. Couldn't process.

"Dr. Bryant said it's far better than me living alone," Beverly continued. "She knows the medical facilities in Seaholly. She can transfer my records. Set up my care with providers there. It's perfect."

"But your house," I managed. "Dad's house."

"Is full of memories. Good ones." Beverly softened her tone. "But I've been alone there too long. Clinging to the past instead of living in the present. Margaret is offering me companionship. A chance to not be lonely anymore. Why would I say no to that?"

"You're really doing this."

"I'm really doing this." She paused. "And Amy set me up with a real estate agent. She's handling everything with the house. I don't have to worry about any of it."

Tears streamed down my face. Maya watched with wide eyes, mouthing *What's happening?*

"When?" I asked.

"Soon. We'll take it slow. Make sure the room is ready. Transfer my things gradually." Beverly sounded happy. Genuinely happy. "Margaret says there's no rush. We have time to do this right."

We talked logistics. Details. Plans.

When I hung up, I stared at Maya.

"What just happened?" she asked.

"She said yes." The words felt unreal. "Mom said yes to Margaret."

Maya's face split into a huge grin. "Are you serious?"

I nodded. Fresh tears falling.

We both screamed. Loud enough that Dali leaped off my lap with an indignant yowl.

"My MOM is moving to SEAHOLLY!" I shouted.

"Your mom is moving to Seaholly!" Maya grabbed my hands, jumping up and down. "This is insane!"

"She said yes! She actually said yes!"

"I can't believe it worked!" Maya was crying now too. Happy tears. "Mrs. Henderson is a miracle worker!"

"Mom gets a friend! I get to stay!" I was laughing and crying at the same time. "This is real! This is actually happening!"

"You don't have to leave!" Maya spun me around. "You get to keep your cottage!"

"I get to keep everything!" My words broke. "My students, my studio, my life here—"

"Ryan!" Maya shouted. "You get Ryan!"

My face went hot, but I was laughing too hard to care. "Maybe! Possibly! If I don't mess it up!"

"You're not going to mess it up!" She squeezed my hands. "This is your moment!"

We collapsed onto the couch, both of us breathless and giddy.

Maya wiped her eyes. "Hey, have I ever told you stories about my brother?"

"A few. Why?"

She refilled our mugs with champagne. "I want to tell you one more. So you know what you're getting into."

I settled against the cushions. "Okay."

"When I first started Celebrations by Maya. My very first event. This huge corporate party. Two hundred people." She smiled at the memory. "I was terrified but trying to act confident."

"What happened?"

"I miscalculated. Badly. Ordered half the shrimp I needed. Didn't realize until the morning of the event when the delivery came." Her face scrunched. "I completely panicked. Called Ryan sobbing. He was an hour away, hiking some trail with friends."

I leaned forward. "What did he do?"

"Left immediately. Called every seafood market on his way back to town. Found one that had enough shrimp in stock. Picked it up, and showed up at my venue two hours before service." She shook her head. "He didn't say 'I told you so.' Didn't lecture me. Didn't act like I'd messed up. That's not how he sees things. He just asked what else I needed."

My throat went tight.

"Then he stayed. Helped me prep. Kept me calm when I started spiraling again." Maya's eyes were soft. "The event went perfectly. When it was over and I tried to thank him, he just said, 'That's what family does.'"

She looked at me. "That's who he is, Rachel. When someone he cares about needs him, he shows up. No questions. No judgment. He doesn't view mistakes like something to hold against you. Just shows up and helps fix it."

Tears spilled down my cheeks again.

"So when I say he's all in with you?" Maya squeezed my hand. "I mean it. He doesn't do anything halfway. And he definitely doesn't give up on people he loves."

I couldn't speak. Just nodded.

Maya threw her arms around me. We held each other, crying and laughing.

I could stay.

The impossible choice was gone.

Everything had just changed.

We drank more champagne. Laughed more. Cried more.

The relief was physical. Like I'd been holding my breath and could finally exhale.

"This is incredible," Maya said. "I can't believe it worked out."

"Mrs. Henderson is a genius."

"She really is." Maya refilled our mugs again. "Two lonely women helping each other. It's perfect."

Her phone buzzed. She glanced at it and smiled.

"Ryan?" I asked.

"Yeah. He's asking if I've heard from you." She looked at me. "Can I tell him? Or do you want to?"

My heart kicked. "You can tell him."

"You sure?"

I nodded. "I want him to know."

Maya grinned and started typing.

She said yes. Beverly's moving in with Mrs. Henderson. Rachel can stay.

Three dots appeared immediately.

Then: *Are you serious?*

Maya typed back: *Dead serious. Your girl gets to stay.*

She's not my girl. Yet.

Maya showed me the screen, grinning. "See? Yet. He's planning ahead."

I grabbed the phone. "Give me that."

I typed: *I'm not your girl. Yet.*

Ryan's response came fast: *Hi Rachel. This is fantastic news.*

Then: *Maya's right though.*

My face went hot. I handed the phone back to Maya.

She laughed. "You two are ridiculous."

"We're not anything."

"Yet," she said pointedly.

We drank more champagne and ate fancy cheese. Dali eventually forgave us for the screaming and curled up between us on the couch.

"Okay, enough about me," I said, refilling our mugs. "What about you? THE WEDDING? Tell me everything."

Maya's face lit up. "Good! Really good, actually. Stressful, but good."

"Have you found your dress yet?"

"Yes!" She pulled out her phone, scrolling through photos. "Look at this."

She showed me a picture of herself in a stunning gown. Elegant, simple, classic lines.

"Maya, that's beautiful."

"Right? I cried when I tried it on. Henry cried when I showed him the picture." She smiled. "He's not supposed to see it before the wedding, but he snuck a peek and got all emotional."

"That's so sweet."

She scrolled to another photo. "Sofia was with me when I tried it on. She asked if I was going to be a real princess now."

I laughed. "What did you say?"

"I told her yes, obviously. Then she asked if that meant she got to be a princess too." Maya grinned. "So I told her she'd be the flower princess. Her face lit up like I'd just given her the moon."

"Flower princess. That's perfect."

"Right? She immediately started planning her 'princess duties' which apparently include throwing petals 'like snow' and wearing sparkles." Maya shook her head fondly. "Henry said we should just lean into it and get her a little tiara."

"Obviously you should."

"That's what I said!" She laughed. "He is sweet. Also completely useless at wedding planning. Last week he suggested we just serve pizza at the reception because 'everyone likes pizza.'"

I laughed. "He's not wrong."

"Right? That's the problem. He makes terrible suggestions that are somehow also perfectly logical." She laughed. "We compromised. Fancy dinner, but pizza at midnight for anyone still dancing."

"That's actually genius."

"He's annoyingly good at compromises." She scrolled through more photos. "Look at the flowers we picked."

Beautiful arrangements. Soft colors. Romantic without being overly traditional.

"And the cake—wait, let me find it." She kept scrolling. "Here. Three tiers. Henry insisted on chocolate because he said 'vanilla is boring.'"

"He would say that."

"The baker told him chocolate doesn't photograph as well. He said, 'We're eating it, not framing it.'" Maya grinned. "I'm marrying a very practical man."

Her joy was contagious. Seeing her this happy, this excited about her future with Henry, made everything feel possible.

Eventually, Maya checked her phone. "I should go. It's late and I have a tasting appointment early tomorrow."

"Another one?"

"Bride keeps changing her mind about appetizers." She stood, stretching. "But that's the job."

We hugged at the door. Long and tight.

"I'm really happy for you," she said. "You get to stay. You get your life here."

"Thank you. For everything. For celebrating with me."

"That's what friends do." She squeezed me once more. "Now go get some sleep. You've had a big day."

After she left, I stood in my living room. Looking around at everything that was mine.

The paintings. The easels. Dali curled in her chair. The life I'd built here that I didn't have to leave—and I was ready to own it.

Mom said yes.

Now it was my turn.

Chapter Thirty

Coral Pier

Ryan

My truck's headlights cut through the darkness as I pulled into the empty parking lot. Late. The boardwalk deserted except for one silhouette at an easel.

I knew where she'd be.

Our spot. The place where everything started.

Moonlight painted the water silver. Waves crashed against the new supports, steady and relentless.

Rachel stood alone, brush moving across the canvas. So absorbed she didn't hear my truck door close. Didn't hear my footsteps on the wooden planks.

I walked toward her slowly. Giving her time to sense my presence.

She kept painting. Lost in whatever she was creating.

I got close enough to see the canvas. The pier. The exact spot where the boards collapsed. Where she'd fallen. Where I'd pulled her from the water.

Looked like she was painting her trauma. Processing it the only way she knew how.

"You're going to ruin your eyes painting in the dark."

Rachel jumped. Spun around. Paintbrush clutched like a weapon.

Then she saw it was me. Her shoulders dropped. A smile broke across her face.

"Ryan." Her voice came out soft. Happy. "What are you doing here?"

"Couldn't stay away." I stepped closer. "Your mom said yes."

Her smile widened. "She did."

"That text exchange with Maya got cut short." I grinned. "Figured we should celebrate in person."

Rachel laughed. "Maya's going to be insufferable about this."

"She already is." I sat on the boardwalk railing. "Called me five minutes after to gloat."

Rachel set down her paintbrush and joined me.

We looked out at the ocean together. The water dark and endless. The new pier supports solid beneath us.

Salt air filled my lungs. Sharp and clean. Mixed with the smell of paint from her canvas and something floral from her hair. The ocean breathed around us, constant and alive.

"Your mom's really moving here," I said. "To Seaholly."

"She is." I heard relief in Rachel's words. "Mrs. Henderson gets a friend. Mom gets companionship. I get to stay."

"You get to keep everything you've built."

"Everything." She looked at me. "My cottage. My students. The mural. This town."

Us, I thought. But didn't say it.

She looked down at her hands. Picked at dried paint on her thumb.

"What is it?" I asked.

"What do you mean?"

"We got through the big barrier. Your mom. The impossible choice." I shifted to face her. "But something's still holding you back. I can see it."

Rachel bit her lip. "It's not about Mom."

"Then what?"

She was quiet for a long moment. The ocean crashed below. Steady. Patient.

"Can we talk about it?" I asked gently.

She nodded slowly. "Yeah. We should."

I waited. Giving her space to find the words.

She looked out at the water. Struggling.

"How about I start?" I said.

She glanced at me. Grateful. Nodded.

"I haven't told you the whole story," I said. "About why I left my last department."

Rachel stayed quiet. Listening.

"I dated my lieutenant's ex-wife." The words came out flat. Direct. "Met her at a community event after their divorce was final. She seemed great. Smart. Funny. We hit it off."

The waves crashed below us. Regular. Predictable.

"The lieutenant didn't like it. Made that clear from day one." I gripped the railing. "But she was divorced. I was single. We were adults. I thought it would blow over."

Rachel moved closer. Set down her paintbrush. Sat on the railing beside me.

"It didn't blow over. She'd talk to him sometimes. About their kid. About logistics. And she'd mention me. Good things. How I helped her fix her car. How I was patient with her son."

My jaw clenched at the memory.

"The lieutenant assumed she was telling me things about him. Department gossip. Things he wouldn't want me to know. He got paranoid. Started making my life hell."

"What did he do?" Rachel leaned closer.

"Worst shifts. Denied my promotion. Wrote me up for things other guys got warnings for. Made it clear I wasn't welcome." I looked at her. "Then I found out the truth. She was seeing someone else the whole time. Wasn't interested in me at all—she was using me as a weapon."

Rachel's hand found mine.

"Every time she mentioned me to her ex-husband, every 'nice thing' she said about me to him, it was calculated. She wanted to make him jealous. Wanted him to see her with someone from his department, someone he had to work with every day. I was just a tool to get back at him."

"Ryan—"

"The politics were poison after that. The whole department took sides. And on top of everything else, the lieutenant had no interest in community outreach. Thought it was a waste of resources." I shook my head. "I believe in that work. Fire safety education, building relationships with the community. It matters."

"So you came here."

"Fresh start. New department. No history. No drama. And a chief who values community programs as much as I do." I held her gaze. "I swore I'd never risk that again. Never trust someone enough to let them destroy what I'd built."

The ocean stretched out before us. Endless and dark.

"And then I met you."

Rachel's breath caught.

"You, with your paint-stained hands and your chaotic life and your fierce heart." I turned to face her fully. "You, setting off fire alarms and needing spider rescues and painting murals that make grown men cry."

Her eyes filled with tears.

"That whole situation taught me something." I squeezed her hand. "It taught me that love without trust isn't love at all. It's just fear wearing love's mask."

I held her gaze.

"And I trust you, Rachel. With everything. With my heart and my life and my future. I trust you."

She was quiet for a long moment. Then: "Can I ask you something about that? About trust?"

"Anything."

She bit her lip. "When Maya and Henry got together... you were upset about your sister being involved with your best friend."

My stomach tightened. I knew where this was going.

"Maya told me she gave us her blessing. But I also know how you reacted when she and Henry first got together. I need to understand that. How you were so against them, but you're okay with us. This time her best friend instead of yours."

I deserved that question. Had been waiting for it, honestly.

"I was a jerk," I said simply. "A complete jerk about the whole thing."

Rachel's eyebrows rose slightly.

"I was dealing with my own stuff. The situation with my lieutenant's ex. The betrayal. The manipulation." I ran a hand through my hair. "I projected all of that onto Henry and Maya. Got overprotective and emotional about my own baggage instead of seeing what was actually happening. And I was scared. Of losing one of them."

"But they're your two favorite people."

"Exactly." I shook my head. "Looking back, I don't know what I was thinking. They're both incredible people. Of course they're great together. It was obvious to everyone except me."

Rachel's expression softened.

"Now they're two of my three favorite people," I said, squeezing her hand. "And watching them together, seeing how happy Maya is, how solid they are... I was wrong. Dead wrong. They're exactly right for each other."

"Maya said it was hard on her. When you didn't approve."

"I know that. And I'm sorry I put them through that stress. Put Maya through it especially. She shouldn't have had to get my permission to be happy." I grimaced. "And I'm embarrassed that you and Maya's other friends had to witness the whole thing. I wasn't exactly subtle about my feelings."

Rachel searched my face. Finding what she needed to see.

She nodded slowly. Then took a shaky breath.

I wanted to pull her into my arms. Kiss her until neither of us could breathe. But something held her back. I could see it in her eyes.

"But..." she whispered.

"But what?"

She looked down at our joined hands. "I'm worried you'll want to change me eventually. That the chaos will get old. That you'll realize I'm too much."

I opened my mouth to reassure her. To promise I'd never want her different.

But she kept talking. Words tumbling out in a rush.

"My ex wanted to change everything about me. And I've talked about him too much already. Like he still matters." She swiped at her tears with her free hand. "But he wanted me to play a role. Be someone I wasn't. Present this perfect persona to the world instead of just being myself."

"Rachel—"

"I tried. Hated every minute. And I'm worried—"

I laughed.

Couldn't help it. The sound came out warm. Affectionate. Maybe a little incredulous.

Rachel looked up at me, startled. Confused.

"I'm sorry." I held her face in my hands. "I'm not laughing at you. I'm laughing because the idea of you being neat and organized and conventional is the most absurd thing I've ever heard."

"Ryan—"

"I'd never survive you being neat." I grinned at her. "Who would give me excuses to come over? Who would set off fire alarms and need spider rescues and leave paint on my kitchen cabinets?"

She let out a watery laugh despite herself.

"I love your chaos, Rachel. I love that you have canvases and multiple easels set up in your living room. I love that you forget to eat when you're painting. I love that you see beauty in a broken pier and turn it into art."

I brushed my thumbs across her cheeks, wiping away tears.

"I love your creativity that sees magic everywhere. Your compassion for your students and your mother, and even my disaster of a dog. The way you love fiercely and completely, even when it scares you."

Her eyes searched mine. Looking for doubt. Finding none.

"I love the paint in your hair and the studios where living rooms should be and the way you make me see the world differently." I held her gaze. "All of it. Exactly as you are. I don't want you neat. I want you real."

Rachel kissed me.

No hesitation. No holding back.

She wrapped her arms around my neck and kissed me like she'd been wanting to for weeks. Like she was done running. Done being worried.

I pulled her close. After weeks of wanting and waiting and hoping.

My hands found her hair—silky and soft, auburn strands sliding through my fingers. I'd wondered what it would feel like. Imagined it more times than I could count. The reality was better.

Her body pressed against mine, warm despite the cool ocean breeze. I could feel her heart racing, or maybe that was mine. Maybe both. I'd lost track of where I ended and she began.

She made a small sound against my mouth. Something between a sigh and a gasp. It sent heat through my entire body.

The ocean crashed below us. Waves against new supports. Everything rebuilt and stronger.

She tilted her head back and I deepened the kiss. She responded immediately, fingers tangling in my hair, pulling me closer like she couldn't get enough.

Weeks of holding back poured into that moment. All the careful distance we'd maintained. Every time I'd stopped myself from reaching for her. Every moment I'd watched her and wanted this exact thing.

Her lips were soft. Salt from tears mixed with something sweet. Heat pulsated through my body.

My hand slid from her hair to her jaw, holding her face, thumb brushing her cheek. Her skin was warm. Impossibly soft.

She pulled back just enough to breathe, forehead against mine. Eyes still closed. Both of us breathing hard.

Then she kissed me again. Urgent. Demanding. Like she was claiming me as much as I was claiming her.

I lost myself in it. In her. The feel of her mouth on mine, her hands in my hair, her body warm and solid against me. The smell of paint and ocean salt. The sound of waves and her breathing and my own pulse thundering in my ears.

This was what I'd been missing. What I'd been searching for in all the wrong places.

Not just a kiss. Not just attraction.

Her. Exactly her. All of her chaos and creativity and fierce, beautiful heart.

We broke apart. Foreheads touching. Both breathing hard. Both smiling.

"Yes," she whispered.

"Yes to what?"

"To staying. To trying. To trusting." Her fingers tangled in my hair. "To believing someone could actually want all of me."

I kissed her again. Softer this time. Slower. Like we had all the time in the world.

Because we did.

We stood wrapped in each other's arms. The ocean watching. Waves crashing with their steady rhythm. Moonlight painting everything silver.

Neither of us wanted to let go.

"Yes to you," she whispered against my lips. "Yes to all of it."

Chapter Thirty-One

Ryan's Cottage

Rachel

I changed my dress three times.

The blue one looked too formal. The green one felt wrong. I settled on the burgundy one Maya had insisted I buy last month.

Makeup took another fifteen minutes. My hands shook while applying eyeliner.

First official date with Ryan Rodriguez.

After everything. After the pier. After the kiss. After saying yes to all of it.

My stomach fluttered.

Dali watched from the bed, judging my outfit choices with typical cat disdain.

"Don't look at me like that. This is important."

She yawned.

The knock came at exactly seven. Punctual. Of course he was.

I opened the door and forgot how to breathe.

Ryan stood on my porch wearing dark jeans and a button-down shirt that made his eyes even more striking. He'd shaved. Styled his hair. Looked like he'd put actual effort into this.

"Hi." His voice came out rough.

"Hi."

We stared at each other.

"You look beautiful," he said.

Heat climbed my cheeks. "You clean up pretty well yourself."

He grinned. Offered his arm. "Ready?"

"Where are we going?"

"The new Italian place on the coast. The one with the ocean view."

Fancy. Romantic. Perfect first date material.

His truck was clean. Actually clean. No construction materials, no Dozer hair covering the seats.

"Did you detail your truck?"

"Maybe." He closed my door, walked around to the driver's side.

We were halfway to the restaurant when his phone rang.

He glanced at the screen, frowned. "It's the contractor. I'm sorry, I have to take this."

"Of course."

He answered on speaker. "Hey, Tom. What's up?"

"Ryan, sorry to bother you. But we've got a situation at your place. Found a water leak behind the kitchen wall. Pretty significant damage. Pipe's been leaking for a while."

Ryan's jaw tightened. "How bad?"

"Wall's got to come down anyway for repairs. But I need your decision on how you want to proceed. Whether to just patch and replace, or if you want to make any changes while we've got it open."

Ryan pulled into a parking lot. Looked at me with frustration clear on his face.

"We can reschedule," I said. "This is important."

"No." He shook his head. "I've been waiting for this date for weeks. I'm not canceling." He looked back at his phone. "Tom, give me a few minutes. I'm bringing someone with me who knows design."

My heart skipped.

"Come with me?" Ryan asked after hanging up. "We can grab food after?"

"Are you sure?"

"Absolutely." He reached for my hand. "Besides, you're good at this stuff. I could use your eye."

Twenty minutes later, we stood in Ryan's kitchen. Still dressed for our fancy date. Surrounded by construction dust and exposed wall studs.

Tom, the contractor, explained the damage. Water had been seeping behind the wall for months. Maybe longer. The whole section needed replacing.

"You want me to just put it back the same?" Tom gestured at the wall between the kitchen and the living room.

Ryan looked at me.

I was already envisioning the space. My design brain kicked into gear without permission.

The wall was unnecessary. Cutting off the kitchen from the living area. Making both spaces feel smaller than they were.

"What if you didn't put it back?"

Ryan turned toward me. "What do you mean?"

"The wall between the kitchen and the living room. What if you opened it up? Made it flow?" I gestured at the space, seeing it transform. "Open concept. More light. Better connection between the spaces."

I kept talking, describing the vision forming. How the kitchen could breathe into the living area. How you could cook and still be part of the conversation. How the whole cottage would feel bigger, more connected.

Ryan listened. Watched me gesture and explain. I could see him visualizing it through my eyes.

"That's brilliant," he said.

Then he kissed me. Right there in his half-demolished kitchen. With Tom the contractor standing in the same room.

Tom cleared his throat.

We broke apart, both grinning.

"So... open concept?" Tom asked, fighting a smile.

"Open concept," Ryan confirmed.

Tom gathered his tools. "I'll start first thing tomorrow. Get the wall down, check the structural requirements. You two figure out the design details."

After Tom left, Ryan and I stood alone in the cottage. Both dressed up for a nice dinner. Standing in a construction zone.

I started laughing. Couldn't help it. The absurdity of it all.

Ryan joined in. "This is not how I planned our first date."

"We could still go. The reservation's probably still good."

He looked down at his dust-covered shoes. At the exposed wall studs. At me in my burgundy dress covered in a fine layer of construction dust.

"Or..." I said. "We could stay here. Order in. Start planning while it's fresh in my mind?"

Relief crossed his face. "You sure you don't mind?"

"Are you kidding? This is way better than fancy restaurant small talk." I grinned at him. "Chinese food and renovation planning?"

"Best first date ever," he agreed.

He ordered delivery while I went to my car for my design materials.

I always kept samples and catalogs in my trunk. Had helped Maya with her apartment. Helped Mom pick colors for her bedroom. Always ready to brainstorm spaces.

When I walked back into the cottage, I froze.

Dali was carefully licking Dozer's ear. The massive puppy sprawled on the floor, completely passed out. His tail thumped occasionally in his sleep.

My heart melted.

"Ryan," I whispered. "Look."

He turned, eyes going wide. We both grinned at each other.

Dali giving Dozer a cat bath. Clear sign of affection. She'd warmed up to him.

"I need my camera. The good one. Not my phone."

I tiptoed toward the door.

BANG BANG BANG.

The delivery driver pounded on the door.

Dozer jolted awake. Barked.

Dali SHRIEKED. Bolted across the room like her tail was on fire.

She crashed directly into the lamp on the side table. The ugly thing toppled, hit the floor, shattered.

Total chaos in two seconds flat.

Ryan opened the door for the delivery driver. I tried to calm Dali, who'd puffed to twice her normal size. Dozer kept barking at nothing.

Both pets retreated to opposite sides of the room. Pretending nothing had happened. Like they hadn't been cuddling moments ago.

"I'm so sorry!" I stared at the broken lamp. Glass everywhere. "I'll replace it, I—"

Ryan handed the delivery driver cash, closed the door. Looked at the lamp.

Then started laughing.

"I always hated it anyway. Had it since college. No idea how I even got it."

"You're not mad?"

"About what? You saving me from having to look at it anymore?" He grabbed the broom from his closet. "This is the best thing Dali's done all week."

I helped him sweep up the glass. Both of us still in our fancy date clothes. Chinese food containers on the counter. A broken lamp. Two sulking pets.

Perfect chaos.

We spread out on the living room floor. Paint samples. Furniture catalogs. My sketchbook.

I showed him color options. Explained how different shades would make the space feel. Sketched quick layouts of where furniture could go.

Ryan watched me transform his house into a home.

I gestured, described, built our future without realizing it at first. When I suggested sage green for the kitchen, he agreed immediately. Trusting my vision completely.

We worked well together. My chaos complementing his order. His practicality grounding my creativity.

"What about here?" I pointed to where the wall would come down. "You could do an island. Seating on one side. Open to the living room."

"I love it." He leaned closer, studying my sketch. "Show me more."

I did. Drew out the whole space. How light would flow. Where art could hang. How the kitchen and living area would connect.

We took a break to eat lo mein straight from the containers.

"Mom moves into Mrs. Henderson's next week."

"How are you feeling about it?"

"Relieved." The word came out on an exhale. "I don't have to choose anymore. She'll be close but independent. We both get what we need."

"You seem different," Ryan observed. "Lighter."

"I am." I smiled at him. "The future feels possible now. Like I can actually plan for it instead of just bracing for the next crisis."

Dozer and Dali had declared a truce. Both on the couch now. Not cuddling, but coexisting in peace.

Small miracles.

This moment felt like home. Sitting on Ryan's floor. Surrounded by paint chips and catalogs. Planning his space. Helping him create something beautiful.

I could see myself here. Not living here. Not yet. But being here. Often. Part of this.

Together.

We went back to planning. I showed him countertop options. Backsplash tiles. Cabinet hardware.

My exhaustion caught up with me somewhere between flooring samples and cabinet colors.

I leaned against Ryan's shoulder. Warm and solid and safe.

My eyes grew heavy. The catalog in my lap blurred.

"Rachel?" His voice came from far away.

"Mmm. Just resting my eyes."

"Come on. Let's get you comfortable."

I felt him move. Felt myself being lifted. But I was too tired to process it. Too content to care.

This. Him. Planning a future together. Breaking down walls literally and figuratively.

I drifted off.

I woke on Ryan's couch.

Covered with a blanket I didn't remember getting.

Morning light streamed through the windows. Warm and bright.

Ryan stood in the kitchen making coffee. His back to me. Hair messed. Wearing sweatpants and a t-shirt.

I stayed still. Watching him. Unobserved.

He hummed quietly. Something I didn't recognize. Looked relaxed. Happy. At peace.

My heart squeezed with how much I loved this view. This moment. This man.

Movement on the couch caught my attention.

Dozer and Dali. Actually cuddling. The cat tucked against the dog's side. Both of them peaceful. Content.

Miracle of miracles.

They'd figured it out before we did. Let go of their differences. Found comfort in each other.

I pulled the blanket closer. Watched Ryan pour coffee into two mugs.

I could wake up like this every day.

Chapter Thirty-Two

The Firehouse

Ryan

"May I?" Rachel gestured at my helmet sitting on the bench.

"Go ahead."

She settled it on her head. Way too big. It slipped down over her eyes.

She pushed it up, grinning at me from under the brim. Then spotted my turnout coat hanging on the hook. Grabbed it before I could stop her.

The heavy protective gear swallowed her frame. She laughed, arms disappearing into the sleeves. "I can't even find my hands."

"How do I look?" She struck a pose, nearly toppling from the coat's weight.

"Like the most beautiful firefighter I've ever seen."

Her cheeks flushed pink.

The firehouse held a low, dull hum. The overnight crew was on duty, most of them in the common room. I'd brought Rachel here after dinner, wanting to show her this part of my life.

"Come on." I steadied her, helped her out of the coat. "Let me show you the rest."

We walked through the bay. I explained as we went.

"This is the ladder truck." I ran my hand along the side. "Extends up to seventy-five feet. We use it for roof access, window rescues, anything elevated."

"How long does it take to set up?" Rachel circled around to see the mechanism.

"Depends on the situation. Under a minute in an emergency."

She pointed at the rescue tools mounted on the side. "What about these?"

"Jaws of Life. For vehicle extrications mostly. Can cut through metal, pry open doors." I showed her how they worked. "We train on old cars in the back lot. Practice until the movements are automatic."

"And this?" She gestured at the communication panel.

"Connects us to dispatch. Gives us real-time updates on calls." I walked her through the system. How information flowed. How we coordinated with other units.

Rachel listened. Asked questions. Sketched quick drawings in the small notebook she always carried.

She was trying to understand. Not the mechanics, but why it mattered to me.

"What made this place right for you?" She leaned against the engine.

I looked around the bay. This place had become home.

"The community outreach. My old lieutenant didn't value prevention programs. Thought they were a waste of resources."

Rachel nodded, waiting for more.

"But where you make the real difference is prevention." I gestured around us. "Teaching kids fire safety before they need rescuing. Building relationships with people before emergencies happen. Chief Patterson gets it. Values it. Gives me freedom to build those programs here."

"Like Safety Day."

"Exactly. Teaching students how to call 911, how to escape a burning building, what to do if their clothes catch fire." I thought about all the kids who'd come through. "Those lessons stick. Kids go home and teach their families. Residents learn to check smoke detectors, plan escape routes. It ripples out."

Rachel's pencil moved across her paper. Capturing more than my face. Capturing something deeper.

"You're not just a firefighter," she said. "You're a teacher. A protector. Someone who invests in people."

Her words hit me.

"I just want to make a difference. Here. In this community. With these people."

"You do." She looked up from her sketch. "You really do."

I pulled her close. Kissed her there in the quiet bay.

The alarm bells blared.

We jumped apart. The sound piercing and urgent.

The crew mobilized. Movement erupting from the common room. Everyone shifting into professional mode.

I was already moving toward my gear. Mind switching focus.

"Structure fire, residential, possible occupants," the dispatcher's voice crackled over the speaker.

Rachel stepped back. "Should I go?"

I pulled on my turnout pants, boots. "You can stay in the common room if you want. Or head home. Up to you."

The crew swarmed around us. Organized chaos.

I grabbed my coat, my helmet. Kissed Rachel quickly. Distracted. Already thinking about the call.

"Be safe," she said.

The crew was already heading for the trucks. I climbed into my seat, caught one last glimpse of Rachel standing in the bay.

Watching me go.

The truck rolled out. Sirens wailing into the night.

Rachel

I stood in the empty bay long after the sirens faded.

The silence felt heavy. Oppressive. Too many thoughts crowding in at once.

I could go home. Should probably go home. But the idea of sitting alone in my cottage, waiting, not knowing—

No. I'd stay.

The crew's common room felt too quiet. Like a waiting room. I couldn't sit still.

I found the kitchen. Made tea in a mug someone had left in the dish rack. Chamomile. The hot liquid helped, but only a little.

Dozer followed me, brown eyes watching my every move. He'd stayed behind, sensing I needed company more than Ryan did right now.

"He does this all the time. He'll be fine."

Dozer's tail gave a halfhearted wag.

I wandered back to the bay. Found the desk tucked in the corner. Someone's workspace, probably for paperwork. An oversized calendar blotter covered the surface, current month showing appointments and notes.

I flipped to last month. The back was blank. Perfect.

The desk drawer held the usual supplies. Pens, paper clips, rubber bands. And there—a ruler. Wooden, worn at the edges. Someone's measuring tool for who knows what.

I grabbed it. Found a pencil. Pulled my notebook from my bag.

The measurements I'd taken at Ryan's cottage. Scribbled in margins, on the back of paint sample cards, anywhere I could find space.

I spread everything out under the fluorescent lights. Flipped the calendar page over. Started drawing.

Kitchen layout. Wall coming down. Island placement.

The ruler became an anchor. Something concrete to focus on. If I could make these lines straight, these measurements accurate, maybe everything else would be okay too.

Dozer settled at my feet. His weight warm against my shoe.

I measured twice. Drew once. The way my dad had taught me years ago, when I was learning technical drafting for art school.

Erased a line. Redrew it. Got the proportions right.

Time passed. I didn't know how much. Didn't check my phone.

The tea grew cold beside me. I took sips anyway. Made another cup. Came back to the plans.

Cabinet configuration. Traffic flow. Where the sink would go. Where the stove could move to.

My hand cramped. I flexed my fingers, kept working.

This was Ryan's space. But I was planning it like it was ours. Like I'd be there. Often. Part of it.

The thought should have scared me. Maybe it did, a little.

But mostly it felt right.

I added another measurement. Double-checked the math. Made a note about electrical outlets.

Dozer's breathing grew steady. Regular. He'd fallen asleep.

I kept drawing. Adjusting. Perfecting.

The ruler's edge made satisfying lines across the paper. Precise. Controlled. Everything the waiting wasn't.

Hours must have passed. The lights seemed brighter. My eyes strained.

But I kept working. Because stopping meant thinking. And thinking meant worrying about where Ryan was, what he was doing, whether he was safe.

Engine sounds broke through my focus.

I looked up. Blinked at the clock on the wall.

After midnight.

The truck was back.

Ryan

The crew piled out. Exhausted. Moving slower than when we'd left.

I climbed down from the truck. Smelling of smoke. Face streaked with soot. Turnout gear covered in ash and water.

The bay looked different. Emptier. Darker.

Then I spotted the desk in the corner.

Floor plans spread across the surface. Precise lines drawn with a ruler. Measurements labeled in Rachel's handwriting. My cottage kitchen laid out in technical detail. Professional. Thoughtful. Complete.

A mug of tea sat beside the papers. Cold now, probably.

She'd stayed. Spent hours drawing plans for my space while I was gone. My throat went tight.

"Ryan." Martinez nudged me. Gestured toward the common room doorway.

I looked up.

Rachel stood there. Dozer at her side. Her hair was messy, pencil tucked behind her ear. She looked tired. Worried.

But she was still here.

The crew noticed. Gave us space. Headed inside to clean up without their usual teasing.

Rachel looked at me.

Not with fear or questions about where I'd been. Not with worry about the danger.

With pride. Understanding. Acceptance.

She saw all of me. The smoke and soot. The exhaustion. The job would always call me away at unexpected times.

And she was still here. Still looking at me like I was everything.

She set down her pencil on the desk. Stepped toward me.

Didn't say anything. Didn't need to.

My throat tightened.

I crossed to her. Still in my turnout gear. Soot-covered. Exhausted.

Pulled her into my arms.

This kiss was different from the others.

Not quick. Not stolen. Not interrupted.

Long. Unhurried. Deep.

I poured everything into it. All the fear I'd felt on the call. The relief of coming back safe. The overwhelming want I'd been carrying for weeks.

Her hands found my hair. My arms wrapped around her. Neither of us pulled away.

We took our time. Finally allowed to.

Graphite smudges on her hands. Soot on mine. Smoke smell clung to both of us now.

Perfect.

She tasted like chamomile. Like someone who'd wait for me. Who'd understand this life.

I kissed her like she was my anchor. My home. My reason for coming back safe.

When we finally broke apart, we were both breathing hard. Both smiling.

The crew had disappeared inside. Giving us privacy.

We stood alone under the fluorescent lights. Her floor plans scattered across the desk. Dozer watching us with approval.

Both pencil-smudged and smoke-covered. Not wanting the night to end.

I looked at her. This woman who'd stayed. Who'd waited. Who'd drawn floor plans for my kitchen while I was out fighting fires.

"Come home with me," I said.

The invitation hung between us. Loaded with meaning.

Not just tonight. Everything it implied. Taking the next step. Choosing this. Choosing us.

Rachel's breath caught. I watched emotions flicker across her face.

Want. Fear. Hope.

"Rachel." I touched her cheek. "Come home with me."

Chapter Thirty-Three

Beverly's House

Rachel

A cold nose pressed against my face.

I yelped, jerking awake.

Dozer wagged his tail, pleased with himself. Mission accomplished.

"He does that to everyone he loves."

Ryan stood in the doorway holding two mugs of coffee. Hair messy. Wearing sweatpants and a t-shirt. Grinning at my startled expression.

Dawn light streamed through his bedroom window, soft and inviting. I'd stayed. Spent the night. Woken up in his bed.

My heart did a little flip.

"Your dog is a menace."

I pushed Dozer's face away.

"He's enthusiastic." Ryan crossed to the bed, handed me coffee. "There's a difference."

I took the mug. Let the warmth seep into my hands.

Ryan sat on the edge of the bed. Close but not crowding. "Morning."

"Morning."

We smiled at each other. Comfortable. Easy. Like we'd done this a hundred times before.

Dozer bounced between us, tail creating a small hurricane.

"We should get ready." The words came out reluctant. "We need to leave soon to get to Mom's."

"Right. Packing day." Ryan stood. "I'll make breakfast while you get dressed."

I borrowed his sweatshirt. Navy blue, smelling like him. Way too big but perfect.

Found my jeans from last night. My shoes by the door.

Dozer ran circles around the cottage. Excited energy radiating from every movement.

"Is he always like this in the morning?" I ducked as he bounded past.

"Pretty much." Ryan flipped pancakes at the stove. "You'll get used to it."

You'll get used to it.

Like this was permanent. Like mornings together were a given now.

I liked the sound of it more than I should.

We ate quickly. Cleaned up together. A rhythm developing between us.

Ryan grabbed his keys. "Ready?"

"As I'll ever be."

The drive to Beverly's took over an hour.

I got more nervous as we got closer.

Ryan was meeting my mom. Properly meeting her. Having actual conversations.

What if she didn't like him? What if they didn't click? What if—

"You're spiraling." Ryan glanced at me.

"I'm not spiraling."

"Your leg's bouncing. You only do that when you're spiraling."

I stilled my leg. "Fine. Maybe a little."

"She's going to love me." He said it with complete confidence. "I'm very lovable."

I laughed despite my nerves. "Oh really?"

"Extremely lovable. Ask Dozer."

Dozer barked from the back seat. On cue.

"See? Expert testimony."

I reached across the center console. Found his hand. Laced our fingers together.

He squeezed. "It's going to be fine, Rachel. I promise."

We pulled into Mom's driveway after nine.

The house looked the same. Small. Well-maintained. Dad's garden still thriving in the front yard, even though he'd been gone for years.

Mom must have been watching for us. The front door opened before we even got out of the truck.

"Rachel!" She hurried down the steps.

I barely got out of the truck before she pulled me into a hug.

"Hi, Mom."

She squeezed tight. Then released me and turned to Ryan.

No awkwardness. No hesitation.

She hugged him too.

"Ryan! It's so wonderful to finally meet you properly. Thank you for helping today."

Ryan returned the hug easily. "Of course, Mrs. Brown. Happy to help."

"Oh, please. Call me Beverly." She stepped back, beaming at both of us. "Come in, come in! I've been up since five packing. I'm so excited I can barely stand it."

She was excited. Genuinely. More energized than I'd seen her in months.

The difference was startling.

We followed her inside. Dozer trotting beside Ryan, well-behaved for once.

"Margaret called this morning." Mom led us to the kitchen. "She's planning the garden for spring. Wants my input on what vegetables to grow. And we're starting a book club! Just the two of us to begin with, but she knows some ladies at the senior center who might join."

She poured coffee without asking if we wanted any. Kept talking.

"There's a pottery class on Tuesdays. And a watercolor group on Thursdays. Margaret thinks we should try both. I haven't done pottery since before your father died."

The house felt lighter. Like the decision to move had lifted a weight I hadn't realized was pressing down on everything.

"That sounds wonderful, Mom."

"It is wonderful." She handed us mugs. "I feel like I'm getting my life back. Does that sound silly?"

"Not at all." Ryan's voice came out gentle.

Mom smiled at him. Really looked at him for the first time.

"You're good for my daughter."

Heat climbed my cheeks. "Mom—"

"I can tell." She patted Ryan's arm. "A mother knows these things."

We started packing in the living room.

Boxes lined the walls. Some sealed, others waiting to be filled.

Ryan surveyed the setup. "These ready to be taped up?"

"Not quite yet, dear." Mom gestured at the bookcase. "Still sorting what goes and what stays."

"What can I do?"

"Strong young man like you? Reach the high shelves." Mom pointed. "I haven't been able to get those books down in years."

Ryan got to work. Stretching to reach the top shelf. Handing books down to me and Mom.

"So, Dozer." Mom watched the dog sniff around the room. "Rachel tells me he's still a puppy?"

"Very much still a puppy." Ryan grabbed another stack of books. "Though you wouldn't know it by the size of him."

"What's the funniest thing he's done?"

Ryan laughed. "Where do I start? He stole my boot the day I moved in. Refused to give it back for two hours."

"What did you do?"

"Traded him for a piece of chicken." Ryan grinned. "He's very food-motivated."

Mom laughed. Genuine. Delighted.

I watched them together. My mom and my... boyfriend? The word felt strange. New.

But right.

They were getting along beautifully. Natural conversation. Easy rapport.

Ryan told another Dozer story. Mom laughed again.

My heart squeezed with how much I loved this. Both of them. This moment.

"Rachel, there's bubble wrap in the garage." Mom waved toward the door. "Can you grab it?"

I headed out. Left them alone.

Came back five minutes later with the wrap to find them sitting on the floor.

Photo albums spread between them.

"Oh no." I stopped in the doorway.

They looked up. Both grinning like conspirators.

"Before we pack these," Mom said, "I thought Ryan should see a few pictures."

"Absolutely not."

"Too late." Ryan patted the floor beside him. "Come look at tiny Rachel."

I sat. Dozer claimed my lap.

Mom opened the first album. "This is second grade. Her first big art project."

The photo showed me covered in paint. Completely covered. Hair, face, clothes. Grinning at the camera with missing front teeth.

"She painted a mural on butcher paper," Mom explained. "The entire solar system. To scale. It was ten feet long."

"Ambitious." Ryan studied the photo like it were precious.

"She got paint everywhere. The classroom. The hallway. Herself." Mom turned the page. "The teacher called me. I thought she was in trouble. But no. The teacher wanted to frame it."

"Did she?"

"Hung it in the school library for five years." Mom's voice went soft with pride.

More pages. More photos.

Middle school Rachel with braces and defiant expression. High school Rachel covered in clay from pottery class. Rachel at seventeen, paint in her hair, standing beside a canvas twice her size.

Ryan was enchanted. Made me tell stories behind each photo.

I obliged. Mortified but laughing.

Mom added embarrassing details I'd forgotten.

The time I painted the garage door. The sculpture exploded in the kiln. The art show where I knocked over an entire display.

Ryan looked at young me like I was already perfect. Like the chaos was a feature, not a bug.

"Here." Mom's voice went quiet.

She'd found a photo of Dad.

My throat went tight.

Dad in his workshop. Sawdust in his hair. Smiling at the camera. One arm around teenage me, both of us covered in wood stain.

"That's my husband." Mom told Ryan. "Rachel's father. He died when she was seventeen."

"I'm sorry."

Mom touched the photo. "He encouraged her art always. From the time she could hold a crayon. Never wanted her to dim her light for anyone."

She looked at Ryan when she said it. Pointed. Meaningful.

Ryan held her gaze. Understanding the weight of the look. The trust being placed in him.

"He sounds like a good man."

"He was." Mom smiled sadly. "He'd have liked you."

My eyes burned. I blinked hard.

Mom squeezed my hand. Then stood. "I need to grab something from upstairs. Keep looking."

She left. Footsteps climbing the stairs.

Ryan and I sat in the quiet.

"Your dad built things?" He looked at the photo again.

"Furniture. Custom pieces." I traced the edge of the album. "He had a workshop in the garage. Made our kitchen table. Mom's bookshelf. My easel."

"The one in your studio?"

I nodded. "He made it for my sixteenth birthday. Adjusted the height perfectly for me. Said every artist needed the right tools."

Ryan was quiet for a moment. "You were lucky to have him."

"I was."

"And he was lucky to have you." Ryan looked at me. "A daughter who sees the world in color. Who creates beauty everywhere she goes. Who's brave enough to chase her dreams."

My lungs forgot how to work.

"Rachel?"

Mom's voice floated down from upstairs. "Can you come help me with this box?"

I stood. Grateful for the interruption. "Be right back."

I climbed the stairs. Found Mom in her bedroom.

There was no box.

"Sorry." She didn't look sorry at all. "I wanted to talk to Ryan alone for a minute."

"Mom—"

"Just a minute. Go label those boxes in the spare room."

I went. Because arguing with Beverly Brown was pointless.

But I left the door open.

Downstairs, I could hear their voices. Quiet. Murmured.

I couldn't make out words. Didn't try.

Instead, I labeled boxes. Master Bedroom. Winter Clothes. Books.

Gave them their privacy.

Five minutes later, I headed back down.

Found them hunched over the photo albums. Whispering. Looking conspiratorial.

They looked up when I entered. Both grinning.

"What are you two doing?"

"Just getting to know each other." Mom's tone dripped innocence.

Ryan's grin widened. Dangerous.

"Oh honey," Mom continued, "I have SO many stories—"

"Nope!" I clapped my hands. "No more stories! We have packing to do! Right now!"

Both of them laughed at my panic.

But I realized something.

Mom liked him.

Really liked him.

She'd never liked Derek. Barely tolerated the guy before him. Been polite but distant with everyone I'd ever brought home.

This was different.

This was the first man I'd dated that Mom actually approved of.

Ever.

Mom stood, still smiling. "I'll make lunch. You two keep packing."

She headed to the kitchen. Humming.

Humming.

I couldn't remember the last time I'd heard her hum.

Ryan caught my eye. "Your mom's great."

"She likes you."

"I like her too." He stood, brushed dust off his jeans. "She reminds me of you. Strong. Creative. Doesn't take any nonsense."

I stepped closer. Smiled.

Ryan pulled me in for a kiss.

"Extremely lovable," I agreed against his lips.

Mom's never liked anyone I've dated. Not once. And now she's bonding with Ryan over my embarrassing childhood like they're best friends.

I didn't know whether to be relieved or terrified.

Chapter Thirty-Four

Mrs. Henderson's House

Ryan

"Watch the camellias! Not on the grass! Turn the wheel!"

Mrs. Henderson's voice rang out sharp and commanding.

The moving truck beeped, backing into her driveway. The driver adjusted, stopping short of her prize camellia bushes.

I parked on the street. Grabbed my work gloves from the truck bed.

Mrs. Henderson stood on her porch with a clipboard. Naturally. Directing operations like a general commanding troops.

Beverly paced the lawn. Excited but nervous energy radiating from every movement.

Dozer bounded out of my truck, supervising the scene. Tail wagging. Nose investigating everything.

"Mr. Rodriguez." Mrs. Henderson descended the porch steps. Handed me a laminated assignment list. "Your tasks for the day."

I scanned it. Unloading truck. Setting up Beverly's bedroom. Heavy lifting as needed.

"Got it."

"Good." She marked something on her clipboard. "The others should arrive shortly."

Right on cue, Henry pulled up in his truck. Coffee carrier balanced on his dashboard. Box of donuts on the passenger seat.

"Fuel for the workers." He climbed out, grinning.

Maya and Rachel arrived next. Rachel's car loaded with organizing supplies. Bins, labels, shelf liners.

Chief Patterson pulled up with Martinez. Both in casual clothes and ready to work.

Everyone pitched in. This was what community looked like.

Mrs. Henderson deployed people efficiently. Assigned tasks. Coordinated movements.

Dozer "helped" by investigating every box. Getting underfoot. Wagging.

The house filled with voices. Laughter. Purpose.

The actual work began.

Martinez and I lifted Beverly's bedroom furniture from the truck. Dresser. Nightstand. Headboard and frame.

Chief and Henry carried the antique desk. Beverly's mother's desk, she'd told us. Watching nervously as they maneuvered it through the door.

"Careful with the corner." Beverly's voice carried from the lawn. "That desk is older than I am."

They placed it perfectly by the window in her new room. Natural light streaming across the surface.

Beverly touched it. Tears welling in her eyes.

"Perfect," she whispered.

Maya and Rachel organized boxes. Creating systems. Deciding what went where.

Beverly's personality blended into Mrs. Henderson's space. Photos appeared on surfaces. Quilts draped over chairs. Books found homes on shelves.

The house transformed. No longer Mrs. Henderson's space alone. Now shared. Now home to both of them.

Dozer "helped" throughout. Stealing soft things. Getting tangled in bubble wrap. Causing general chaos.

Everyone laughed. Worked together. Made progress.

Cooper arrived late with more coffee. "Sorry. Got called in for an hour."

"You're forgiven." Mrs. Henderson gestured toward the stairs. "Third bedroom. Boxes labeled 'books.'"

He saluted. Headed upstairs.

By noon, Mrs. Henderson called a break.

"Everyone outside. I've made lunch."

Of course she had.

We collapsed on the porch. The lawn. Wherever there was space.

Sandwiches. Lemonade. Cookies still warm.

Dozer sprawled in the grass. Exhausted from "helping." Tongue lolling out.

Martinez started it. "Remember that cat in the tree last month?"

Cooper groaned. "The one that didn't actually need rescuing?"

"Lady called 911 because her cat was stuck." Martinez grinned. "We get there with the ladder truck. Full response. Cat's sitting on a branch about eight feet up."

"Could've jumped down anytime." Frank shook his head.

"So what happened?" Beverly leaned forward.

"Cooper climbs up." Martinez couldn't contain his laughter. "Gets almost to the cat. Cat jumps. Lands perfectly. Walks away."

"Left me on the ladder looking like an idiot." Cooper's tone was dry.

Everyone laughed. Beverly included. She fit into the circle naturally. Asking questions. Engaging with the stories.

Chief told one about a false alarm at the grocery store. Henry shared a story about Dune stealing evidence at a crime scene.

Rachel sat with Maya across the lawn. Organizing labels. Hair falling out of its bun. Focused on her task.

I watched her. The way she moved. The way she solved problems. The way she belonged here as much as I did.

Our eyes met. She smiled. Soft. Private. For me.

Henry caught me watching. Grinned. Nudged Maya.

They knew. Everyone knew.

This was belonging. Community. Home.

After lunch, I carried the last box to Beverly's room.

Found Mrs. Henderson standing by the window. Holding a photo frame.

She and Harold on their wedding day. 1960s based on the fashion. Both young. Both smiling.

"You were beautiful, Mrs. Henderson."

She looked up. Surprised. Then smiled. "I was terrified."

"Of getting married?"

"Of loving a firefighter." She set the photo on Beverly's dresser. "Harold was with the department for thirty years. Every time the alarm bells rang, I wondered if he'd come home."

I stayed quiet. Listening.

"But I also felt pride. Purpose. I chose to love him anyway." She looked at me. "I could have chosen someone safe. I would have been bored to tears."

Her voice went firm. "Love requires courage, Mr. Rodriguez. The courage to choose someone even when you're afraid."

She paused. Let it settle.

"Your Rachel? She's finding her courage."

Another pause. Her eyes sharp and knowing.

"Don't let fear make your choices for you."

She squeezed my arm. Turned back to arranging photos on the dresser.

I stood there. Letting the wisdom settle into my bones.

Mrs. Henderson had chosen courage. Had chosen love despite the fear. Had lived with a firefighter for decades.

And she was telling me Rachel was choosing the same thing.

Choosing me. Choosing us. Despite the fear.

"Thank you."

"Don't thank me yet." She adjusted a frame. "You still have work to do. Those boxes in the hall won't unpack themselves."

I grinned. Headed back to work.

By late afternoon, Beverly's room was complete.

Familiar quilt on the bed. Photos on the dresser. Her mother's antique desk by the window with her knitting supplies already arranged.

Books on shelves. Everything in place. Everything home.

Beverly stood in the doorway. Taking it all in. Tears streaming down her face.

Rachel touched her arm. "Mom? What's wrong?"

"Nothing's wrong." Beverly's voice broke. "Everything's right."

She stepped into the room. Touched the quilt. The desk. The photos.

"I was so scared of being a burden. Scared you would sacrifice everything for me."

"Mom—"

"But this." Beverly gestured around. "This is friendship. Companionship. Mutual support. Not burden. Not sacrifice."

Mrs. Henderson appeared in the doorway.

Beverly crossed to her. Pulled her into a tight hug.

"Thank you for giving me my daughter back."

Mrs. Henderson's voice went gruff but tender. "Thank you for giving me a friend."

They held each other. Two widows who'd found companionship. Who'd solved each other's loneliness.

Rachel's eyes filled with tears. She looked at me.

I pulled her close. Both of us misty-eyed watching them.

Evening came. The work done. Everyone'd gone home.

Rachel and I walked to the beach. Dozer trotting between us.

The sun hung low, casting everything in amber light. Waves gentle. The light perfect.

We walked in comfortable silence. Our hands finding each other.

Rachel stopped. Looked out at the ocean.

"When did you know?" Her voice came out quiet.

"Know what?"

"That you loved me."

I thought about it. "The mural. When you were explaining the light angles. How each firefighter had their own light source to tell their story." I smiled at the memory. "You were so focused. So passionate. And I realized I wanted to watch you create things for the rest of my life."

She turned to face me. "The firehouse. When you came back from that call covered in soot. I'd spent hours waiting, drawing floor plans for your kitchen." Her voice went soft. "And when you saw what I'd done, you didn't think it was presumptuous. You looked at me like I'd given you a gift."

"You had."

"I almost missed this." Her eyes filled with tears. "I was so close to leaving. To choosing duty over happiness. To running away because it felt safer than staying."

"But you didn't run."

"No. I didn't." She stepped closer. "And that's new for me. Staying. Choosing something that scares me because I want it more than I fear it."

I understood. "I've spent two years keeping people at a distance. After the betrayal. After the politics. I told myself it was safer to stay uninvolved."

"What changed?"

"You changed me." I caught myself. "No. That's not right. You didn't change me. But loving you made me want to be braver. Made me willing to risk getting hurt again because the alternative was missing this."

She smiled through her tears. "I'm not smaller with you. I'm more myself. But also more than I was. Does that make sense?"

"Perfect sense." I touched her face. "You make me want to build instead of just protect. To create a life instead of just survive one."

"I don't love you in spite of your chaos." I framed her face with my hands. "I love you because of it."

"Because of it?"

"Because your chaos is creativity. Passion. The way you see beauty everywhere. The way you make the world more colorful just by existing in it." I held her gaze. "I will always be here. For the chaos and the beauty and everything in between."

The sun set behind us, wrapping us in fading light.

I pulled her close. Kissed her.

No hesitation. No walls. No fear.

This was freedom. Choice. Commitment.

Rachel kissed back with everything she had.

When we broke apart, both breathless, she was laughing.

That joyful, unrestrained laugh I loved.

"I'm staying. In Seaholly. With you."

I spun her around. Lifted her feet off the sand.

Dozer barked. Ran circles around us. Tail wagging chaos.

I set her down. Pressed my forehead to hers.

"I love you. Chaos and all."

"I love you." Her smile was radiant. "Order and all."

We walked back hand in hand.

Finally free to be exactly who we were.

Together.

Chapter Thirty-Five

The Community Center

Rachel

"Where does this one go?"

I looked up from taping a portrait to the wall. Sarah held her artwork in both hands, protective and proud.

"Wherever you think it should go, sweetheart."

She studied the wall like she was curating a museum. Nodded. Placed her portrait of the school librarian next to Tommy's firefighter piece.

Hero portraits covered every available surface in the community center. The kids had each created their own vision of heroism. Pride radiated from every crooked line and smudged fingerprint.

My hands shook as I smoothed another piece of tape. Nervous energy coursed through me.

This had grown beyond anything I'd imagined when we started the project months ago.

Tommy's portrait of Ryan held the center position. I'd placed it there on purpose. Detailed. Loving. Powerful. Ryan in his firefighter gear, Dozer at his side, both rendered with such care it made my throat tight.

Other portraits surrounded it. A teacher helping a struggling student. A mail carrier delivering medicine in a snowstorm. A librarian reading to children. A parent holding a newborn. A crossing guard stopping traffic with her stop sign raised high.

Heroes came in all forms.

The door opened. Kids started trickling in early. Bouncing with barely contained excitement.

"Miss Rachel, where's mine?"

"Can my mom sit in the front?"

"Is Mr. Ryan coming?"

I answered each question. Directed traffic. Tried not to let my nerves show.

"Breathe."

Maya appeared at my elbow. Held out a bottle of water I hadn't realized I needed.

I took it. Drank.

"They're going to love it."

"What if they don't? What if the parents think it's silly? What if—"

"Rachel." Maya gripped my shoulders. "Look what you created with these kids. Look at this room."

I looked. Really looked.

A collection of portraits. A collection of stories. Children who'd learned to see heroism in the everyday people around them.

"You did this." Maya's voice went soft. "You and Ryan together. This is incredible."

The door opened again.

Ryan walked in with Dozer on a leash. Still in his uniform. Must have come straight from shift.

His eyes found mine across the room. He smiled. The soft smile meant for me.

Dozer immediately pulled toward a group of kids, tail wagging. Ryan held firm on the leash.

My nerves settled. Not gone, but manageable.

He crossed to me. Stopped close enough I could smell smoke still clinging to his gear.

"You've been on a call."

"Small one. Kitchen fire. Everyone's fine." He looked around the room. "This is amazing, Rachel."

"The kids did all the work."

"You taught them how." He touched my hand. Squeezed. "I'm going to change and tie up Dozer in the back room. Be right back."

He disappeared toward the bathroom with his duffel bag, Dozer trotting beside him.

Parents started arriving. A trickle became a flood.

The room filled with voices. Laughter. The sound of families together.

Kids pulled parents to their artwork. Explained with pride what they'd created. Why they'd chosen their particular hero.

Sarah dragged her mom to a portrait of a nurse. "That's Miss Johnson from the hospital. She gave me a shot last year, but she was really nice about it. See? I painted her with a smile."

Her mom's eyes filled with tears. "It's beautiful, baby."

Another child showed off a portrait of his grandmother. Gray hair in a bun. Hands holding a mixing bowl.

"She makes the best cookies." His tone was serious. "And she always listens when I'm sad."

His father ruffled his hair. "Grandma's going to love this."

I circulated through the room. Answering questions. Accepting compliments I didn't quite know what to do with.

Ryan returned in jeans and a button-down. Clean. Smelling like soap instead of smoke.

He moved through the crowd. Talked to kids and parents. Crouched down to eye level with the children. Made everyone feel important and seen.

He kept looking at me. Pride clear in his expression every time our eyes met.

My heart squeezed. This was it. This was the life we were building. Together.

The community center director moved to the front of the room. Raised her voice over the chatter.

"Can I have everyone's attention, please?"

The crowd quieted. Turned toward her.

"First, I want to thank Miss Rachel Brown for this incredible showcase." She gestured at the walls. "And Mr. Ryan Rodriguez for partnering with us on the fire safety program that inspired these portraits."

Applause filled the room. My cheeks burned.

"We have someone who'd like to say a few words." The director's voice carried warmth. "Mr. Watson, Tommy's grandfather."

My pulse jumped. I hadn't known this was happening.

An older man stepped forward. Weathered face. Kind eyes crinkled at the corners. Tommy stood beside him, beaming with pride.

Ryan's hand found mine. Held tight.

"I won't take much of your time." Mr. Watson's voice stayed steady but carried emotion underneath. "But I needed to say something tonight."

He looked at Ryan. Then at me.

"A few weeks ago, there was a fire at my house. Kitchen fire. Started small. Got big fast."

The room went silent. Everyone listening.

"Tommy smelled the smoke. Came to wake me." Mr. Watson's voice grew stronger. "I was stubborn. Told him to wait while I grabbed my wife's photo albums. But Tommy did exactly what Mr. Rodriguez taught him."

Tommy ducked his head. Shy under the attention but smiling.

"He didn't wait for me. He got himself out of the house immediately. Then called 911." Mr. Watson's voice cracked. "If he'd tried to help me, if he'd waited, we both might have died. But he did the smart thing. The hard thing. The thing that saved both our lives."

He paused. Let it sink in.

"The firefighters got there in time because Tommy called immediately. Because an eight-year-old boy stayed calm enough to do exactly what he'd been taught." Mr. Watson looked directly at Ryan. "That fire safety program didn't just save my life. It saved Tommy's life, too."

Ryan's grip on my hand tightened.

"But that's not all." Mr. Watson continued. "After the fire, Tommy was scared. Had nightmares. Didn't want to talk about what happened. Didn't want to be alone."

He put his hand on Tommy's shoulder. Protective. Loving.

"Miss Rachel's art class helped him process what he was feeling. Drawing what he couldn't put into words. Creating something beautiful out of something scary."

Tears blurred my vision. I blinked hard.

"These two young people are building something special here." Mr. Watson looked between Ryan and me. "Teaching our children to be brave. To be creative. To be heroes in their own ways. To save lives and to heal hearts."

He paused. Let it settle over the room.

"Thank you both. From the bottom of my heart. You gave me my grandson back twice."

The room erupted in applause.

Tommy ran over. Threw his arms around me first. Then Ryan. Both of us trying not to cry in front of everyone.

"Thank you, Miss Rachel," Tommy whispered against my shoulder.

"You're the brave one, Tommy."

He pulled back. Grinned. Ran back to his grandfather.

Parents swarmed us after.

Questions came rapid-fire.

"Could we do this at other schools?"

"What about summer programs?"

"My daughter wants to take art classes from you. Do you have openings?"

"Can you teach the older kids, too?"

Ideas flowed. I fielded questions. My brain spun with possibilities I hadn't considered.

Ryan added his perspective on the fire safety side. We built on each other's thoughts. Natural partnership. Finishing each other's sentences without realizing it.

"We could coordinate with the school calendar," I suggested.

"And tie it into our seasonal safety themes," Ryan added. "Water safety in summer. Fire safety in fall."

"Art as a processing tool year-round."

"Exactly."

The community center director appeared with a tray of cookies and punch. "Please, everyone, help yourselves to refreshments."

Parents migrated toward the food table. Kids grabbed cookies with enthusiastic hands.

The energy shifted from intense to social. Conversations continued over paper cups and napkins.

Ryan excused himself. "Going to check on Dozer. Make sure he hasn't destroyed anything."

He headed toward the back room.

I was answering a mom's question about supply lists when I heard it.

Ryan's voice. Sharp. "Dozer, NO."

Then laughter. The kind that comes from complete resignation.

I excused myself. Followed the sound.

Found Ryan in the back room where they'd stored the extra refreshments.

Dozer sat in the middle of the floor. Blue frosting smeared across his snout. A demolished cupcake wrapper beside him. And somehow—impossibly—a cone-shaped party hat stuck on his head at a jaunty angle.

The backup desserts Maya had stored here were in shambles. Three cupcakes missing. Frosting everywhere.

Dozer's tail wagged. Completely pleased with himself despite the evidence of his crimes.

I pressed my hand over my mouth. Trying not to laugh.

"This is not funny," Ryan said. But his mouth twitched.

"It's a little funny."

"He ate three cupcakes. THREE." Ryan gestured at the destruction. "And I have no idea how he got that hat on his head."

Dozer tilted his head. The party hat slipped further sideways. Made him look even more ridiculous.

I lost it. Laughed until tears streamed down my face.

All the emotion from the evening. Mr. Watson's speech. Tommy's hug. The weight of being called heroes. It all released in helpless laughter at this ridiculous dog wearing a party hat and covered in frosting.

Ryan watched me. His expression softened. Started laughing too.

"I'm so sorry," he managed between laughs. "I tied him up. I don't know how he—"

"Stop apologizing." I wiped my eyes. "This is perfect."

"Perfect?"

"Chaos and order." I gestured between Dozer and Ryan. "This is us. This is our life."

Ryan looked at his frosting-covered dog. At me laughing with mascara probably running down my face. At the destroyed dessert table.

"Yeah." His smile was soft. Genuine. "I guess it is."

We cleaned up together. Paper towels and whispered laughter so parents wouldn't hear.

Dozer supervised. Still wearing his party hat. Unrepentant.

Ryan tried to remove the hat. Dozer ducked away.

"Leave it," I said. "He's earned it."

"He's destroyed property."

"He's providing comic relief." I scratched behind Dozer's ears. "Good boy. Very dramatic entrance."

Dozer licked my hand. Left blue frosting on my fingers.

Ryan caught my eye. Both of us covered in frosting now. Both grinning like idiots.

"I love you," he said. Simple. Easy. True.

"I love you too." I kissed him. Tasted sugar and coffee, and home. "Chaos and all."

We finished cleaning. Smuggled Dozer back to Ryan's truck before anyone noticed the cupcake situation.

The party hat came with him. Still stuck at a jaunty angle.

Across the room, Ryan circulated through the remaining crowd.

I watched him crouch beside a little girl. Listen to her explain her portrait of her big brother. Nod like her words mattered more than anything.

Chief Patterson appeared at my side. Watched Ryan with the same expression I probably wore.

"You two make a good team."

"We do."

"He's different since he met you." Chief's voice went thoughtful. "More settled. Like he finally found what he was looking for."

My throat went tight. "He makes me braver."

"Good partnerships do that." Chief smiled. "My wife and I have been married for forty-two years. Best teams make each other better."

He wandered off to admire more portraits.

I watched Ryan stand. Ruffle the little girl's hair. Move to the next family.

This was who he was. Not with me alone. With everyone. Creating connection and safety wherever he went.

And somehow, he'd chosen me. We'd chosen each other.

Evening settled. Most people gone.

A few stragglers remained. Maya folding chairs. Parents collecting the last of their children.

Kids left carrying their artwork home. Proud. Beaming.

Ryan and I moved through the space. Straightened remaining chairs. Took down the decorations we'd hung earlier.

Worked side by side in comfortable silence. The good kind of quiet from being at ease with someone.

The good kind of exhausted from doing meaningful work.

Maya stacked the last chair. Grabbed her purse from the table.

"You two really are building something beautiful here." She smiled at both of us. "Not just the programs. Everything."

"I'm just saying." She headed for the door. "I'll see you guys later."

She paused at the door. "I'm really happy for you both. You know that, right?"

"We know." Ryan's voice came out soft.

She left. The door closing behind her with a soft click.

Me and Ryan in the community center.

I moved behind the display table to grab my bag.

My foot knocked against something propped against the wall.

I bent down. Picked it up.

Another portrait. One I hadn't seen before.

My breath caught.

It showed Ryan and me. Together. Side by side.

Tommy's careful artwork rendered both of us in loving detail. Ryan in his firefighter gear. Me with a paintbrush. Both of us smiling. Dozer between us, tail mid-wag.

Labeled in his precise printing: "MY HEROES"

Not Ryan alone. Both of us.

Tears filled my eyes. Spilled over before I could stop them.

"Rachel?" Ryan's voice came from across the room. "You okay?"

I couldn't speak. Held up the portrait.

He crossed to me quickly. Took it from my shaking hands.

His expression transformed. Softened. Eyes going bright with emotion.

"He made this for us." My voice broke.

"For both of us." Ryan touched the portrait. Traced the careful lines Tommy had drawn. "His heroes."

We stood there looking at it together.

The weight of being seen this way by a child we'd both helped. The gift of knowing we'd made a difference. The responsibility of living up to this innocent trust.

"We should frame this." Ryan's voice came out rough with emotion.

I nodded. Wiped my eyes with the back of my hand. "Where?"

"The cottage." He said it like it was obvious. "Maybe in the living room? Above the couch once the renovation's done?"

The words hung there.

THE cottage.

Not "my cottage."

Not "your cottage."

THE cottage. Singular. Shared. Ours.

My pulse stuttered. Heat flooded my face.

We hadn't talked about this. About living together. About sharing space permanently.

But he said it so naturally. Like it was already decided. Like of course we were building a life together in every sense.

"The cottage?" I barely whispered.

Ryan realized what he'd said. His eyes widened. Then he met my gaze. Didn't take it back. Didn't backtrack.

"Yeah." His voice was steady. Sure. "Ours. If you want."

The question loaded with everything.

Moving in together. Sharing mornings and evenings. Building a home instead of visiting each other's spaces.

My answer came through tears and laughter tangled together.

"Yes." I stepped closer. "Ours."

Ryan set the portrait down on the table. Pulled me into his arms.

Kissed me there in the empty community center. Surrounded by evidence of what we were building together.

More than art programs and safety initiatives.

A life. A home. A future.

AVIANNE ASH

Piece by piece.

Chapter Thirty-Six

Ryan's Cottage

Ryan

"Hand me the paintbrush?"

Rachel stood below me, ocean-blue paint streaking her forearms. Her overalls were splattered with different colors from previous projects. Hair pulled back in a messy bun held together by what looked like a pencil.

I climbed down the ladder. Handed her the brush.

"This blue is perfect." She dipped it into the paint tray. "Like the ocean right before a storm. All that depth and energy."

"You picked it."

"We picked it." She glanced at me, smiling. "I suggested six shades. You chose this one."

I stepped behind her. Close enough to feel her warmth radiating through the cool air. Close enough to catch the scent of paint and her shampoo.

"Looking good," I said, watching her smooth strokes across the shutter.

She turned her head. Grinned up at me. Paint streaked her left cheek. "The shutters or me?"

"Both."

Her laugh made my pulse kick up. She leaned back into me. Testing.

I put my hands on her waist. Steadied her. Pulled her closer.

The kiss tasted like coffee, but sweeter. Her paint-smudged fingers found my collar. Dozer wedged himself between our legs, tail wagging hard enough to knock us both off balance.

"Your dog has terrible timing."

"Always has."

She kissed me again. Longer this time. Her hand sliding to the back of my neck.

Dozer whined. Pushed his massive head between us.

I laughed, breaking away. "Dozer, down."

He sat. Tail still wagging. Looking pleased with himself.

Rachel wiped her mouth with the back of her hand, spreading more blue paint across her face. "I think he's jealous."

"Definitely jealous."

Gravel crunched in the driveway.

We both turned. Henry's sedan pulled in.

"UNCLE RYAN!"

Doors burst open. Henry's kids, Lucy and Max, spilled out first, followed by Maya's twins Sofia and Leo. Four kids exploding like confetti from a cannon.

Maya followed at a more reasonable pace, shaking her head with the fond exasperation of someone who'd been managing chaos for the past hour.

Sofia got to me first. Ten years old and pure energy. She threw her arms around my waist. "Uncle Ryan!"

Leo barreled into my legs right after. Her twin. "We're going to the amusement park!"

Lucy and Max, Henry's kids, went straight for Dozer.

"MISS RACHEL!" Sofia threw her arms around Rachel's waist, getting blue paint all over her pink shirt. She didn't seem to notice or care.

Dozer lost his mind.

Complete chaos.

He spun in circles, knocked over the paint tray with his tail, barked loud enough to scare seagulls off the beach. Blue paint splattered across the grass.

"Oh no." Rachel lunged for the tray. Too late.

Maya reached us, laughing. Pulled Rachel into a hug. "Sorry. We're on our way to the amusement park. Thought we'd stop and say hi first."

"I'm so glad you did." Rachel hugged her back, then bent to hug Sofia properly. "Look at you! You're getting so tall!"

Henry was already grinning at the scene unfolding in my front yard. "Hey, man." He clapped my shoulder. "Place is looking great."

"Thanks to Rachel." I gestured at the shutters. At the paint supplies organized on the porch. At the general state of renovation surrounding us. "She's doing most of the work."

"I see that." Henry's grin widened. His eyes tracked to the paint streaks decorating both of us. "Very hands-on project."

I turned my head. Ignored him.

Sofia had climbed onto Dozer's back. Straddling him like a horse, bouncing.

"Sofia!" Maya's voice went sharp with maternal alarm. "Stop trying to ride the dog!"

"But he's so big!" Sofia bounced again. Dozer stood there wagging his tail, thrilled by the attention and unconcerned about being used as transportation.

"He's not a horse!" Maya started toward her daughter.

Max grabbed a tennis ball from the grass. "Dozer! Fetch!"

He threw it. Hard. It sailed across the yard.

Dozer forgot about Sofia. Sent her tumbling onto the grass as he took off after the ball at full speed.

Sofia landed with an "oof!" Then laughed. Got up. Brushed herself off and grabbed another tennis ball. "My turn!"

Leo joined in. Both of them throwing balls in different directions. Dozer racing back and forth, trying to catch all of them, succeeding at catching none.

Lucy stood apart. Arms crossed over her chest. Watching the chaos with her usual twelve-year-old judgment.

Too old for this. Too mature for playing with dogs and tennis balls.

Except Dozer had other ideas.

He trotted over to her. Sat in front of her. Looked up with those big brown eyes.

Lucy ignored him. Checked her phone.

Dozer reached up. Grabbed her hair tie right out of her ponytail. Snatched it with his teeth in one smooth motion.

Her hair fell around her shoulders. Dark and long and messy.

She froze. Stared at Dozer.

He wagged his tail. Hair tie dangling from his mouth like a trophy.

We all held our breath.

Then Lucy laughed.

Threw her head back and chased Dozer around the yard, playing for the first time in months. Maybe years.

"Lucy?" Henry's voice caught. "Did she just—"

"Yeah." Maya squeezed his arm.

I couldn't stop grinning.

Rachel caught my eye across the chaos. Her whole face soft with delight. She mouthed: "He's magic."

I mouthed back: "Best dog ever."

Dozer sprinted past with kids chasing him. Lucy in the lead, laughing so hard she could barely run.

"Coffee?" I called out to the adults.

"Please." Henry's voice carried relief.

I headed inside. Grabbed the pot I'd made an hour ago. Still warm. Poured four mugs.

When I came back out, Maya and Rachel had claimed the porch chairs. Henry leaned against the railing. All three watching the kids and dog with fond amusement.

I distributed coffee. Settled into the chair beside Rachel.

She leaned into me. Natural. Easy. Like we'd been doing this for years instead of weeks.

"So," Rachel said, wrapping both hands around her mug. "How's everything? How's wedding planning?"

Maya groaned. "Don't ask."

"That bad?"

"I'm trying to plan my own wedding. Be the bride AND the event coordinator." Maya shook her head. "Every decision feels like I'm working, not celebrating. Should the centerpieces be ivory or cream? Who cares? Except apparently I do because I'm the planner."

Henry sipped his coffee. "I keep telling her to hire someone."

"And spend money we don't have?" Maya looked at him. "I AM someone. I can do this."

"But should you?" Rachel's voice was gentle.

"Exactly." Henry gestured with his mug. "You deserve to enjoy your own wedding."

"I will enjoy it." Maya's tone went defensive. "Once everything's planned perfectly."

They smiled at each other. The easy affection of two people who'd figured out how to navigate conflict without losing themselves.

"If we survive the planning process." Maya laughed. Took a long drink of coffee. "I saw your mom at the market last week. She and Mrs. Henderson were picking out ingredients for some recipe. Debating garlic versus shallots very passionately."

Rachel grinned. "That sounds like them."

I squeezed her hand.

"Mrs. Henderson called Ryan last week," Rachel said. "Said it was urgent."

"What happened?" Maya asked.

"She needed me to get a jar down from the top shelf." I grinned. "That's it. The emergency. A jar of pickles."

Everyone laughed.

"Did you give her grief about it?" Henry asked.

"Are you kidding? I was happy to help. Got her pickles, stayed for tea, listened to her theories about some cold case podcast she's into." I shrugged. "Best emergency call I've had all week."

Rachel pressed her face against my shoulder. "My mother's never had it so good."

"Speaking of partnerships," Henry said, looking at me with a grin. "I'm losing business."

"What?"

"Mrs. Henderson doesn't come to The Grind nearly as much anymore." He gestured with his coffee mug. "She used to be there every morning. Seven-thirty, one scone, pot of tea, knitting for two hours."

"And now?"

"Now she comes in maybe twice a week. Orders two scones to go, tells me she can't stay and chat." Henry grinned. "Then proceeds to tell me exactly where they're going. Last week, it was a historical society lecture."

Maya nodded. "They've got their own routine now."

"Pretty sure I make up for it. My daily visits."

Henry grinned. "You really do. You and your emotional support dog."

On cue, Dozer crashed into the porch railing. Children on his heels. One tennis ball in his mouth, two more on the ground behind him.

The railing held. Barely.

We all laughed.

"I should probably reinforce that," I muttered.

"Add it to the list." Rachel patted my knee.

The easy friendship settled over us. Comfortable silence between words. The knowledge our lives had woven together in ways none of us expected.

Maya checked her watch. "Alright! Time to go! Amusement park's waiting!"

The kids groaned in unison. A chorus of complaint.

"But we just got here!"

"Five more minutes!"

"Dozer needs me!"

"Now." Maya's voice went firm. "We have a two-hour drive, and I promised you'd be there by noon."

More groaning. Dragging of feet.

But they came. Eventually.

Sofia hugged Dozer goodbye. Wrapped her arms around his neck and whispered something in his ear. Dozer's tail wagged.

Max and Leo did the same. Both of them promising to come back soon.

Lucy—miracle of miracles—knelt. Wrapped her arms around Dozer's massive neck. Buried her face in his fur.

My throat went tight.

She stood up. Looked at me. "Can we come back next weekend, Uncle Ryan?"

"Absolutely." I ruffled Max's hair. "Dozer would be devastated without you guys."

More hugs. Rachel got pulled into the chaos. Kids clinging to her like she was family too.

She was family. To them. To Maya. To all of us.

Car doors slammed. Windows rolled down. Goodbyes shouted.

They drove off. The sound of the engine fading down the road toward the highway.

Sudden quiet.

Rachel and I stood in the yard. Surrounded by tennis balls. Overturned paint supplies. Grass torn up from kid-and-dog play.

Dozer collapsed on the porch. Passed out cold. Exhausted. His sides heaving with deep, satisfied breaths.

I looked at Rachel. She looked at me.

We both started laughing.

"They're wonderful kids." Rachel bent to pick up tennis balls.

"They are." I grabbed the paint tray, set it upright. "Exhausting, but wonderful."

We worked together. Straightening furniture. Cleaning up the chaos. Picking up scattered toys Dozer had dragged from inside.

Comfortable silence settled over us. The kind from being at ease with someone.

But I could feel it. The weight of the unspoken conversation hanging between us.

Both thinking the same thing.

"You're really good with them." Rachel's voice came out careful. Not looking at me. Focusing on the tennis balls in her hands.

I paused. Studied her profile. "I love being an uncle." The words came out slower than I meant. Choosing each one. "But my schedule isn't exactly family-friendly." I watched her face. "And I like my life. The way it is."

Her shoulders dropped. Visible relief.

But she still didn't look at me. Still didn't say anything.

"Rachel."

She turned. Eyes wide. Scared.

"I don't want kids." The words came out in a rush. Like she'd been holding them in for weeks. "Never have. I was terrified that would be a dealbreaker for you."

Air rushed out of my lungs. Relief matching hers.

I crossed to her. Took her hands. "I thought I was supposed to want them. Everyone assumes firefighters want the whole package. House, wife, kids, white picket fence." I squeezed her fingers. "But I don't."

"You don't?"

"No. I want what we have. You, me, Dozer. The cottage. Our work. This community. That's enough. That's everything."

We both laughed. The tension breaking like a wave hitting shore.

"We're really good with other people's kids, though." Rachel gestured at the destroyed yard.

"Best aunt and uncle in Seaholly."

"Is this okay?" She searched my face. Looking for doubt. For hesitation. "Are we okay?"

I pulled her close. Kissed her forehead. Her temple. Her mouth. "We're more than okay."

She wrapped her arms around my waist. Held tight. Face pressed against my shoulder.

Relief and promise and future spreading between us.

When we broke apart, both grinning like idiots, I tugged her toward the porch steps.

We sat. Rachel leaning against me. Both of us watching the ocean-blue shutters dry in the autumn sun.

Dozer snored beside us. Exhausted and content.

Pale light filtered through the trees. The ocean rolled steady in the background. Salt air mixed with coffee and the lingering sweetness of children's chaos.

"You know I'm robbing the cradle." Rachel's voice came out teasing. "You're my younger man."

"One year doesn't count."

"Still counts." She poked my ribs. "I'm a cougar."

I laughed. Kissed the top of her head. "Thirty-eight and thirty-nine. Real scandalous."

"People will talk."

"Let them."

She tilted her face up. Smiled at me. Paint still streaking her cheek. Hair falling out of its bun. Beautiful, chaotic, and here.

"The mural dedication is next week," I said.

The smile faded. "I know." Her voice went soft. Nervous. "I'm terrified."

"You're going to be amazing."

"What if nobody comes? What if they hate it? What if—"

I kissed her. Cut off the spiral before it could start.

When I pulled back, she was smiling again.

"Robert Vanderson is coming." I reminded her. "Your hero. The artist you've admired for years. He's coming to see your work."

"That makes it worse."

"He wouldn't come if he didn't think it was worth seeing."

She absorbed that. Nodded. Some of the tension easing from her shoulders.

"We're really doing this," she whispered.

"Yeah." I threaded my fingers through hers. Held on. "We really are."

The future stretched before us. Unconventional and perfect and ours.

Chapter Thirty-Seven

The Easel

Rachel

I adjusted the painting for the hundredth time. The wire on the back refused to sit level.

"They're perfect." Vivian's voice carried from across the gallery. "Stop fussing."

"This one's crooked."

"That one's been level for ten minutes. You're stalling."

I stepped back. Studied the wall. The firefighter series displayed prominently. Six large canvases showing different moments, different angles, different stories.

But the centerpiece drew every eye.

Ryan's portrait. Not the formal mural study. The intimate one.

Him laughing. Guard down. Eyes soft and warm, crinkled at the corners. The exact moment from moving day when Dozer had stolen his boot, and he'd given up trying to be serious.

I'd captured something raw. Something real. Something I hadn't meant anyone else to see.

My hands shook as I reached for the lever again.

"Rachel." Vivian's voice went firm. "Come down from there."

"I need to—"

"Now."

I climbed down. My legs unsteady on the ladder rungs.

Vivian pressed coffee into my hands. From The Grind. Still warm. She must have gone out while I was obsessing over placement.

She wore a scarlet red paneled sheath dress. Gallery owner professional. Confident in a way I'd never quite manage.

I'd put effort into tonight. The black sleeveless dress skimmed my curves. A long gold necklace hung down the front, geometric and bold against the fabric. Heels that made me hyper-aware of every step. My hair fell loose past my shoulders instead of tangled in a bun. I checked my hands one more time. Clean. No paint under my nails or dried on my knuckles.

I felt like I was wearing a costume.

"This is your biggest show yet." Her voice came out gentle. "It's normal to be nervous."

"I'm not nervous." I took a sip. Burned my tongue. "I'm terrified."

"The work is brilliant. The online buzz has been incredible. We've had pre-orders from fire departments in seven states."

"That's insane."

"That's talent." Vivian gestured at the walls. "You're documenting something important. Everyday heroism. The people who show up when we need them."

I looked at Ryan's portrait again. My throat went tight.

"He doesn't know about this one." The admission came out quiet. "The intimate portrait. I told him I'd only be showing the mural studies."

Vivian raised an eyebrow. "And why did you include it?"

"Because it's the best work I've ever done." The truth came out vulnerable. "Because when I look at it, I see everything I feel about him. Everything I can't quite say."

"Then it belongs here."

"What if he hates it?"

"What if he loves it?" Vivian squeezed my shoulder. "Either way, he deserves to see how you see him."

The gallery door chimed. I jumped.

Too early. We didn't open for another hour.

But the entire Seaholly Fire Department came through the door in dress uniforms.

Chief Patterson led the way. Martinez, Cooper, Frank. The whole crew. Polished and professional and grinning.

My throat went tight. They came. For me.

"Couldn't miss this." Chief shook my hand. "We're honored to be part of your work."

They spread through the gallery. Finding themselves in the preliminary mural sketches. The action shots. The candid moments I'd captured during station visits.

"That's me!" Cooper pointed at a sketch. "Look at how she got the equipment detail!"

Martinez laughed. "She made you look good, man. That's real talent."

"Is that from the training day?" Frank studied one of the larger paintings. "The hose drill?"

"Yeah." I moved beside him. Nervous. "I tried to capture the teamwork. How you all move together."

"You nailed it." His voice went soft with awe. "This is exactly what it feels like."

Frank appeared beside me. He studied the paintings with quiet intensity. He'd been with the department for decades. Seen everything.

"You got it right," he said. Voice low. "Most people see the trucks and the gear. The action." He gestured at the canvases. "But you painted what matters. The waiting. The worry. The relief when everyone makes it home."

My throat went tight.

"My wife looks at me the way you painted Ryan." Frank's eyes stayed on the centerpiece portrait. "Like we're worth the fear. Worth the risk." He looked at me. "Thank you for seeing that."

I couldn't speak. Just nodded.

The door chimed again.

Tommy burst through. His grandfather following at a more sedate pace. Both dressed up. Tommy's hair combed flat, his shirt tucked in.

"Miss Rachel!" He ran over. Threw his arms around my waist.

I hugged him back. Blinking hard against tears. "Hey, Tommy. You look very handsome."

"Grandpa said we had to dress up for your fancy art show."

"It's not that fancy."

Mr. Watson smiled. Extended his hand. "Wouldn't have missed it. Not after everything you've done for Tommy."

More people arrived. A steady stream through the door.

Mom and Mrs. Henderson arrived together. Of course. Both beaming with pride.

Mom wore a navy blue dress I hadn't seen in over ten years. The one she used to wear to Dad's work events. Fitted and elegant. She looked radiant.

"That's my daughter!" Beverly announced to anyone within earshot. "She painted all of this!"

Mrs. Henderson squeezed my hand. "Beautiful work, dear."

Henry and Maya came next. The kids in tow. Lucy, Max, Sofia, and Leo all scrubbed clean and uncomfortable in their nice clothes.

"Can we look at everything?" Max asked, already bouncing toward the paintings.

"Of course." I gestured at the gallery. "Be careful."

They scattered. Dragging their parents along. Pointing out details. Asking questions.

The gallery filled. Collectors Vivian had invited. Town council members. Other artists I knew. People from the community who'd followed the mural project.

But Ryan hadn't arrived yet.

I checked my phone. No messages.

My stomach twisted. What if he didn't come? What if he'd seen the portrait and was angry I'd displayed it without asking?

Vivian touched my elbow. "He's on shift. He texted me an hour ago. He'll be here."

"He texted you?"

"To make sure I saved him a spot for the opening." She smiled. "He's coming, Rachel. Relax."

I tried to relax. Failed.

I circulated through the crowd. Answered questions about technique. Explained my process. Accepted compliments that made my face burn.

Then the door opened.

Ryan.

Still in his uniform. Hair combed. Clean-shaven. Gorgeous.

Our eyes met across the crowded gallery.

Everything else faded. The noise. The people. All of it.

Him. Me. The space between us crackling with everything unsaid.

He smiled. That soft smile meant only for me.

Then he navigated through the crowd. Stopped beside me. Close enough to catch the scent of his cologne.

His eyes swept over me. The dress. The necklace. My styled hair. "You look incredible."

His hand found the small of my back. Warm. Grounding. "Wouldn't have missed this."

A collector approached. Older woman, sharp eyes, expensive clothes. "Miss Brown? I'm interested in the lighthouse series. Can we discuss pricing?"

I started to answer. Ryan squeezed my hand.

"I'm Ryan." Easy. Confident. "Rachel's boyfriend."

The word sent heat flooding through me. Boyfriend. He said it with such certainty. Such pride.

The woman smiled. "Lucky man. Her work is extraordinary."

They chatted. Ryan explained the mural project without being asked. Described the community connection. The firefighter program we'd built together.

His pride in my achievement written all over his face.

I watched him. This man who understood my vision. My process. My art. Who could discuss it with collectors like he'd been studying it for years.

Because he had been. Studying me. Learning me. Supporting me.

More collectors approached. Ryan stayed beside me. His hand never leaving my back. Anchoring me through the overwhelming attention.

"The centerpiece is stunning." One man gestured at Ryan's portrait. "Who's the subject?"

Ryan turned. Saw his own face staring back at him.

He went still.

I held my breath. Waiting for his reaction.

"That's me." His voice came out quiet. Looking at how I'd painted him. How I'd captured that moment of pure joy and vulnerability.

The collector nodded. "She's captured something remarkable. The intimacy. The humanity. This is museum-quality work."

Ryan didn't respond. Kept staring at his portrait.

I touched his arm. "Are you okay?"

He looked at me. Eyes bright with emotion. "You painted me like that."

"Like what?"

"Like I'm someone worth painting."

My throat went tight. "You are. You're—"

Vivian tapped a glass. The sharp sound cutting through conversation.

"Can I have everyone's attention, please?"

The crowd quieted. Turned toward her.

"First, thank you all for coming to celebrate Rachel Brown's extraordinary new work." Vivian gestured at the walls. "The firefighter series has generated incredible interest. We've had inquiries from departments nationwide wanting similar tributes."

Applause rippled through the gallery.

"But before Rachel says a few words, I have an announcement." Vivian pulled me forward. Ryan came too, his hand still in mine. "We've been approached by a collector from Portland. Robert Vanderson."

My pulse jumped. I knew that name. Major collector. Museum connections.

"He wants to commission an entire series." Vivian's voice carried excitement. "Everyday Heroes of America. Documenting first responders, teachers, healthcare workers across the country. A multi-year project with national exhibition potential."

The room erupted. Congratulations. Questions. Excitement.

I couldn't process it. Multi-year project. National recognition. Career-defining work.

Ryan squeezed my hand. Leaned close. "This is amazing. You deserve this."

Vivian smiled at me. "Take time to think about it. But Rachel, this is your moment."

The crowd waited. Expectant. Vivian gestured for me to speak.

I hated public speaking. Always had. My mouth went dry.

Ryan's hand tightened in mine. Grounding. Steady.

I stepped forward. Took a breath.

"I moved to Seaholly three years ago." Voice shaking. "Thinking it was temporary. A place to hide. To heal."

Beverly smiled at me through tears. Mrs. Henderson nodded encouragement.

"But I found something I wasn't looking for." My voice grew stronger. "A home. A community. People who showed up when I needed them."

I looked at Ryan. Couldn't help it.

"I found inspiration in unexpected places. In heroes who see beauty in chaos. Who run toward danger while everyone else runs away."

The fire crew straightened. Pride clear on their faces.

"This work isn't about firefighters alone. It's about anyone who chooses to show up. To help. To care when it would be easier not to."

My eyes found Tommy. His grandfather's hand on his shoulder.

"It's about teaching our children to be brave. To be kind. To be heroes in their own ways."

I looked back at Ryan. My voice breaking on the next words.

"Thank you for showing me that love doesn't require changing who you are. It's about expanding who you can become together."

The room erupted in applause.

But I only saw Ryan.

He stared at me with such intensity. Such love. Such promise.

I crossed to him through the applause. Didn't care that everyone was watching.

Kissed him in front of the entire gallery.

The fire crew whooped. Cheered. Made ridiculous noises.

Mom cried happy tears. Mrs. Henderson nodded with satisfaction.

When we broke apart, both grinning, the celebration continued around us. Sales happening. Contacts exchanged. Future planned.

But I floated through it all. Untethered. Overwhelmed. Happy.

The fire crew took selfies with their portraits. Comparing notes on who looked best.

"She made me look like a superhero." Martinez studied his portrait. "Look at this angle."

"That's your regular face." Cooper shot back. "She made ME look good."

Tommy dragged his grandfather around. Showing everyone his favorite paintings. Explaining details with the seriousness of a professional curator.

Beverly told anyone who would listen about my childhood. How I'd always loved art. How proud she was.

Mrs. Henderson critiqued my technique with the loving precision of someone who'd taken art classes in the sixties. "The brushwork here is excellent, dear. Very controlled."

Henry bought a piece for The Grind. A seascape that reminded him of early morning beach walks with Dune.

Ryan never left my side. His hand on my back, my waist, my hand. Always touching. Anchoring me through the overwhelming success.

Evening settled. The crowd thinned. A few stragglers examining paintings in the corner.

Vivian appeared with paperwork. Sales figures. Commission contracts.

"You sold eight pieces tonight." She set the papers down. "Three more on hold pending framing decisions. The licensing interest is substantial. And Robert Vanderson's commission—" She paused. "This changes everything, Rachel."

Ryan and I stood together looking at the firefighter series. At his portrait. At the work that had grown from simple mural studies into something neither of us expected.

"This is going to change everything," I said.

"Good change?" Ryan asked.

I turned to face him. "The best change. I get to document heroes. I get to stay in Seaholly." I touched his face. "I get you."

Ryan pulled me close and whispered, "I love you."

The words hit me like lightning. Perfect. True. Everything.

"I love you too."

First time we'd said it. Private. Perfect.

He kissed my forehead. My temple. My mouth. "You've always had me."

The gallery hummed with conversation around us.

I pressed closer to Ryan. "One down."

"One to go." He kissed the top of my head.

Tonight was mine. My vision. My art on these walls.

Tomorrow belonged to Seaholly.

Chapter Thirty-Eight

The Firehouse

Ryan

I stood in front of the covered mural, hands clasped behind my back in dress uniform parade rest.

The firehouse bay packed with people. More people than I'd expected. Way more.

Press cameras. Local news crew with their van parked outside. Town council members in their best clothes. Half of Seaholly, it seemed, crushed into the bay and spilling out onto the street.

The mural loomed behind me under a massive tarp. Navy blue canvas covering months of Rachel's work. Months of planning and collaboration. The biggest project either of us had tackled.

My pulse hammered. Dress uniform felt too tight across my shoulders. The collar strangling me.

Rachel stood beside me. Also nervous. Paint still visible under her fingernails despite obvious scrubbing. She wore a dress I'd never seen before. Dark green. Simple. Beautiful.

Her hand found mine. Squeezed.

I squeezed back. Grounding us both.

Chief Patterson stepped up to the microphone. Tapped it twice. The feedback screech silenced the crowd.

"Thank you all for coming today." Chief's voice boomed through the bay. "We're here to celebrate something extraordinary. A partnership between art and service. Between our department and this community we're honored to protect."

The crew stood in formation behind us. Dress uniforms pressed and polished. Families beside them. Kids fidgeting in their nice clothes.

This was bigger than I'd expected. More official. More real.

Dozer sat at perfect attention beside me. Actual miracle. He wore one of Beverly's handmade bandanas around his neck. Navy blue with an embroidered fire department logo in gold thread.

The dog hadn't moved in ten minutes. Sat there looking noble and well-behaved and nothing like his usual chaotic self.

I made a mental note to give him extra treats later.

"Rachel Brown moved to Seaholly three years ago." Chief continued. "Since then, she's become an integral part of our community. Teaching our children. Supporting local businesses. And now, creating something that will stand as a testament to who we are as a town."

Rachel's grip on my hand tightened. Her breathing shallow.

I leaned closer. Whispered. "You've got this."

She nodded. Didn't look convinced.

"And Ryan Rodriguez." Chief gestured toward me. "Our newest firefighter has proven himself invaluable not in emergency response alone, but in community education and outreach. Together, these two have created something we're incredibly proud of."

Chief and Rachel moved toward the covered mural. They each grabbed a corner of the cord attached to the tarp.

"Seaholly. Your mural."

They pulled.

The tarp fell away.

A collective gasp from the crowd.

Cameras flashed. Press surged forward. People leaning, craning their necks for better views.

The mural was stunning.

I'd seen it in progress. Watched Rachel paint for weeks. Knew every brushstroke, every color choice, every detail she'd agonized over.

But seeing it complete, revealed, whole, took my breath away.

Vibrant colors exploded across the firehouse wall. Massive scale. Thirty-two feet wide, seventeen feet tall. Breathtaking detail demanded you step closer, look harder, see more.

My throat went tight.

The crew erupted in cheers. Families applauding. Martinez whistling loud enough to hurt ears.

Cameras kept flashing. The news crew filming everything.

I couldn't look away from the mural.

My portrait did anchor the center. Rachel had warned me about it. But it wasn't me alone.

The whole crew in action around me. Martinez hauling hose. Cooper on the ladder. Frank directing operations. Captain helping an elderly woman to safety.

But also the community we served.

Tommy painted calling 911 on a phone. His face determined. Brave. Doing exactly what I'd taught him.

Mrs. Henderson, with arms full of groceries, helping an elderly neighbor up porch steps.

Henry visible through The Grind's window, handing coffee to exhausted firefighters after a long call.

Teachers. Mail carriers. Nurses in scrubs. Crossing guards with their stop signs raised. Construction workers rebuilding after the hurricane.

It wasn't a mural about firefighters.

It was a mural about Seaholly. Everyone who showed up. Who helped. Who served in their own way.

Heroes everywhere, in every act of service.

My throat tightened with emotion. Pride. Gratitude. Overwhelming love for this woman who saw things I couldn't see.

Rachel understood what I did this job for. Not glory. Not recognition. But community. Connection. Being part of something bigger than myself.

She'd painted it onto the firehouse wall for everyone to see.

Chief stepped back to the microphone. "Rachel Brown, would you like to say a few words?"

Rachel's hand trembled in mine. She hated public speaking. Always had. But she stepped forward anyway. Took the microphone.

Her voice came out strong. Clear. No hesitation.

"Three years ago, I moved to Seaholly thinking it was temporary. A place to hide while I figured out what came next."

The crowd quieted. Everyone listening.

"But I found something I wasn't looking for. A home. A community. People who showed up when I needed them."

She paused. Found my eyes across the small distance between us.

"I learned that heroes don't wear capes. They wear turnout gear, yes. But also aprons. Scrubs. Name tags. Uniforms of every kind. They're teachers who stay late. Mail carriers who check on elderly residents. Neighbors who help carry groceries."

Beverly stood in the front row beside Mrs. Henderson. Both of them holding hands. Both crying happy tears.

"Communities don't have one hero." Rachel's voice grew stronger. "They have hundreds. Thousands. People choosing every day to show up. To help. To care when it would be easier not to."

When she talked about courage, she looked at me.

When she talked about showing up, her eyes found Tommy's grandfather.

When she talked about service, she gestured to the crew.

Everyone knew this was a love letter. To the town. To the people.

And when she looked at me again, everyone knew it was also deeply personal.

"Thank you for letting me be part of this community." Rachel's voice broke. "For showing me what real heroism looks like every single day."

The crowd erupted. Applause loud enough to rattle the bay doors.

Chief Patterson wiped his eyes. Tried to hide it. Failed.

Beverly and Mrs. Henderson squeezed each other's hands tighter.

Mayor Milford stepped forward. Broad smile. Official-looking folder in her hands.

"Before we open this up for photos and refreshments," the Mayor said, "I have a surprise announcement."

Rachel glanced at me. Confused. I shrugged. No idea.

Mayor Milford opened the folder. Pulled out an official-looking document. City seal at the top.

"The town council convened last week. We were so impressed with this mural, with the community response, with the partnership between Ms. Brown and our fire department, that we voted unanimously."

She paused for effect. Smiled at Rachel.

"We're commissioning Rachel Brown for a series of murals throughout Seaholly. The elementary school. The library. The community center. Other public buildings. Documenting the heart of our town through her art."

Rachel's mouth fell open. Actual shock.

"Funding has been approved through a state arts grant." Mayor Milford's voice carried pride. "This is years of work. Paid work. Official town artist position."

The crowd cheered. Louder than before.

Rachel stood frozen. Tears streaming down her face.

I stepped beside her. Took her hand. Squeezed.

She looked at me. Eyes wide. Overwhelmed. Disbelieving.

"This is your dream," I whispered. "You get to stay. You get to create. You get to honor this place."

She nodded. Couldn't speak past the tears.

Mayor Milford handed her the official proclamation. They posed for photos. Cameras flashing. Press asking questions.

Rachel's dream expanding beyond what she'd imagined.

The ceremony ended. Crowd milling around. Taking photos with the mural. Kids pointing at different details. Adults discussing their favorite parts.

Tommy broke free from the crowd. Ran straight to me.

He threw his arms around my waist. Squeezed hard.

His grandfather followed at a more measured pace. Hand on Tommy's shoulder when he caught up.

Both of them looking at me with expressions that made my throat tight.

"You're in the painting!" Tommy's eyes were bright with excitement. "You're really a hero!"

I knelt to Tommy's level. Met his eyes.

"You're the hero, buddy. You remembered everything. You stayed calm. You saved your grandfather."

Tommy beamed with pride. Threw his arms around my neck again.

I held him. This brave kid who'd learned fire safety because I made it fun. Who'd used it when it mattered most.

This was why we did what we did.

Rachel watched from a few feet away. Her throat working. Eyes bright.

She understood. She always understood.

Mr. Watson shook my hand. Didn't say anything. Didn't need to. The gratitude clear in his eyes.

They melted back into the crowd. Tommy still bouncing with excitement.

The local news crew approached. Reporter with perfect hair and practiced smile.

"Mr. Rodriguez, Ms. Brown, could we get a quick interview?"

We stood together. Natural partnership. My hand found her back. Her shoulder pressed against mine.

Comfortable. Easy. Right.

"Tell us about the community impact of this project." The reporter's camera rolled.

I credited Rachel's art program. "She taught these kids to see heroes everywhere. Not in uniforms alone, but in everyday people doing extraordinary things."

"Tommy learned fire safety in my class," I added. "But he learned to be brave in hers."

The reporter turned to Rachel. "And the artistic vision behind the mural?"

"Ryan doesn't fight fires alone. He prevents them. He teaches. He connects. He builds relationships. That's what I wanted to capture. The community we're all building together."

We built on each other's answers. Natural rhythm. Finishing thoughts. Adding context. Making each other better.

The reporter smiled. "You two make quite a team."

I didn't hesitate. "We do."

Total certainty in those two words.

They positioned us for photos. My arm around Rachel's waist. Her hand on my chest.

We looked at each other. The camera forgotten. The crowd forgotten.

Her. Me. This moment of everything coming together.

The reporter got her shot. Thanked us. Moved on to interview Chief Patterson.

The crowd thinned as evening approached. Sunset caught the mural, made the colors richer. Deeper.

Rachel and me standing in front of it.

Dozer at our feet. Exhausted from all the attention. Bandana askew.

Rachel leaned against me. My arm came around her.

"We did it," she said.

"You did it. This is all you."

"No." She looked up at me. "It's us. All of it. The mural. The programs. The future. Us."

Comfortable silence settled. The kind from being in sync.

I'd been working up to this. All day. All week, maybe.

"Your toothbrush is at my place." Casual. But my heart pounded. "I know you can feel my pulse right now."

She smiled. "I can."

"Your clothes are in my closet. Your coffee mug in my cabinet. You're there more than you're at your cottage."

"I know."

I turned to face her. Both hands on her waist. Eyes serious.

"Move in with me."

Her breath caught.

"Officially. Let's live together. In our cottage."

Our cottage.

The words sent warmth flooding through her. I could see it in her eyes.

She'd been staying there most nights. Leaving more things. Creating space for herself in my life. I'd done the same in hers.

But this was different. Official. Permanent. Choosing each other completely.

"Our cottage." She tested the words. "I love the sound of it."

"Is that a yes?"

She kissed me instead of answering. Long. Deep. Pouring everything into it. All the love. All the certainty. All the yes.

When we broke apart, both grinning like idiots, she whispered against my mouth.

"Yes. Absolutely yes."

Chapter Thirty-Nine

The Cottage

Rachel

My clothes exploded out of the box.

Not metaphorically. Exploded.

The cardboard gave way under the weight of every sweater I owned crammed into one space. The contents erupted across Ryan's renovated hardwood floor in a chaos of color and fabric.

Ryan's boxes sat stacked against the wall. Each one labeled in his tidy handwriting. "KITCHEN - POTS AND PANS." "BATHROOM - LINENS." "OFFICE - FILES A-M."

The contrast was immediate and hilarious.

My boxes said things like "STUFF" and "PAINT THINGS MAYBE?" and one had a question mark drawn on it in Sharpie.

Ryan emerged from the bedroom carrying another stack of his meticulously organized containers. He looked at the sweater explosion. Looked at me. Looked at his perfect boxes.

Then he started laughing.

"This is our life now," he said.

"You knew what you were getting into." I threw a sweater at him.

He caught it. Folded it. Set it on the growing pile.

I threw another one. He folded it too.

"You're not supposed to fold them. That's not the game."

"What game?"

"The throwing game."

Dozer bounded through the door. My favorite paintbrush clamped in his jaws. Still wet with cerulean blue.

"DOZER!" I lunged for him. "That's expensive!"

He dodged. Sprinted back toward my cottage. Paint dripping on both floors.

I chased him. Ryan followed.

My cottage door stood open. I'd been moving back and forth all morning. Bringing things over. Deciding what stayed where.

Dozer dropped the paintbrush in the middle of my studio. Blue paint now decorating a path between the cottages.

Dali sat on the windowsill. Watching. Deeply offended by the chaos. Her tail flicked with irritation.

"Your dog is a menace."

"Your cat is judging us."

"She has standards."

Ryan grabbed paper towels. Started cleaning up paint. I rescued my paintbrush. Wiped it down. Assessed the damage.

Salvageable. Barely.

"We should establish rules." Ryan scrubbed blue paint off the hardwood. "For Dozer. And the cottages. And moving."

"Rules are overrated."

"Rachel."

"Fine. One rule. Dozer stays out of my wet paint."

"Good rule." Ryan pointed at Dali. "Can we add: Dali doesn't knock over my coffee?"

"She can't help being expressive."

"She knocked over three cups yesterday."

"She's establishing dominance."

We looked at each other. Both grinning despite the paint disaster.

This was us. This chaos. This beautiful disaster we were building together.

I surveyed the two cottages. Our arrangement taking shape.

Ryan's renovated cottage would be our main living space. The wall between the kitchen and the living room gone like I'd suggested. Open. Bright. Balanced.

Perfect blend of his order and my creativity.

My cottage was staying as my studio. The ocean views. The north light. The space I'd built my career in. Too perfect to give up.

Ryan's office would go in the other room at my cottage. His organized heaven. Filing systems. Labeled everything. A place for his precise firefighter brain to do its thing.

We were keeping both. Using both. Making it work.

The luxury of space. The comfort of proximity.

Dozer and Dali could have their own territories. Mostly.

I started unpacking kitchen boxes. Trying to find some system in the chaos.

Ryan watched me put a colander in the utensil drawer.

"That goes—"

"I know where it goes in a normal kitchen. But I need it near the forks."

"Why?"

"I don't know. It feels right there."

He opened his mouth. Closed it. Opened it again.

"You're not going to fight me on this?"

"Picking my battles." He moved the colander to the cabinet above the stove. "But it's going here. Where you can reach it while cooking."

"I don't cook."

"Exactly my point."

That evening, I decided to contribute. Be a good partner. Cook dinner.

How hard could it be?

Ryan was on shift. I had the cottage to myself. Plenty of cooking shows existed. I'd watched people make pasta a million times.

I boiled water. Added pasta. Easy.

Then I got distracted by the light coming through the kitchen window. Late afternoon sun. Perfect for painting.

I grabbed my sketchbook. Started capturing the way the light hit the new countertops. The shadows. The warm tones.

Lost track of time.

The smoke alarm shrieked.

I bolted back to the kitchen. The pot boiling over. Water everywhere. Pasta welded to the bottom. Black smoke pouring from the stove.

"NO NO NO!"

I grabbed the pot. Burned my hand. Dropped it. Water and ruined pasta splashing across the floor.

The alarm kept screaming.

I opened the windows. Waved a towel at the alarm. Tried to salvage something from the disaster.

The front door burst open.

Ryan rushed in. Still in his turnout pants and department t-shirt. Must have been close by. Must have gotten some kind of alert on his phone.

"Rachel!" He scanned the room. Assessed the situation. "You okay?"

"I'm fine. The pasta's dead."

He looked at the disaster. The burned pot. The water everywhere. Me standing in the middle holding a towel, covered in pasta water.

His mouth twitched. Fighting a smile.

"Don't laugh," I warned.

"I'm not laughing."

"You're about to."

He pressed his lips together. Lost the battle. Started laughing.

"I can paint a masterpiece, but I can't boil water."

"That's why we're a team." He grabbed paper towels. Started cleaning. "I cook. You create. We're happy."

"I wanted to contribute."

"You contribute plenty." He kissed my forehead. "Maybe not in the kitchen."

That evening, I painted him while he cooked.

Sat at the kitchen counter with my sketchbook. Watching him move through the space we'd created together.

He chopped vegetables with precision. Added them to the pan with timing I didn't understand. Everything coordinated. Controlled. Beautiful.

I captured the concentration on his face. The confidence in his movements. The way his shoulders relaxed when he cooked.

This was our rhythm. He cooked. I created. We were happy.

"What are you drawing?" He didn't look up.

"You."

"Again?"

"I'll never run out of ways to see you."

He glanced over. Smiled. Went back to cooking.

Dozer sprawled at my feet. Dali claimed her perch on the bookshelf. Both pets in their respective territories. Mostly peaceful.

Later, we christened the rooms.

Made every space ours.

Building memories. Building home.

I learned his rhythms. He learned mine.

He started his days at five AM for early shifts. I painted at three AM when inspiration struck.

We passed like ships sometimes. Him leaving coffee ready for me. Me leaving notes in unexpected places.

In his gear bag: "You're my hero."

In his truck: "Drive safe. I love you."

In his shaving kit: "Still the most handsome firefighter in Seaholly."

He left notes too. Found them when I least expected.

On my easel: "Your art makes the world better."

In my paint box: "Don't forget to eat lunch."

On my coffee mug: "I love you. Even at 3 AM."

One morning, unpacking the last boxes, I found his iron.

"You have an iron?" I held it up like an alien artifact.

Ryan looked up from organizing his closet. "How else would I crease my pants?"

"I'm not going to iron them."

He laughed. "I wouldn't want you to."

But the chaos had limits.

Two weeks in, I left paint on his tools. Again.

Cerulean blue on his wrench. Crimson on his hammer. A whole rainbow on his screwdriver set.

Ryan found them in the garage. Brought them inside. Set them on the kitchen counter.

"Rachel."

I looked up from my sketchbook. Saw the paint-covered tools.

"Oh. Sorry. I was using them to open paint cans and—"

"You have palette knives for that."

"I couldn't find them."

"Because I organized your studio." His tone went tight. Frustrated. "And you un-organized it."

"I need my chaos!"

"I need SOME order!"

We stared at each other. First real fight as cohabitants.

My paint supplies scattered everywhere. His tools ruined. Both of us frustrated. Both right.

The moment stretched. Tense. Worried this wouldn't work.

Then we sat down. On the floor. Like adults.

"I'm not trying to ruin your tools."

"I know. And I'm not trying to destroy your creative process." He took my hand. "But I need to be able to find my things."

"And I need to be able to find mine."

We looked at each other. Both stubborn. Both willing to compromise.

"One junk drawer," Ryan offered. "For you. You can organize it however you want. I won't touch it."

"Really?"

"Really. And I get one closet in the garage. Mine. You don't put paint supplies in there."

"Deal."

We shook on it. Then kissed. Then laughed at ourselves.

The cottage found its balance.

Always messier than Ryan preferred. Always neater than I naturally maintained.

The perfect middle ground.

Paint smudges on unexpected surfaces. Ryan's tools precisely placed in his garage closet. My canvases leaning against walls. His firefighter gear by the door.

Dozer's toys everywhere. Dali's climbing tree in the corner. Both pets carving out their territories.

It was chaotic and organized and perfectly us.

That evening, we walked to the beach.

The sun setting. Warm light painting everything orange and pink. Perfect temperature.

I went barefoot. Laughing. Free in ways I'd never been before.

Ryan put on music from his phone. Something slow. Something perfect.

He pulled me into a dance on the sand.

No one watching. Us and the ocean. The life we were building together.

He held me like I might float away. I held him like an anchor.

"I love you," I whispered. "Messy and complicated and forever."

"I love you too." He spun me under the stars beginning to emerge. "Chaotic and beautiful and here."

We danced while the sun finished setting. Both knowing every rescue, every paint spill, every moment of chaos had led us exactly where we needed to be.

Together. Finally. Home.

Chapter Forty

Coral Pier

Ryan

Rachel's hand trembled in mine as we walked down the aisle.

Her auburn hair caught the afternoon light. Long sleeveless navy blue dress flowing behind her. Heels making her nearly my height.

She looked beautiful. Nervous. Determined.

The aisle stretched down the rebuilt Coral Pier. White chairs lined both sides. Flower petals scattered across new boards. The ocean rolling beneath us. Salt air mixing with roses and jasmine.

Henry and Maya had chosen the perfect venue. The pier connected our little beach community to the ocean beyond. The pier held all our stories.

Rachel was walking toward the spot where she had fallen. Where I caught her. Where everything started between us.

Her hand steadied in mine as we walked. Small triumph. Quiet courage.

My pride in her swelled. She conquered this fear. Stood here for Henry and Maya. For family.

"When Henry asked me to be his best man, I knew I'd have to give some kind of speech today."

Rachel glanced up at me. Eyes bright with unshed tears. Trying not to cry before the ceremony even started.

"But I didn't know I'd also be walking down the aisle with the most beautiful bridesmaid in Seaholly."

She squeezed my hand. Color flooding her cheeks.

This was Henry and Maya's wedding. Their day. Their moment.

But walking here with Rachel, watching her face her fear, seeing her smile through happy tears, made it feel like ours too.

The ceremony space glowed in perfect spring weather. May sunshine. Gentle breeze. Ocean rolling steady in the background.

Henry stood at the end of the pier. Looking nervous and happy, and ready. His eyes found Maya when the music started.

Maya walked down the aisle. Looking stunning in her simple white dress. Flowers in her hair. Radiant.

She reached Henry. He took her hands. Neither of them could stop smiling.

Rachel stood beside me as bridesmaid. I stood beside Henry as best man. The positions we'd earned through years of friendship and love.

But I couldn't stop watching Rachel.

The way the navy dress complemented her skin. The way she wiped tears with her free hand. The way she smiled when Maya said her vows.

The officiant spoke about love. About partnership. About two people choosing each other every day.

Henry and Maya exchanged rings. Voices strong. Certain. No hesitation.

"I do."

"I do."

The kiss drew cheers from the crowd. Applause. Whistles from the fire crew.

Beverly and Mrs. Henderson sat in the front row. Both crying. Both beaming.

Dozer sat perfectly beside them. Wearing a navy blue bandana with embroidered wedding bells. He hadn't moved in the entire time. Actual miracle.

The ceremony ended. Henry and Maya walked back down the aisle as husband and wife. Everyone cheering. Throwing flower petals.

The reception moved to the beach. Shoes abandoned. Sand between toes. Music playing. Food and drinks and celebration.

Rachel kicked off her heels the second we hit the sand. Sighed with relief.

"Those were torture," she said.

"They were beautiful."

"They were both." She wiggled her toes in the sand. "Much better."

Toasts began as the sun started its descent. Warm light painting everything orange and pink.

I gave my best man speech. Kept it short. Told the story of how Henry and I became friends in third grade. How he'd shared his lunch with me that first week when I forgot mine. How the friendship had lasted through decades and distance.

"And then he fell for my sister. Which was terrifying at first. But now I can't imagine anyone better for Maya. They're perfect together. They make each other better."

I raised my glass. "To Henry and Maya. May you have a lifetime of coffee dates and terrible puns and love that gets stronger every day."

Everyone drank. Cheered. Henry hugged me.

Rachel gave her bridesmaid toast next. About meeting Maya that first week after the hurricane. How Maya had welcomed her. Made her feel like family.

"Maya taught me that family isn't blood alone." Rachel's voice came out thick with emotion. "It's the people who show up. Who stay. Who choose you every single day."

She looked at Beverly. At Mrs. Henderson. At Maya and Henry.

Then her eyes found mine.

"Thank you for choosing me. For teaching me what belonging feels like."

The crowd erupted. Maya was crying now. Henry handed her tissues.

Dancing began as the sun touched the horizon.

I watched Rachel laugh with Maya. Watched her hug Beverly. Watched her move through the crowd with confidence and joy.

The ring sat in my jacket pocket. Had been there for weeks. Custom made. Designed for her.

I'd been waiting for the right moment. The perfect moment.

Tonight felt right. Perfect.

The wedding party dance started. Traditional pairings. Best man and maid of honor.

I took Rachel's hand. Led her onto the makeshift dance floor in the sand.

My hand found her waist. Hers rested on my shoulder. We fit together perfectly. Like we'd been designed for this.

"What are you thinking?" She read my expression.

"Nothing." I deflected. Not ready yet. "Happy for them."

"You're a terrible liar."

I smiled. Spun her under the stars beginning to emerge. "Maybe."

We danced while the ocean watched. While our friends and family celebrated around us.

She was beautiful. She was everything. She was mine.

Almost time.

After several dances, I pulled her away from the reception.

"Where are we going?" She laughed. Barefoot in the sand. Hair coming loose from its pins. Navy dress flowing in the breeze.

"Walk with me."

I led her down the beach. Away from the crowd. Away from the music and lights and celebration.

Us. Moonlight. Waves.

My heart pounded like a fire call. Adrenaline and nerves and certainty all tangled together.

I led her back to Coral Pier. The rebuilt structure strong beneath our feet.

Stopped at the exact spot where she fell that first day.

"Do you remember?" I asked.

She looked around. Recognition dawning. "This is where I fell."

"This is where it started." I took both her hands. "The day you fell, I caught you."

"You did."

"That moment changed everything." I held her gaze. "I've been catching you ever since."

"Ryan—"

"And you've been catching me too." My voice went rough with emotion. "My life before Seaholly was ordered. Lonely. Safe. Everything in its place. Everything controlled."

I touched her face. Traced the line of her jaw. "My life now is chaotic. Full. Complete. You brought color to my black-and-white world."

"Literally." She laughed through tears. "Paint everywhere."

"Everywhere." I smiled. "Art. Beauty. Joy. You showed me that life isn't about control. It's about connection."

The waves crashed below us. The moon painted silver across the water.

"I love your chaos. Your creativity. Your heart." I squeezed her hands. "I want forever with you."

I dropped to one knee right there on the pier.

Rachel's breath caught. Tears streaming down her face.

I pulled out the ring box. Hands steady despite my racing pulse.

"Rachel Brown, will you marry me?"

The ring caught the moonlight. Silver. Geometric patterns. Elegant and unique.

Custom designed to coordinate with her favorite artwork. With her aesthetic. With everything made her, her.

"It's perfect." She whispered. "How did you—"

"I paid attention." I smiled up at her. "So what do you say? Will you marry this firefighter who can't stop watching you paint? Who loves your beautiful chaos? Who wants to spend every day catching you when you fall?"

"Yes." She nodded. Laughing and crying. "Yes. Absolutely yes."

I stood. Slid the ring on her finger. It fit perfectly.

She threw her arms around my neck. Kissed me while the ocean watched. While the stars witnessed. While the pier where everything began held us steady.

Both crying. Both laughing. Both knowing this was exactly right.

When we broke apart, both grinning like idiots, she held up her hand. The ring catching moonlight.

"We're engaged." Wonder in her voice.

"We're engaged." I pulled her close again. Kissed her forehead. Her temple. Her mouth.

We walked back to the reception hand in hand. Rachel kept looking at her ring. Touching it. Making sure it was real.

"Should we tell them?" She asked. "Or wait?"

"It's Maya's day. We should—"

Maya screamed.

Loud enough to startle seagulls. She ran across the sand. Henry following. Both of them grinning.

"You did it!" Maya threw her arms around us both. "Finally!"

"How did you—" I started.

Maya grabbed Rachel's left hand. Held it up. "The ring, genius. Kind of hard to miss."

The crowd converged. Everyone congratulating us. Hugging us. Celebrating our news along with Maya and Henry's wedding.

Beverly cried happy tears. Hugged us both. "I knew it. I knew from the moment I saw you two together."

Mrs. Henderson squeezed my arm. "Well done, Mr. Rodriguez." Her eyes twinkled. "Don't make her wait too long for the wedding."

"Yes, ma'am."

Chief Patterson clapped my back. "Congratulations, Rodriguez. You found a good one."

"I know, sir."

The celebration continued. Doubled now. Wedding and engagement. Henry and Maya. Rachel and me.

I watched Rachel laugh with my sister. Watched them hug. Watched the two most important women in my life celebrating together.

My family. Her family. Our community.

Everything I'd wanted without knowing I wanted it.

Later in the evening, Maya called all single women to the dance floor for the bouquet toss.

Rachel protested. "I'm engaged now!"

"You're not married yet!" Maya grabbed her hand. Dragged her to the group. "Get out here!"

Rachel laughed. Joined the other women. Barefoot in the sand. Navy dress dirty at the hem. Hair loose now. Ring catching the light.

Maya turned her back to the group. Raised the bouquet.

"Ready?" She called.

"Ready!" The women shouted back.

Maya threw. The bouquet sailed through the air. Perfect arc.

Landed in Rachel's hands.

Everyone laughed. Cheered. The perfect cliché of it.

Rachel held up the bouquet and her ring hand. Both catching the light.

Looking right at me.

I stood at the edge of the dance floor. Grinning. Heart full. Life complete.

Every moment of order I'd given up was worth it.

This was our life now. Chaotic. Beautiful. Perfect.

Epilogue

One Year Later

Rachel

I stretched out on the beach blanket. Early June afternoon. Sun warm on my skin. Dali curled beside me, purring. Journal open, pen in hand.

Down the beach, Ryan threw a frisbee for Dozer. Their laughter carried on the wind. The dog bounded through the surf, joyful and chaotic, still acting like a puppy.

I turned a page in my journal. Found the section on career decisions.

Robert Vanderson's national commission. I'd said no. I chose Seaholly instead.

```
June 10
The elementary school mural went up in
September. Library project starts next week. Then
the community center.
Smaller stages. Local impact. Work that
matters to people I know.
Ryan made lieutenant six months ago. More
responsibility. More late nights. But he loved
it.
Once a month we loaded up his truck. Drove to
small towns around Seaholly. Taught fire safety
through art. Kids painting fire trucks and smoke
detectors and escape routes. Learning to stay safe
while Ryan told them stories. While I showed them
```

how to make something beautiful from something scary.

We built something. Together.

Dozer completed his therapy dog certification two months ago. The giant puppy who destroyed my pansies on day one now visited hospitals and nursing homes with Ryan. Comforted people through their worst moments.

Mom and Mrs. Henderson spent most days at the local senior center. Inseparable. They had their book club and their craft group and their opinions about everyone else's business.

We visited every Sunday for lunch. Listened to their stories. Watched them bicker. Watched them care for each other. It warmed my heart.

Mom was okay. Really okay. Not just managing or surviving. Thriving.

I got to witness that instead of carrying it alone.

These eighteen months since I met Ryan taught me that I was allowed to want things. To build a life that made me happy instead of small. To take up space and paint loud and love hard.

Some days I still couldn't believe this was real. That I got to keep my life in Seaholly. That I got this man who looked at me like I hung the moon. That in four months I'd walk down that pier toward him.

The pier where I fell. Where he caught me. Where everything started.

A small ceremony on Coral Pier in October. Just family and close friends. The reception afterward would fill the fire department ballroom.

I wouldn't be scared. Wouldn't be looking for exits or second-guessing or wondering if I deserved this.

I'd just be walking toward him. Toward us. Toward this life we built together.

The real choice was never Mom or Seaholly. Duty or happiness. Sacrifice or love.

The real choice was whether to believe I was worth fighting for. Worth staying for. Worth loving.

I'm worth all of it.

Warm breeze in my hair. Sand under my feet. Ryan's laughter in the air.

This. Right here.

Ryan called from down the beach. "Rachel! Come play!"

Dozer barked agreement. Both soaking wet. Both grinning.

I set down my journal. Stood. Stretched in the warm sun.

Dali followed me down the sand.

Ryan threw the frisbee to me. I missed. Of course. Laughed at my terrible catch.

Dozer retrieved it. Brought it to my feet. Tail wagging. Ready to play again.

We played until the sun lowered. Amber light painting everything warm.

Walking back to the cottages, Ryan's arm around me. Dozer and Dali ahead of us. Unlikely friends who'd figured out how to coexist.

I wouldn't change a thing. Not a single paint spill. Not a single choice.

Ryan pulled me close. Kissed my temple. "Shower?"

"Yeah." I smiled. "Then dinner?"

"Perfect."

THE END

Thank You

Thank you for reading *The Grumpy Firefighter Next Door*!

Reviews are the best way to help sweet romances like this one reach new readers—and every single one makes a difference. If you enjoyed your time with Ryan and Rachel, I'd be so grateful if you left a short review. Your words keep these small-town love stories alive.

Scan this QR code with your camera to leave a quick review!

With heartfelt thanks,

Avi

P.S. Want to spend more time in Seaholly Beach? Keep turning the page to see what else is waiting for you.

Also by Avi

Off Limits with my Brother's Best Friend

"Trapped by a hurricane with my brother's best friend, I swore I wouldn't fall for his rough edges and quiet warmth—until one night, one touch, and one breath too close made breaking the rules feel inevitable."

Meet Henry and Maya, two supporting characters you met in The Grumpy Firefighter Next Door. Their undeniable chemistry and intertwined fates in this friends to lovers happily-ever-after, despite Ryan's interference. Dive into this standalone love story with witty banter, small-town comfort, and sizzling tension. Ready to return to Seaholly Beach? Scan this QR code with your phone camera to purchase and download instantly.

About the Author

As a child, Avianne Ash often found solace in reading beneath a maple tree. Those early bookish adventures planted seeds for her storytelling journey. Now, with grown children, Avi brings her ideas and plots to life.

Her formative fictional voyages grew into a passion, further enriched by studies in quaint European villages and urban U.S. cities. These experiences shaped her blend of sweet romance and messy, lovable characters, often found thriving in communities like Seaholly. The most important lesson Avi learned from graduate writing courses was perseverance.

She writes from a countryside farmhouse with her hubby, lazy dogs, and cuddly cats. In her downtime, Avi dreams up fictional flings from their vintage boat, reads, oil paints, travels, and enjoys family time.

Escape with Avi on her path of sweet romance, with pages of swoony banter and heartwarming, tender connections. Join Avi's reader community for great book deals, new release alerts, and exclusive content: Scan the QR code with your camera!

Made in United States
North Haven, CT
28 February 2026

89291871R00198